Murder
on a
Crooked Path

1 /⅓0/⅓⅓

Publishing

American Quilter's Society
5801 Kentucky Dam Rd,
Paducah, Kentucky 42003

Library of Congress Cataloging-in-Publication Data Pending

Names: Velarde, Kay, author.
Title: Murder on a crooked path / by Kay Velarde.
Description: Paducah, KY : American Quilter's Society, [2016]
Identifiers: LCCN 2016030988 (print) | LCCN 2016039119 (ebook) | ISBN
  9781683390060 (pbk.) | ISBN 9781683395072 (e-book)
Subjects: LCSH: Murder--Investigation--Fiction. | Quiltmakers--Fiction. |
  Tennessee--Fiction. | GSAFD: Mystery fiction.
Classification: LCC PS3622.E434 M86 2016 (print) | LCC PS3622.E434 (ebook)
|
  DDC 813/.6--dc23
LC record available at https://lccn.loc.gov/2016030988

Editor: Gina Schade
Book and Cover designer: Chris Gilbert
Production Manager: Sarah Bozone
Assistant Editor: Adriana Fitch
Director of Publications: Kimberly Holland Tetrev

Murder
on a
Crooked Path

A Sewanee Mountain Series

KAY VELARDE

Ⓐ Ⓠ Ⓢ Publishing

PADUCAH, KENTUCKY

CHAPTER 1

"This. Is. Not. Happening," I said, spitting each word through gritted teeth as I tugged on the doorknob with all my might. A sudden gust of late autumn wind through the open window of my office had slammed the door shut, jamming it tight. "Not today! Please, please." I glanced at the wall clock. In about ten minutes my boss would arrive at the Heritage Craft Center to tour the progress I'd made in getting it ready for the grand opening. Janice Price would expect her director—her recently hired director—to be standing on the porch greeting her with an eager smile. She certainly would not expect to find me locked in my own office.

I pounded on the door, but it felt as solid as stone. "Donnie? Donnie! Can you hear me? Help!" I shouted and then waited with my ear pressed to the panel. There were no noises of the handyman I'd hired last week racing up the stairs to rescue me. There were no sounds at all from the first floor where he was painting today. With renewed vigor, I banged my fists against the wood, but everything in the hundred-plus-year-old log building was substantial oak, rough with the marks of hand tools and dark with age.

Letting my hands fall to my sides, I stepped back to assess the situation. That meant I stared at the stubborn door wishing it would open. Maybe if I muttered the magic words, but I only huffed in frustration.

Then I twisted in a circle, taking in the room, searching for something, anything, to use as a tool to free myself. The assortment didn't look promising. New shelves, recently installed, were filled with books on crafting and Tennessee history. Several quilts, one of which I'd made with my own hands, hung on the walls. An antique chair with a newly caned seat was poised in front of my desk, waiting for visitors. Plus, I couldn't forget the smiling black bear in its primitive carved glory, standing in the corner, waving with one paw and hugging a honey pot with the other. I'd bought Pooh, as I called the statue, from an old man demonstrating his talent with a chain saw on the side of the road. He worked most sunny days beside his Ford truck, the front seat his office.

In spite of my ridiculous present circumstances, I felt my own smile blossom. In only six short weeks I'd managed to turn this space, my office, into a creative haven for myself. That had seemed necessary to me to reflect the purpose of the Heritage Craft Center, soon to be opened by the Tennessee Department of Tourism in my hometown of Sewanee. Although the hope was to lure tourists and their dollars, I thought of the Center's role in my community as being more about education and pride. Here, high on the Cumberland Plateau, the traditional crafts were our lifeblood and our history, and I desperately wanted to be a part of by living a creative life.

It had been a sudden change for me when I'd decided to move back home to Sewanee Mountain after my mom had faced down a murder charge, and I'd caught the real murderer. Going back to my old life in Nashville had not been appealing, and I'd immediately started looking for a job. Work turned out to be scarce in Sewanee, at least for jobs that didn't involve flipping burgers or flapjacks. Of course, I didn't just want a paycheck but a profession. This position as director was the only opening that both filled that need and interested me.

Now, as new state employees were subject to four months of probation, I needed to prove that I could do a great job. During my interview with Ms. Price, she had been cold and snooty, and she hadn't struck me as someone who would laugh at my current situation. No, I imagined her whipping a mini tablet out of her handbag, digitally flicking to a page for jotting down a note, and, fingers flying, recording my transgression. Later, she'd tally the list to use in my evaluation for permanent employment.

The grand opening, in only two weeks, would be a test, the final exam, and more hard work than I'd ever put into anything in my life.

That thought caused me to break out in a cold sweat and sent me rushing forward. I snatched at the doorknob again in haste, as if getting a jump on my problem would make my efforts more likely to succeed this time. Balancing on one foot, I planted the other one against the door frame and positioned my hands for a good grip. One mighty effort and surely I'd be free. Holding my breath, I heaved, but instead of the door opening, the hardware broke free. I staggered backward as the knob flew out of my hands. It landed on the floor with a clunk and rolled in an aimless circle with a decidedly drunken wobble.

I stood, still rubbing my stinging hands together while listening to the noise from the street through the open window. My tense muscles began to relax until I heard a car slow to a stop in front of the building. I crossed the room in long strides, making it to the window in time to see the driver's side door swing open. My boss's tall, trim form unfolded from the vehicle. I knew I should just stick my head out the window and call down to Janice that I needed some help. Instead I found myself ducking out of sight. I let the moment slip past and waited until I heard the old-fashioned bell over the front door signal that she had entered the Center.

With the office door jammed closed, there was only one way out. Before I could think twice and change my mind, I popped the screen out of the window and sat on the sill. With a quick twist my legs dangled outside. Although my office was on the second floor, the roof of the porch over the entrance was only two inches below my feet. It was nice and wide so I shouldn't be afraid, but I suffered from acrophobia.

"Jeez, get a grip," I mumbled. Standing took all my willpower and even then I gave a couple of little bounces to test the soundness of the structure.

I gritted my teeth as I side-stepped, shuffling and hugging the big logs, toward the other window on the front of the building. There was no way I could look toward the edge of the metal ledge, although I could now hear voices from down at street level.

"Hey, ain't that Stella Hill way up there? Hey, Stella," a woman's warbling soprano called out.

I wasn't brave enough to let go and turn around. All I could do was wave my hand behind my back. The owner of the voice probably took my motions for a greeting, but I wanted whomever it was to hush in case Janice came back outside or maybe someone like my brother Gibb, the town sheriff, came along. If he saw me, he'd never let me live this escapade down.

"Whoo-hoo, Stella," a male voice called out. "What ya looking for? Need any help?"

Now I recognized the voice of Elmer Colley, so the woman had to be his wife Emily.

"Hey, Elmer. Hey, Emily. No, thanks. I'm just inspecting the condition of the wall here. I'm 'bout done, but it was right nice of you to offer to lend a hand." I slid open the other window that would lead me to a small broom closet and, beyond it, the stairs. I shouted good-bye to the elderly couple as I scooted through the opening.

I think if I hadn't put my foot into the mop bucket, I'd have made it downstairs in time to meet with my boss. As it was, I bounced around wasting precious seconds until I jerked my shoe free and raced down the stairs. All I got was a glimpse of the back of her car surging away when I ran out onto the front porch.

"Oh, shue." I stomped my foot.

"That boss lady of yours is a snob." A big voice boomed from behind me, and I whirled around to find Donnie Clark, the handyman I'd hired, standing in the doorway. He wore his usual dirty denim overalls with a sweatshirt beneath and carried a paint tray in one hand and a brush in the other.

"I offered to let her help me paint while she waited on you," Donnie said. "Told her I hadn't seen you in a couple of hours." He barked a deep laugh that rolled up from his belly.

"Shoot, was she mad? No, don't tell me. It won't help to know. I was working upstairs and then I got locked in my office." I explained how the door had blown shut and about the knob coming loose in my hand.

"Probably the shank broke and jammed against the frame." Donnie turned back inside, put the tray on the floor, and started up the stairs while I trotted behind. When he took hold of the door knob on the outside of my office, it fell into his hand, and the door swung open easily. "See. Say, what kind of room has no door?"

"Huh? I don't know, Donnie." I'd learned to just let him give me the answers to the riddles he loved, or I wouldn't be able to get the man's mind back on business. "What kind?" I asked.

"Boy, you never know the right answer, Stella. A mushroom." He laughed with a high-pitched girlish giggle. When he finally wound down, he asked, "You want me to go buy you a new knob and install it now or keep painting?" He dumped the broken parts into the wastebasket with a ringing clatter of metal on metal.

"I can live with things the way they are for a while," I said, not wanting to deal with that particular problem for another second. I tried to keep the irritation out of my voice. It wasn't Donnie's fault that my boss had taken off so quickly, although actually maybe it was. Had he really asked her to help him paint? I knew he was always joking around, but she might have been offended. "Donnie, didn't you say you need to leave early today?"

Maybe getting a break from Donnie for a few hours would make me feel better.

"Oh, yeah. Reckon I keep forgetting 'cause I wasn't wanting to remember. My brother Ronnie is getting out of prison today. Out of Lebanon Maximum Security. He's supposed to come by the house tonight."

"How's he going to get here from Lebanon?" I asked. It was forty miles between the two towns. I knew it was none of my business, but as usual for me, the first thing that came into my head popped right out of my mouth. This bad habit had gotten me into trouble more than once, but Donnie didn't seem to mind that I asked him.

"That's a good question. I never thought about it. You think he woulda' asked me to pick him up, but he just called last week and said he'd be coming by the house tonight. First thing he wants to do," he said.

With that puzzling thought, Donnie scratched under the baseball cap he always wore, causing the hat to bob in time to the motion. He used it to hide his mostly bald head, which still sported a fringe of lank brown hair. He had more hair on his face with a scrappy growth of whiskers that wasn't generous enough to be called a beard. I figured the man was just too lazy to shave every day.

He asked, "Did I tell you he robbed a bank and shot the guard? It's been ten years since I seen him. My own brother." His head tossed back and forth with the words.

Not knowing how to reply, I shuffled around, stooped over, and picked up the papers that had blown off my desk earlier. Donnie must have told me his news at least two dozen times since I'd hired him. The man didn't seem a bit happy about the upcoming reunion, and I guess I could see his point of view.

"If you need to take tomorrow off, it's okay. Your brother's probably going to need some help getting back into society." I spoke to Donnie's back as he fitted the window screen into the opening and lowered the sash.

Donnie turned, his face twisted into a quizzical expression.

"You know," I said. "A car. Job. I believe he'll probably have to register with a probation officer." I guess I'd heard that tidbit of information at some point from Gibb.

"Nope. I'll be here bright and early as always. Got to keep up my sterlin' reputation. See you tomorrow, Stella." Donnie stuffed his hands deep into the pockets of his overalls. He ambled out of my office, leaving me with only the sound of his heavy footsteps as they slapped each tread on the staircase.

I sighed and hurried down after him, following him through the large showroom and into the back room used for storage and as a mini break area. He lifted a jacket off a hook on the wall.

"Don't forget, Donnie. Eight o'clock in the morning. No later than 8:30." I bit my lip, instantly regretting being such a pushover without the handyman even saying a word. "Seriously, eight sharp."

Donnie acted as if he hadn't heard a word I'd said. "This here," he said, pointing to the light switch by the back door, "I think you'd better get a *cer-t-ified* electrician to fix it. I taped over it so nobody could get hurt. Remember, I never advertised myself as no electric man." He stepped outside without giving me another look.

I leaned around the door to where I could call after him. "Eight."

When I jerked the sticky back door closed, I noticed that Donnie had used at least four or five overly long strips of duct tape to prevent anyone from using the switch to the overhead light fixture. We'd had a problem earlier today when I asked him if he could figure out why the light would not come on. I'd already changed the bulbs and discovered that wasn't the answer.

To say that he wasn't a qualified electrician was an understatement. The sparks flying when he'd poked a screwdriver into the switch had been clue enough. I frowned at the memory of Donnie hopping around after receiving a minor shock.

I frowned again, knowing I had bigger problems. I'd hired Donnie about ten days ago, and so far he had yet to show up before nine when I'd specifically told him I arrived at eight and wanted him to get an early start too. I paid him by the hour, but the deadline for the grand opening loomed in my mind. This building still needed a lot of work to turn it into the Heritage Craft Center.

When I had phoned Donnie's business references, most people said Donnie was adequate at best. Others, who hadn't been as kind, outright said I'd regret doing business with him. I hadn't in the end had any choice. He'd turned out to be the only handyman I could afford with my stingy state budget. As bad as Donnie's work was, putting up with his childish riddles and practical jokes at least five or six times a day, had been even more difficult. Just yesterday he'd placed a fake cigarette butt on my sandwich when I'd left it for a moment to sign for a delivery. The bit of plastic hadn't bothered me half as much as the thought of Donnie's usually dirty hands on my food.

I shivered. This arrangement would only be for a couple of weeks more, and until then I wouldn't let my packed lunch out of my sight. I'd get this building cleaned up, the repairs complete, my displays in place, and my days of wheedling Donnie through each and every task would be behind me.

Then the fun would start. I would find creative new crafts to sell, and I would prepare the displays of historical craftwork that had already been donated. For now all those items were safely stored, but I needed more, many more, items that showed the rich heritage of the mountain.

Just thinking of the search made me rub my hands together. I especially wanted things like corn cob pipes, straw brooms, dried apple-head dolls, handmade pottery, and, of course, quilts, quilts, quilts. The pièce de résistance—and I hadn't revealed my plan yet to my boss—was going to be a moonshine still, one that had actually seen use. I worried a bit that Janice might not agree with my opinion that making one's own spirits was truly a craft. I wanted the still right in the front window, sitting up on a platform for better viewing. Talk about a tourist attraction!

CHAPTER 2

My next task was to call Janice and explain why I hadn't been around to meet her. I smiled, thinking I could wait for at least another hour until she'd be off the road and back in her Nashville office. At least I could enjoy a last meal before finding out if Janice was in a mood to fire me. My stomach growled, making the decision for me.

I grabbed my sweater off the coat rack and checked my pockets for money before bustling out the front door. While I had been busy today, the air had turned much cooler, but it was, after all, November. Our Indian summer had lasted longer than usual so no one should complain that it was time to dig out the coats. Truly this was my favorite time of year, and now that I'd returned to the mountain, I couldn't be happier.

With a glance both ways for cars, I shuffled through the crisp leaves littering the gutter and hurried across the two lanes. At my last job in downtown Nashville, I would have been taking my life in my hands to cross the busy streets without a traffic light.

The gate of a cute white picket fence surrounding the restaurant, converted from an old house, creaked pleasantly when I opened it and the spring snapped it closed behind me. Either side of the walkway contained what had once been a front yard but was now completely covered by JoAnn's herb garden. Come spring, neat furrows would sprout dill, parsley, basil, and more. For now the soil rested under a layer of mulch.

Eager to eat, I hurried up the steps of the porch and into JoAnn's Café. A blast of the crisp air following close behind caused several diners to look up from their plates. One face lit up, and I felt my heart do a little square dance in my chest. It was my old friend and new boyfriend Lamont Wythe, Lam for short. Unfortunately, the surge of happiness I felt also carried a twinge of guilt. Somehow last month I had attracted the attention of two men and now found myself dating both of them. Confusion over which one I liked best had my emotions swinging a do-si-do.

Lam sat across one of the small tables from my brother and it looked as if he left Gibb hanging in mid-word when he jumped from his chair and crossed the room with quick strides of his long legs.

"Hi, Stella. You look cold, baby." He wrapped an arm around my shoulders in a gesture that could have been just friendly except that he then dipped his head to my ear and whispered, "I've been experimenting with flavors of homemade ice cream. Why don't you come over tonight and we'll make a batch? I'm thinking strawberry and lavender for you."

Oh, boy. Lam knew my weakness for sweets, and he loved to cook. I leaned away. "I thought you just said I look cold and you want to serve me ice cream? In November?"

"Well, I was thinking we'd eat snuggled in front of the fireplace."

His gaze swept my face, and as usual, the intensity of his blue eyes caught my breath and whisked it away.

Lam had been my brother's best mate forever so I'd always thought about him just as a friend. For some reason, though, Lam had started to flirt with me when I'd come home early last month. At first I thought he was teasing me. After all, the closest we'd ever come to a date was playing in the tree house together when I was ten and he was seven. Several recent passionate kisses had let me know that Lam definitely wanted to be so much more.

The other man in my life, Harley Morgan, had been on my short list of possible suspects during the murder ordeal. A stranger in town, he kept showing up in the nick of time. That had made me suspicious, but it turned out that Harley also was working to find the murderer. We'd finally joined forces and gotten to know one another better during the process. He had even saved my life.

"Lam, you don't have a fireplace in—" I gasped. "You didn't! Did you? You bought that cute cottage on Lake Drive?"

"Not yet, but I am pretty serious. I have the key though. I told the realtor I wanted to take some measurements while I'm making a final decision." Lam brushed a strand of my hair back from my face and used the opportunity to trace his fingertips lightly along my jaw. "What I really want is for you to come look at it again, darlin'. I want to know that you like the place."

I swear Lam could switch a sexy Southern accent on and off at will, and I always fell for it. When the word darlin' formed on his lips, I tingled from head to toe. It wasn't that he didn't already have a perfectly adorable Tennessee hillbilly twang that was as cute as a June bug, but when he'd gone away to college, choosing Ole Miss, he'd broadened his mind and come home with sharpened womanizing skills too.

"Owww," I cooed. "That sounds so nice. Strawberry and lavender." Suddenly the fog that attacked my brain at the closeness of Lam lifted. Maybe my growling stomach helped. "Hey, is lavender even edible?"

Lam sighed. Even as persistent as he was, Lam knew the spell was broken. "Come and sit with Gibb and me. Did you come for a late lunch or an early supper?" He guided me around the floor of full tables as deftly as if the café were a dance studio and the jukebox sounded a waltz instead of Elvis. Lam slid one of the extra chairs beside my brother out for me and then took his seat. It looked like he had only ordered a glass of tea, and I knew it would be sweet. Who in the South didn't take iced tea sweet and drink it all winter too?

I shrugged out of my sweater since it was cozy-warm in the restaurant. The dining area—actually what had once been the original front parlor and the library of the house—still retained the working fireplaces and pine flooring. The wide boards glowed from the smooth finish that only a hundred years of use can achieve. Having the fire going on each end of the room made me want to sit here for hours curled up with a good book or some hand sewing.

"Hey, Sis, couldn't face Mom's cooking tonight?" My brother asked, shoving the bread basket with one lone bun toward me across the green plaid tablecloth. The golden top glistened with butter, and I knew that being homemade its fluffiness would melt in my mouth. "I'd guess all the fresh vegetables out of Mom's garden are gone, except maybe some cabbage, and now you're into canned okra, stewed tomatoes, and zucchini?" He grinned. "There's nothing like a good vegan diet." He rubbed his flat belly.

Since I'd quit my job and moved back to Sewanee, I'd been living with our mother. She was somewhat famous as an innovative quilter and quilting teacher, but she was infamous for her awful vegan cooking. The only good thing I could say about it was that over the last few weeks I'd lost seven pounds.

"Don't forget the tofu. Boiled. Pickled." I let the aroma of the warm bread guide my hand to the basket and briefly reveled in a vision of throwing it at him. Instead I borrowed Gibb's knife sitting on the edge of his plate. I was jealous. Since he had his own home, my brother could eat anything, anytime he wanted, without Mom complaining that he was ruining his health.

"What did you have, Gibb?" I asked, looking at his plate which had practically been licked clean.

"The special. Chicken fried steak, mashed potatoes, white gravy on both," he replied.

I moaned just as JoAnn came up and slapped a paper place mat and silverware in front of me. I told her I'd have the special also. The woman, a legend in the county, was absolutely the best cook in Tennessee. Maybe the whole South. Lately I'd been sneaking over from work after her morning breakfast rush for a couple of biscuits with apple butter spooned thick onto the split halves. Since Mom had recently declared her house a gluten-free zone, I felt desperate.

"Extra bread, hon?" JoAnn asked, knowing me well.

I nodded and she headed back to her kitchen domain. I watched her slim figure retreat with a bit of envy. Who could cook that well and not gain a pound a day? I glanced back at Gibb to see him smiling because I hadn't been able to resist JoAnn's offer.

Although he and I had grown up with the usual little brother versus big sister spats, we were actually close and I respected the man he had become. He'd been a sheriff's deputy of Sewanee for the last eleven years. It was the career he had wanted since age four. I knew he worked hard, but he was also a fun-loving bachelor.

"Are you guys here plotting something?" I asked, thinking I was making a joke until I noticed Gibb's face brighten as only a redhead's could. Much to my delight growing up, he had never been particularly good at lying, and for a second I thought about badgering him to find out what the two of them were up to. Being three years older, I had always been able to bully my brother into revealing secrets, but I realized I'd do better to wait until I had Gibb alone. Then I could really turn up the heat when he didn't have Lam to turn to.

Lam jerked forward in his seat and asked, "How's the clean-up going? That building hasn't been occupied for close to twenty years."

"Remember, it was a shoe store when we were kids," I said. "When I first got started cleaning, I found about thirty pairs of sneakers in the broom closet and took them over to Goodwill. I guess the ol' log place has been about everything at one time or another."

"When Ennie Pickens died, his widow told the townsfolk to go in and help themselves and then afterward she locked the door. Didn't need the money and didn't want the bother," Gibb said.

"I'd forgotten that." Lam finished the last swallow from his glass. "But I know Lona Pickens died last year and that's when the For Lease or Sale sign went up in the window."

"Their daughter put it up. She's somewhere down in Florida now," Gibb said.

"It's amazing how dirty and rundown the inside is, I mean was. The first weeks of work were basic scrubbing, things like window washing and using a broom to get the dust off of the log walls, but I'm getting it into shape." I tried to inject a positive note into my voice before taking another bite of bread.

"Of course you will." Lam flashed a smile.

Gibb asked. "How's that no-good Donnie working out?"

"Well, he's lazy and slow and loves bad practical jokes and stupid riddles. Actually," I frowned, "he's not a very handy handyman. This morning he just about electrocuted himself trying to figure out why a light fixture doesn't work." I tore open a sugar packet, which I poured into my coffee along with two creamers. "So, overall, just great," I added, not being able to suppress my laughter.

"Just don't let him rob you blind," Gibb said. "Make sure you nail down anything you want to keep."

"I know. I know. You and half the town have already warned me that he's not the straightest arrow in town," I said.

Gibb stood and pulled on a jacket over his uniform and, by habit, made sure it didn't cover the gun holstered on his hip. Next, he picked up his hat from the extra chair pushed up to the table. "Let me know if you have any trouble with him. Maybe he's smart enough not to cheat the sheriff's sister."

He bent and gave me a peck on the cheek but then made a move so typical of him, mussing my hair. I swatted his hand.

"Git," I said, finger-combing my shoulder-length brown hair.

"See you tomorrow, buddy," Gibb said to Lam as he walked away.

"So what were you guys scheming about? I know when Gibb turns the color of a fire engine you two are up to something someone will regret." Right then JoAnn set a heavy plate in front of me, handling it with a folded dish towel to protect her hand from the heat. I leaned over and breathed in the wonderful aroma.

"Do you know what that gravy does to your arteries?" Lam asked after the cook was out of ear-shot.

"You sound like Mom."

"I'm not that far gone done the path of nutrition, but I'd have to run an extra two miles today to burn it off and I'm way too lazy."

Not wanting to think about exercise, which I wasn't getting except for cleaning, I pointed at the bread basket JoAnn had replenished. Lam picked up a roll and buttered it for me.

I said, "No, really. I want to know what you and Gibb are up to." I cut off a tender piece of the breaded steak and pushed it through the gravy to get it good and coated before popping the bite into my mouth. "Oh, Lordy, JoAnn is just the best cook."

Instead of answering my question, Lam countered with one of his own. "Why'd you rent that building? It's so much older than some of the others available. The old lawyer's building is only half a block down and it's just a few years old. Been empty since Mr. Moree realized he couldn't make a living here. Mountain men tend to settle their problems out of court with shotguns."

I know I frowned because Lam had sidestepped my question, but then I decided to give up. I was just too happy with this plate in front of me to spoil the moment. The thing about Lam was that he was always so nice, but he definitely had a mind of his own. If the boys were up to something, he wasn't going to be the one to spill the beans.

"My gosh, Lam. It's a log cabin and it was built in the late 1800s! One of the first buildings put up by settlers in the area. That's perfect for the Heritage Craft Center. Building with logs is one of Tennessee's most famous crafts."

"You're right. I didn't think about it like that. It's good to see you excited about this job."

"Oh, I am. If I can just get past this probation."

"What can happen? I mean, you're smart and hard-working. Of course they'll want you on a permanent status."

"No, don't say that. You'll jinx me. You should have seen me earlier—" I clamped my lips together. No use playing up my bad points with my boyfriend by tattling on myself. I mean, who gets trapped in her own office? I pushed my plate back, having devoured the meat and potatoes but leaving most of the string beans uneaten. I got more than my share of vegetables at home and now hated the color green.

Right then JoAnn hurried past with a tray of desserts for a table of four near us. I couldn't tear my gaze from the apple pie that I knew was made with her blue-ribbon-winning recipe.

"I wish you'd look at me like that," Lam said with a wistful sigh.

"Oh, I do. I just wait until your back is turned so you don't get a big head."

I didn't want to upset Lam, but if anything, I was more confused than I'd been weeks ago when he asked me out for our first real date. I'd had an incredible time when he'd taken me dancing at our local dance and beer joint called the Honky Tonk. Lam knew everyone in Sewanee and beyond, including the band members. Throughout the evening he'd requested they play all my favorites, and we'd danced until I'd gotten a stitch in my side. When we weren't dancing, we'd talked to dozens of my old friends whom I'd missed terribly while living in Nashville. It turned out that Lam had put the word out that we'd be there so everyone would come. It was quite a party.

For the life of me I couldn't remember why I'd been so anxious at eighteen to get away from home. I had chosen Ohio State for college and then the big city for a career. Now, being back on the mountain with my family outweighed all the excitement.

Lam grinned. "Me? A big head."

"Yes, you are the county's resident ladies man."

"Nope. I've turned over a new leaf," he said, the joking tone leaving his voice. "You know that, don't you, Stella?"

I felt my mouth open and close, but my brain couldn't quite decide what to say, and then the moment swept away with the opening of the door of the café. Mom stepped over the threshold with Harley Morgan following close behind. His hand rested on her back like the gentleman he was as he held the door for her.

"What the heck?" I said. My mother would never eat at JoAnn's Café where every entrée featured meat.

When I looked at Lam, I could see him arrange a smile on his face. "Wow, the earth just tilted." He stood and motioned for Mom and Harley to join us. So far he had been civil with his rival.

"Cele, come and sit with us." Lam tugged a chair out for my mother. "I don't think I've, uh, ever seen you here in JoAnn's before. Hello, Harley."

My head spun as I watched Mom take the seat after slipping off her coat. She looked from side to side, obviously taking in the room. I could even see her sniff the wonderful aromas of good home cooking, but then she turned her nose up and I saw the moment her gaze settled on the green beans left on my plate. At that same instant JoAnn, who was well aware of my mother's opinion of her cooking, came through the door from the kitchen. The woman saw my mother, and in her shock at seeing Cele in her establishment, dropped a full tray of food onto the floor.

CHAPTER 3

The next morning I climbed into my new-old Jeep, settling onto a seat that felt like a block of ice aiming to freeze my butt. Knowing my former car couldn't handle the mountain's winter weather, I'd traded it for a four-wheel drive that had high mileage but which Lam assured me had been well-maintained. The previous owner, a top mechanic, worked in Lam's big truck repair shop, so he ought to know how to keep an engine running smoothly. The vehicle would be just the ticket when Sewanee had its signature heavy snows, or even worse, the beautiful but treacherous ice storms. It had been sweet of Lam to make sure I'd gotten a fair deal.

A heavy layer of frost etched interesting patterns on the windshield so beautiful that I almost hated to erase them with the defroster. With the top of the plateau reaching an elevation almost twice as high as Nashville's paltry eleven hundred feet, the winter weather always struck harder and faster. It was only early November, but snow could come anytime.

With a shiver, I turned the key and then cranked the heater to high while making a mental note to order some kind of Sherpa-style seat cover. Sipping from my Thermos coffee cup while I waited until I could see to drive, I thought about the events of yesterday that had been puzzling me. My evening had been spent mulling over the scene at the café while I was supposed to be recording receipts into a spreadsheet.

I had to wonder what Lam and Gibb were up to. When that pair, closer than brothers, put their minds to some scheme, they were a force to be frightened of. I remembered the week I had spent with my face dyed blue, the time they convinced me that Loretta Lynn was coming to my ninth grade talent show—I'd worn my favorite Grand Ole Opry dress to school and sung my heart out—and the time ... well, I shuddered. I wouldn't think about that one.

More importantly, what had brought Mom and Harley into the café together? Here was a woman who once vowed never to put a vegan toe across the threshold of what she called that palace of lard. When I'd asked the pair, Mom and Harley, what they were doing, the hemming and hawing rang a bit too loud and ran too long for me to believe they were telling the truth. Most people would ask what's the big deal? So what if mom and Harley met up for a coffee? I knew Mom too well though. She liked Harley plenty and could have coffee with him all she wanted as far as I was concerned, but she'd never pick JoAnn's Café to do that. Harley said they just met up on the sidewalk, and he'd asked her to step in and join him. Cele—short for Celestial—Hill would have stood outside facing down a tornado before she would have come through that door. She believed JoAnn's cooking could clog arteries with a single bite of chicken and dumplings.

What had Harley told Mom he wanted to talk about that could get her to go into the restaurant?

After Mom and I had gotten home, she'd refused to confess, saying she had to finish a quilt. It needed to be mailed tomorrow to a magazine for a feature article. When I'd slipped into bed last night, I could still hear the clack of her antique treadle sewing machine from the studio located in the attic of the old family log cabin. I happened to know that she'd finished hand sewing the binding onto that particular quilt yesterday. The box with the quilt already sealed inside sat on the dining room table ready for its trip to the post office.

So what was the secret?

It wasn't my birthday any time soon so Harley wasn't getting gift ideas from Mom. In fact it wasn't anyone's birthday any time soon. Well, I didn't know Harley's birth date, did I? I'd have to find out and it seemed odd to realize I could Google the man's name. A search would probably bring up dozens, maybe hundreds, of hits. I'd never dated anyone famous before, if you called former trial lawyers famous. He'd taken an early retirement just a few months ago and left all the glamour behind him.

Such flimsy evidence wouldn't raise most people's suspicions, but I knew my family. What I needed was more information, and I planned to be on the lookout for clues.

The windshield cleared, and I drove the Jeep toward work. In only a few miles the first businesses dotted the sides of the road breaking the vista of forest. Lam's garage, Plateau Towing and Repair, was one of them. I liked that it gleamed neat and clean as any restaurant, maybe more so than some. Not far from the garage was the old Baptist Church with the new one still under construction right beside it. I'd almost been killed there. The memory sent a shiver through my body, and I concentrated on the road to distract myself.

I continued on Route 41 and soon drove into the proper downtown of Sewanee, although, if I had kept driving, the little town would have disappeared in only four blocks. Locals always told tourists not to blink.

When I reached the Center, I turned into a narrow alley between the log building and the jewelry store next door. It led to a small cleared area in back that I'd started using as a parking lot for employees and delivery trucks. I couldn't keep feeding the parking meters out front all day, or I'd soon go broke. In fact, I planned to lobby the town council to allow me to enlarge the graveled area and make an official parking lot for customers and tourists.

As I steered around the corner, I got a surprise. Donnie's battered old van sat parked near the back door. I glanced at the Jeep's dash, showing that the time was only 7:30 because I'd gotten an early start this morning. That seemed even odder, since I had not given Donnie a key to the building. I'd been afraid to. He couldn't start work until I arrived and let him in.

Gathering my things, I slipped off the driver's seat and slammed the door shut with my hip. That's when I noticed that something was sticking out of the open back doors of the van. A glint from the pale morning sunlight gave the impression of copper pipes. As soon as I took a few steps forward on the frozen ground, I could see what was wrong. Rain gutters, twisted, battered, and badly bent, poked out over the bumper. The whole lot had been shoved roughly into the cargo space of the van. I peeked inside, but the interior was too dark to make out details.

I knew Donnie's van hadn't been full of gutters yesterday. It seemed odd that it would be loaded now after he had planned to spend the evening with his brother. When had Donnie found time to fit in another job for someone else? I certainly hadn't authorized any work on the outside of this building.

A small, nagging alarm bell dinged in my head. Recently I'd heard that copper prices had skyrocketed, and items made from the metal were becoming a target for thieves. That meant copper electrical wiring and gutters, at least very old ones. Newer gutters were made of aluminum. I looked up to the edge of the roof to see that the gutters of the Heritage Craft Center had been ripped away. Only the brackets remained, torn and twisted.

"No," I wailed. This couldn't be happening. Donnie was actually stealing the copper off the building right from under my nose or rather from over my head. Why, I'd ...

I'd been about to finish that thought with the usual promise to kill him when I realized that Donnie had to be around here somewhere. Suddenly, I wasn't nearly as interested in confronting him, and a shiver ran up my spine. Although I'd been here at least five minutes, I hadn't seen him. Shouldn't he have seen me? If he was in the van, he hadn't gotten out to tell some lie. He hadn't started the vehicle and raced away, never to be seen again. Was he even in the van? Donnie would be expecting me to arrive by eight, and surely he planned to be long gone by then since he was stealing from me.

I saw that a piece of blue denim clothing and the van's seat belt had been caught in the driver's door when it shut. The fabric looked like the bottom edge of a coat. I realized that I'd been creeping backward while I'd been thinking. It took effort, but I forced my feet forward while I gulped in a mouthful of the cold air. I breathed it out slowly through my nose to keep myself from hyperventilating and maybe even fainting.

Now I could see a man's shoulder. No movement. Then his profile came into view. I knew Donnie wasn't going to move, and he wasn't going to hurt me. He was dead.

Hot coffee splashed my ankle and painted my shoe. The tote bag also slipped from my hands, landing upside down and spilling the contents. The thing I needed most right now—my cell phone—bounced under the van. I dropped to my knees and snatched the phone up, and then with feet scrambling like a cartoon character, I hurried to stand at the backdoor to the building. My back pressed hard against the screen of the screened door, stretching it taut. Inside it would be warm, but my keys now lay near the front tire of the van. I'd just have to be cold because I wasn't going near the body again.

"Ninny," I hissed at myself, feeling a surge of anger at my behavior, but I'd never seen a dead body like this before. When a man had been killed in Mom's house weeks ago, the crime scene had been scrubbed clean by the time I'd arrived home. All the corpses I'd seen had been neatly dressed in their Sunday best with their hair combed. Donnie looked the worst I'd ever seen him, which was saying a lot. His face, slack and, well, dead white, was wiped free of expression. His ever-present hat was nowhere to be seen, and the fringe of dark brown hair stood out thin and wispy, making him look older than the thirty-three years he had been in life. And those sightless eyes!

One thought scrolled through my mind over and over, I needed to call the sheriff. Must call the sheriff. But I couldn't remember the phone number of the police station. Gibb's personal cell number was stored in my phone, and I giggled when I finally reasoned through my shock that Gibb was the sheriff regardless of which number I punched in to reach him.

The numbers on the keypad seemed to jump around like pinto beans in a pot and I fumbled the task three times before getting it right. As the ringing echoed in my head, I couldn't keep my gaze from returning again and again to the still figure behind the steering wheel. Sorrow that I hadn't liked or even trusted the man swept over me, leaving me with strong feelings of guilt.

I wanted to shout to the world that Donnie wasn't likable. I wasn't the only one who had felt that way and certainly not the only one who hadn't trusted the man, but I still felt the need to redeem my mean words of yesterday.

Gibb's voice from the phone shocked me from my guilty reverie. "What's up, Sis?"

"Dead. Oh, Lord, Gibb! I didn't know before what they meant by sightless eyes. I mean they're open and at the funeral home, you know the viewings, their eyes are always closed so we can pretend they're just sleeping. I mean, the dead aren't going to wake up. That's crazy."

"Stella, speaking of crazy, what are you babbling about? You sound upset."

Gibb's tone was calming. I knew then that I was speaking the first thoughts to come into my mind. I had to get a grip and settle my spinning thoughts.

"Okay." I pulled a deep breath in. "Donnie's dead."

"What? A car accident?" Gibb asked.

"No. Was there a car accident?" I immediately began to worry about Mom, Lam, and Harley. Had someone I cared about been hurt?

"I'm asking you. Was Donnie in a car accident?"

"How would I know?" How could the man have been killed in a car accident with the van sitting here? Who knew it could be so difficult to report a murder? Exasperation made my next words more sharp than intended. "You're the sheriff."

"Stella, how did Donnie die?"

"Oh, I understand. He was murdered."

Suddenly Gibb was all business. "Where are you and are you safe?"

"I, I guess." I hadn't even let myself think about the blood I'd seen on my handyman's chest. The back of my neck prickled, and it seemed like murderers were now everywhere: in the Center peeking out the window, crouched against the van, maybe hidden behind a tree. "I'm at work. Out back. Hurry, Gibb."

There was no answer. I knew my brother would be here in minutes.

CHAPTER 4

"So tell me again, Ms. Hill."

Gibb's newest deputy, Melissa Mann, led me another few steps away from the van. She was trying to position me so I could no longer watch what was happening with the investigation. She'd noticed that I couldn't tear my gaze from the crime scene where Gibb and the coroner were talking quietly while taking turns leaning into the front compartment of the van. Neither of them had yet to move or touch the body as far as I could see, except the doctor had placed two fingers on Donnie's neck, just in case life remained. Gibb had used his ink pen to gingerly shift the clothing. Police work required too much patience.

I knew the new deputy was just doing her job, but she gripped my shoulder tighter than I thought necessary and I felt myself stiffen and resist. I didn't care for how she towered over me either. The woman looked to be at least six feet tall and reminded me of the stories of Amazon women warriors, but she would also look right at home on the stage of any beauty pageant. What bothered me the most was how unfriendly she seemed. Maybe it was just the northern accent throwing me off.

"Ms. Hill, please go over your story again."

"It's not a story."

"I'm sorry. I'm not passing judgement. Just tell me again what happened exactly as you remember it. You might think of something that will help us find the murderer."

"But the whole thing only took maybe five minutes. I drove up and parked behind Donnie's van, and I was surprised."

"What was it that surprised you?"

"Well, he was on time, early even for once, and Donnie was a pretty bad employee." My words burst out more sharply than I'd intended, and I cringed when Deputy Mann's eyes narrowed. In fact, it seemed she had a permanent disapproving look on her features that included a scowl on her lips and a deep wrinkle between her eyebrows which could use a tweezing. This event reminded me that my family had been through a harrowing experience with last month's murder of one of Mom's neighbors. I didn't want to relive that by being accused of killing my handyman. For a second I wondered if I should demand a lawyer.

Just about as upsetting was the knowledge that I would need to call my boss yet again today. Worry nagged in the back of my mind with the thought. Yesterday, after fortifying myself with lunch at JoAnn's, I'd finally spoken to Janice and explained why I hadn't been there to keep my appointment with her. I told the truth even though I'd longed to invent an excuse that sounded normal, something like a flat tire. Now I would have to tell her that the handyman I'd hired had robbed the Center of its copper gutters and managed to get himself killed. Not just that. I'd have to ask for more money so that the damage could be repaired. Janice had told me several times during my initial interview that she needed a director who could pinch pennies. It looked like I wasn't measuring up.

I said, "That's when I noticed that he'd stolen the gutters right off the building."

"And you're sure that it was this Donnie Clark who did that?"

"Who else?" Again my words sounded too emotional to my own ears. "Uh, I saw right away the ruined gutters were stacked in the back of the van. You can see where he ripped them off the roof. They were there yesterday. I think."

"Right." She continued to write in a small notebook, the pen tip scratching against the paper.

"I mean, it had to be Donnie," I said, using my words as an excuse to turn around and see if anything was going on yet. I pointed upward toward the roof but only for her benefit. I used the motion to steal a glance at the van and nothing was happening. I couldn't stand it any longer.

"Look. I have to go to the restroom. I'll be right back." I stalked across the grass to where I knew my keys to the Center lay in the gravel by the van. I could ask Gibb what the coroner had said while I retrieved them. I wanted to know how Donnie had died. It should be easy, but I could hear the deputy following me, the over-grown grass swooshing with her steps.

As I approached, Gibb turned from his conversation with the doctor. "Sis, I need you out of the way," he said.

"I just need my keys." I pointed to them on the ground and then tried to pantomime that I wanted information. Deputy Mann hurried up behind me, interrupting my efforts.

"I'm sorry, Sir," she said.

She tried to take my arm, but I shook the grasp off. I put on my most authoritative older sister voice. "Gibb, I have to pee."

My brother blushed. "The keys are evidence right now. Look, just go over to the café and then get back here quick. Don't talk to anyone."

Deputy Mann placed her hand on the butt of the gun in its large leather holster. "You want me to escort her, Sir."

I shot him a look that swore revenge. He'd better not embarrass me like that.

"Uh, no. I think I can trust her." My brother's gaze swung back to me. "I mean it. Don't even think about saying a word about this." He pointed his finger at me. "No one."

I twisted on my heel, trying to project some dignity as I hurried on my mission to the restroom. Surely my brother wouldn't mind if I grabbed a coffee on my way out. JoAnn knew I was good to pay her later and would Gibb notice, I wondered, if I grabbed a ham biscuit? All this worrying had made me hungry.

As I rounded the corner, I ran smack into someone and bounced off a protruding belly. I hadn't seen a face, as I had been deep in thought about breakfast with my head bowed to a cold breeze. I landed on the frozen ground on my back, knocking the breath out of my lungs. It took a second, but my eyes focused on the person I'd run into. My view started with the dirty, scuffed cowboy boots that I'd seen Donnie wear every day for the last ten days. The denim overalls came next, again just like I'd seen my handyman wearing to work. Then I saw Donnie's face almost six feet above me, an expression of concern on his features.

"Sorry. You okay, Miss Stella?" He stuck his hand down toward me in an offer to help me stand.

My scream hung in the air.

Deputy Mann reached me first, but Gibb skidded around the corner a close second. I watched my brother take a staggering step backward when he saw the same face as on the murdered man. Well, this one had more color.

It wasn't until Gibb spoke to a woman standing beside this man who looked like Donnie that I realized anyone else was there. My gaze had been locked on the face that only a few minutes ago I'd seen dead.

"Mrs. Clark." Gibb's voice broke. "What brings you here? I was just fixing to visit."

"Well, what the heck do you think brings me here, Sheriff?" The woman shoved past the man who looked like Donnie until she stood close enough to poke Gibb in the chest with her finger. "I was trying to eat my breakfast in peace when the police scanner went crazy. Your Deputy Mullins ordered a hearse for my husband. Are you crazy? Any idiot can see Donnie is right here bigger than life." She slapped the man's beer belly without even looking at him. He flinched.

Thin, but just average height, she had a way of scowling that turned a somewhat pretty face into one you didn't want to focus on. Her hair was cut short and worn spiked. It definitely matched her prickly personality.

I'd met Mrs. Clark last week when she'd shown up at the Center wanting grocery money from her husband. Donnie and she had stood toe-to-toe arguing for a few minutes until he'd given her half of the amount she had asked for. His wife had departed in a huff, ignoring me all the while. If I hadn't been on a ladder holding a shelf bracket in place for Donnie to do the nailing, I'd have high-tailed it out of the room.

Gibb knelt down and helped me to my feet, as he could see that this doppelganger's outstretched hand had freaked me out completely. Now the morning's cold temperatures plus the fright had started a shiver that shook my whole body. I stepped back and eased behind my brother.

Then it dawned on me that this man had to be Donnie's brother Ronnie just released from prison. Donnie never once mentioned that they were identical twins, but hadn't Mrs. Clark said this was Donnie? Somehow I couldn't shake the thought that Donnie was dead in his van just feet away from where we were standing.

"You're, are you, um, I mean, you're Ronnie?" I wasn't sure if I was asking a question or making a statement.

"Is your sister a dolt?" Donnie's wife asked Gibb.

I already knew that Mrs. Clark was difficult to deal with. So far she'd called my brother crazy and thought me stupid.

"This here is my husband." She shook Donnie's arm. "He ain't been outta my sight since he got home from working for you yesterday, Stella. It was four o'clock. I know exactly 'cause he was early and woke me from a nap. I'd worked the early shift and was dead on my feet."

"So, Donnie, we have a body around back," Gibb said.

Donnie gulped, and the color drained from his face.

"Could you take a look and tell me if it's your brother? And I'm going to need to talk to you both down at the station."

Mrs. Clark laughed one short hoot. "Does this body happen to look just like Donnie?"

Gibb blushed, the blood instantly rushing under the skin. "You wait here." He pointed at her but then had to tug on Donnie's arm to get him to step forward.

CHAPTER 5

"You want another slice, hon?" JoAnn asked. "Never thought I'd discourage a customer, but maybe two slices is enough." The cook tucked her tray under her arm and patted me on the shoulder.

It took a second, but her words sank into my addled brain, where for the last few hours nothing had made a lick of sense. I glanced at the fork in my hand and the empty plate in front of me.

"I ate two pieces of apple pie? JoAnn, please tell me I didn't. I don't even remember."

"You said something is bothering you, but that you can't talk about it."

"No, it's hush-hush for the time being."

"I just figured you was upset about Ronnie Clark getting himself murdered behind your craft center."

"Uh. How'd you know?"

"I've heard it from every customer that's been in today."

"JoAnn, did you know Ronnie and Donnie back before the bank robbery?"

The cook slipped into the seat across from me and massaged first one calf and then the other with a work-reddened hand. "No, never met any of that clan. I've just known of Donnie since he sometimes works up here. You know, don't you, they live only halfway up the mountain? Those people tend to drive down for jobs and groceries."

Her words implied that everyone who didn't live on top of Sewanee Mountain was doomed to desperation and dandruff.

I nodded absentmindedly. That was what I'd thought. If I wanted to know more about my handyman, I'd have to ask others, but finding out who'd killed Ronnie was Gibb's job. I had way too much work to do in the remaining two weeks before my grand opening. All I wanted from life right now was to do well as Director of the Heritage Craft Center. I needed that permanent employment status more than I wanted, well, apple pie. I pushed the plate all the way across the table, feeling my stomach churning from too much sugar.

She glanced past me to the door. "Sheriff just walked in. He's going to need some coffee." JoAnn trotted over to a beautiful old sideboard where she keep essentials like coffee and ketchup close at hand and returned with a thermal pot before Gibb could sit down.

"Thanks," he said and blew across the steaming cup she'd poured. Once JoAnn was out of earshot, he said, "Boy that Mrs. Clark is one tough character. She didn't shed a single tear over her brother-in-law."

"Did Donnie? I mean, did he seem sorry to lose his brother?"

Gibb shifted in his seat. "Cried like a baby two or three times. At one point I thought he was going to break down completely. Sis, I need you to come in and make a statement."

"You don't think I did it, do you?" I said with my voice a squeak. "I don't even know how Donnie, uh, Ronnie was killed."

"He was shot and, no, I don't think you did it."

I sighed and felt tense muscles relax that I hadn't even realized were stiff with fear. Of course, my very own brother didn't believe I could kill anyone.

"Doc puts time of death at between seven and midnight yesterday evening. Mom says you were at the house that whole time."

"You already checked my alibi? That feels like a slap in the face."

Gibb slipped down into the chair so that he more reminded me of when he was a teenager. For the most part my little brother had been an easygoing kid. The only rough patch had been when he was seventeen and he'd fallen hard for the local bad girl. Running with her crowd meant late nights, drinking, and pot smoking. Mom never said a word, but when he had been picked up by the sheriff at that time, she had left Gibb at the jail for over a day to, as she said, reflect. It was years before Gibb learned she'd talked old Sheriff Linder into not actually arresting her boy so he wouldn't have a record. The image of him dragging his sorry self home that day, totally ashamed, flashed in my mind.

I leaned forward and patted him on the arm. "I'm sorry. I understand." After Gibb gave me a wavering smile, I asked, "Any idea why Ronnie would be in Donnie's van behind the Center? I wasn't surprised when I thought Donnie was robbing me, but Ronnie Clark? How did he even know I had copper gutters?"

"I'd thought of that. Mrs. Clark says they all spent a pleasant evening catching up and Donnie talked a lot about his business and what he was doing for you. He told his twin about the old log building. He—Donnie—kept saying Ronnie really pumped him for info and then he suggested the two of them go get the copper. Said it would be his seed money to get going again. The missus says Ronnie threatened them when Donnie refused to go along, but then he said he was just kidding about the whole thing."

"Not much of a joke."

"She says they all went to bed ... well, they offered the couch to Ronnie. When the couple got up this morning, Ronnie and the work van were gone."

"What did they think?"

"Mrs. Clark said they thought he'd stolen the van and skedaddled. Didn't expect to see him again." Gibb reached over and removed the fork from my hand. "You're clutching that utensil like it's your lifeline."

I leaned forward and lowered my voice. "Uh, don't tell Mom, but I ate two pieces of pie."

"Your secret is safe with me, Sis."

Still keeping my voice low, I asked, "Any theories?"

Gibb leaned forward as if he were going to share a secret. "No, and stay out of it. Come by for that statement any time today, okay?" His chair scrapped against the wooden floor as he stood.

I only nodded. "My keys?"

"Sorry. Here you go and thanks for the coffee." Gibb dropped the ring on the table before leaving.

I pulled them toward me and fiddled with the quilt charm on the ring as I thought about what to do next. The charm, a brass Sunbonnet Sue block with the dress and hat colored in blues and yellows, reminded me that I had recently subscribed to an online quilting instructional show where I could learn on my laptop from experts. Of course, I had my own resident expert at home, but Mom had never been too interested in appliqué, and I was dying to learn.

My lips turned down in a frown at the thought of that word. Dying. Dead. Somehow I couldn't get it out of my mind that it was Donnie who was gone and not his brother. I obviously wasn't thinking rationally yet after my fright, and going back to the Center to work didn't sound too appealing right now. I'd go to the library and use one of the free computers there. The internet for the Center hadn't been installed anyway, and I wanted to submit a grant application for some federal money. In my previous career I'd written grant proposals for a large university. With my years of experience I could complete this task in my sleep, and just the possibility of recouping some of my lost budget money made me cheerful again.

In fifteen minutes I stood outside the door of the library, peeking through the glass and hoping to find the librarian away from the front desk. Alma Fleck had been a fixture at the Sewanee Library for almost fifty years. The minuscule woman probably weighed in at under ninety pounds and only came up to my chin, but she terrified me, as well as every child and most of the adults in the county. She ruled her kingdom with an iron will and occasionally a fly swatter. Most maximum security prisons were more lax.

After finding the coast clear and dashing across the entry, I settled onto a hardback chair pulled up to one of the five cubicles holding ancient computers. I logged on and listened to the grinding noises emitting from the CPU which was as big as a suitcase. As I waited for the icons to appear on the desktop, I peered over the top of the partition erected to ensure privacy. I saw that Ms. Fleck had returned to her station, where I knew she stood on an old apple crate to be able to command over the tall checkout counter. Hoping she hadn't spied me, I ducked my head and scrunched down in my seat as I began typing.

A hand fell with a thump onto my shoulder, causing me to jump.

"Well, if it isn't Cele Hill's daughter. Has your mother gone to prison yet?"

I certainly didn't have to look around to identify who that croak belonged to.

"She's fine, Ms. Fleck, and you know that murder charge was all a mistake. My mother would never hurt anyone. Ummm, how are you?" As a Southern girl, I knew my manners.

She certainly looked the same as always. The woman probably owned a dozen jumpers, mostly in shades of green, tan, or brown. This time of the year the shapeless garment was layered over a sweater while summer saw a lighter-weight shirt. The shoes matched her face, being leathery and wrinkled from years of use.

"I'd be a lot better if I still had my assistant working for me. As you know, I had to fire Patty and just last week my budget got cut. Now I can't afford to hire a replacement. Those state weenies expect me to do the job of two people." Her words came with a huff of disgust.

"I understand exactly what you mean. My budget for the Heritage Craft Center is also too small for me to hire anyone."

"Since you understand, you can help me out for a few minutes." The librarian executed a perfect about-face and marched away without waiting to see if I was willing to assist her.

I glanced around the one-room library, hoping to find another able-bodied adult whom I could enlist in my place.

No one else looked capable. They were either too young or old, so I shuffled along as Ms. Fleck led me around to the magazine reading area. A couple of quilts lay folded across the back of a winged-back chair. The piece of furniture, covered in a faded and worn red fabric, had seen better days, probably when Lyndon Johnson was President. A small matching foot stool, even more threadbare and showing sprouts of stuffing, waited for the next patron.

"I had my neighbor come in this weekend and put more quilt hangers up on the walls, but he didn't stick around to hang the quilts. Trot on up that ladder." She snapped her fingers twice at me.

Ms. Fleck certainly didn't know I had acrophobia, and probably wouldn't care, but the ladder was only a six-footer. Surely I could handle this simple task.

I cleared my throat, climbed the first three steps, and stretched out toward the wooden rack screwed into the drywall next to a shelf holding the current issues of dozens of magazines. I found I would need to position the ladder closer before I'd be able to reach the quilt holder.

"I can't reach it," I said.

"Climb up a couple more steps." She swatted at my ankles.

"No. I'll be okay if I just move the ladder a bit closer," I said, backing down to the floor. I strained to drag the chair a few inches to the side to get it out of my way. Using my foot, I shoved the stool a foot or so. "Okay. That should do it."

I climbed the rungs again after adjusting the ladder and turned to have Ms. Fleck hand me the quilt, although she hardly looked strong enough to lift the few yards of fabric above her head. To say the woman was thin and frail was an understatement.

"No, first you need to take that bar down." Ms. Fleck pointed with an ancient finger. "It has to slip through the sleeve on the back of the quilt."

"Oh, right. I just hung two in my office, but they were a lot smaller. Guess there are different kinds of hangers." I lifted the wooden bar from the brackets. Designed to hold at least a twin-bed sized quilt, it was heavier than I'd expected. I balanced the five-foot bar across my forearms and climbed down the ladder again.

As I turned, Ms. Fleck shook out the first quilt, and I saw that it was one made by Mom. This quilt had once hung in the dining room of our family log cabin twenty years ago. Not only was she prolific in her craft, but sooner or later Mom gave away almost everything she made.

Anyone who knew Mom recognized that her quilts had become more and more modern through the years, and she had gone through many color palettes. With those two pieces of information, the quilts could be dated as if by a quilt-crafty anthropologist. Her first works in the seventies were reminders of those psychedelic days. Purple dominated. When I arrived, she briefly favored pink. Gibson's birth spurred a trend for bright primary colors. Then Mom, ahead of others, linked earth tones to the growing awareness of ecology and recycling. Recently she had fallen in love again with the vivid hues of batiks. To Cele Hill, all things in life intertwined.

"When did Mom give you this?" I asked. I sneaked a peek at the label on the back.

"At least six months ago. I'd meant to get it on display before."

I watched as the old woman traced one of the pieces of

fabric with a light touch. Her lips curved up at the corners, easing the deep frown lines around her mouth, and I'd swear, her eyes misted over. Even just that ghost of a smile made her look like a friendly old grandmother. Then as quickly as I thought I'd seen enjoyment on her features, she scowled.

"Quit standing there gawking. It's not an attractive quality, young woman," she said.

Ms. Fleck twisted the coverlet so the backing was facing us, and she held open the sleeve for me to insert the bar. It slid through smoothly, but now I held the full weight of the bar as well as the bulk of the quilt.

"Here, help me gather all the fabric, and we can put it over my shoulder so I won't step on it as I climb the ladder," I said.

Ms. Fleck grumbled but did as I asked. Being so short, though, she had trouble and mostly she just shoved the quilt at me. "You're too blasted tall," she said.

That wasn't something I'd ever heard before, being only five foot five inches tall. I squatted, and we soon had my burden arranged so that I felt I could climb the ladder again without being in too much danger of falling.

"That's good," I said, twisting to see the librarian. As I turned, I felt the right end of the wooden hanger hit the ladder. I swiveled to the opposite direction and felt the stick shove something else.

A shriek told me I'd found Ms. Fleck. I spun and saw her stumble back a step and then bang into the foot stool, which was no longer in its usual spot. She toppled over it, landing in a heap. Her piercing cry split the air.

"My leg! You've broken my leg!"

CHAPTER 6

"So you broke Alma's leg," Mom said.

She moved around her kitchen like a ballerina doing a carefully choreographed number for an audience of one. At the pantry she twirled and grabbed, without pausing, a home-canned jar of green beans and then transported it to the old soapstone countertop. The snap of the vacuum seal being broken and the sizzle of the greens hitting the hot cast iron frying pan made me rethink my ban on vegetables.

We'd already discussed my awful find this morning behind the Center and decided that the chief suspect in Ronnie's murder must be some criminal he'd met in prison. Maybe Ronnie had even invited this fellow inmate to Sewanee, telling him they would pull some job, but not knowing he was placing himself in danger. Maybe he'd outsmarted himself by bringing the murderer along to help shake down Donnie and Debbie.

"Hey, you daydreaming?" Mom broke into my thoughts as she walked over and kissed me on top of my head. "Did Alma really say you'd broken her leg instead of it being an accident?"

"Well, she certainly told everyone that I did it. She stopped just short of saying I pushed her on purpose."

I'd been sitting at the kitchen table holding one of Mom's cats in my lap. Sweet little Baby gave a soft meow of protest as I lifted him to the seat of one the chairs so I could help Mom. I pulled two glasses and stoneware dishes from a cabinet to set the table and then poured Mom and me each a glass of cold water from a jug kept in the refrigerator. The spring water came straight from an artesian well which Mom visited every week to refill her pottery jugs. She didn't believe in drinking soda. Said she didn't trust the bubbles. Caffeine in any form, like tea or coffee, never passed her lips.

"First, Ms. Fleck yelled her accusation loud enough for everybody in the library to hear, and that included Mr. Heath. So by now the whole county knows the librarian's version of what happened. Then the ambulance techs got an earful all the way to the hospital."

Mom spooned the now-hot green beans onto our plates. I knew she wouldn't say anything, but she was getting me back for wasting food at the café yesterday. She topped the servings with pine nuts and something that looked like a palmful of twigs. When Mom went to the oven to pull out the casserole, I picked as many of them off the top as I could and hid them in my pocket. I hadn't asked what the main course was, and when I caught a whiff, I was sure I didn't want to know. Maybe Mom should serve her cooking with a clothespin.

"So you rode with her in the ambulance. That was nice of you, sweetie."

"She insisted," I said, not able to tamp down the irritation in my voice. "Ms. Fleck certainly wasn't going to let me get away without complaining more. All the way to Manchester and the doctor couldn't get her to shut up either. I suggested he sedate her, but he refused."

"Well, I hope she didn't hear you say that."

"No, he'd asked me to go out into the hall with him. He thought I was her granddaughter and wanted to ask me if she was senile."

Mom giggled, and it made me smile for the first time during this whole horrible day. In seconds we were laughing so hard we both had to hug our sides.

"What's going on?" Gibb asked, having slipped in the back door without us hearing his arrival over the gales of laughter. Now out of uniform, he wore faded jeans and a sweater I knew Mom had knit for him. After he sniffed the aroma of supper, Gibb frowned but covered the expression with a question, "Stella, how can you laugh after the day you've had?"

"How can she not laugh?" Mom asked the rhetorical question as she moved to pull another plate from the cabinet. "Stella's had a tough day what with finding a body and dealing with Alma."

Gibb shivered. "I agree but, uh, no supper for me, Mom. I'm stuffed."

Mom shoved the stoneware back onto the stack with a sigh but didn't say anything.

"How's the investigation going?" I served a small helping of the casserole for myself and a large one for Mom. I was pretty sure I still had a half pack of peanut butter crackers hidden in my room. As I plopped the spoonful onto my plate, the bright reds and greens of diced peppers glowed between chunks of unappetizing grey that I'd come to know was tofu.

"Alma's not pressing charges, is she?" I asked, meaning it as a joke, but when Gibb didn't answer right away, I gave him a hard stare.

"No, but I wanted to let you know they've released her from the hospital." He took an apple from a bowl sitting at the center of the table and bit into it. He grinned around the large bite. "You're going to love this," he said with his mouth full. "She wouldn't stay overnight for observation like they wanted, and the doctor couldn't send her back to her house because she lives alone, so they took her to the Sewanee Nursing Home."

"Gibb, that's not funny," Mom said. "We should never revel in anyone's misfortune in life regardless of how unpleasant a person they are."

"I agree, and that's not what I'm smiling about. You raised me better," Gibb said.

I could tell from his smile that I wasn't going to like the next bit of news.

"The head nurse from the home called me right before I left work. She didn't know how to reach you, Sis. Didn't know you were living here with Mom. Seems Ms. Fleck expects you to come by and help her out bright and early tomorrow." He fished a piece of paper out of his pocket and unfolded it. "Here's a list of what she wants you to pick up from her house and bring to her tomorrow. Said the neighbor has a key."

I snatched the page from his hand so hard it ripped. "Well, the nerve. Who does she think she is? Does Ms. Fleck think I'm her servant?"

"Honey, who else would she ask? Alma doesn't exactly have any friends, and she lost her family so long ago." Mom took a delicate bite of her meal.

"Family? What family?" I asked. "I thought she was an old maid."

"It was in the mid-sixties, and nobody ever talks about it because it was so horrible. I'm barely old enough to remember. Her husband and two children died in a house fire. He, Bill I think was his name, tried to save the little twin girls.

The firemen found him only a few feet from the door with a child in each arm." Mom wiped at the corner of each eye. "Terrible tragedy."

"Did you know that, Gibb?" I carried my plate to the sink to hide what I knew must be a look of horror and shock on my face. I felt like the world's most insensitive fool.

"Yeah. One night the guys at the fire hall were rehashing some of the worst cases," Gibb said. "Not a job I'd want."

"Okay. Okay." I scraped my plate and rinsed it. "I'll get an early start tomorrow. Better grab a box to put everything in. Are there any empties in the basement, Mom?"

"Sure. Always," she said.

I was already on my way down the stairs.

In the morning I allowed extra time for the errand before my trip into work. Gibb had given me directions to Ms. Fleck's house, and I had no trouble finding it, but I was having trouble readjusting my image of the older woman. All these years I'd been terrified of her because she was downright mean. Like the time she'd embarrassed me by making me recite the Pledge of Allegiance to the library patrons. All by myself! As a shy child that was seared in my memory. Then there was the incident when she'd picked up Nate Thrower by his ear. Okay, I knew that had to be a false memory, but I never wrote in a library book again after that and I'm sure he didn't either. But now that I knew she had good reason to be so unhappy, I just felt plain sorry.

Her house turned out to be a tiny ranch in an area known as Bean Town. It lay just outside of Sewanee down Jump Off Road but still in the county. No one could remember anymore how the locale came by that name. Generally the families there were lower income but honest and hard-working. The few streets were unpaved but scraped and graveled often enough so as not to be rutted out by bad weather. There were no disabled cars up on jacks, no appliances on the porches. Most yards contained kids' toys but no trash. I parked in front of 507 Holler Road and blinked in surprise at how ordinary it seemed. Her place was neat but not distinctive. Maybe I'd been expecting the witch's house. After checking the address Gibb had given me once more to keep from making a mistake, I stepped out of the Jeep.

"You the lady coming for Alma's stuff?" A tired voice called across from the next house.

"Yes." I waved in case the woman hadn't heard as I veered across the grass toward her walkway. "I was worried about waking you coming by this early."

"With four little ones I never sleep," the woman said.

She looked as if she spoke the truth. I'd never seen bags so large under the eyes of someone that young before. Probably in her early thirties, if I had to guess.

"Sorry you had to make the trip," she said. "I'd have taken her things over to her, but we have one car barely limping along right now."

"No, it's okay." I took the key which she held out. "What's Alma like as a neighbor?" I felt nosy asking but was too curious to pass up the chance for some information.

"Oh, not bad like you might expect. At first, when we rented this place, I figured she'd complain about the kids screaming when they play outside, but she never has. Brought me a pie once." The young woman looked down when a child tugged her hand.

"Mommy, Charlie's eating the cat's food again."

She rolled her eyes at me and let her shoulders rise and fall. "It's never hurt him before but I'd …" She started to back away.

"No problem. Thanks for your help. Really."

I crossed back to Alma's house and made quick work of finding the items on her list. I hunted down cough drops, lip balm, a heavy lavender robe, socks, and house shoes. There were other items, and as I worked, I found myself trying not to look around at the details of this woman's life. I didn't want to see pictures of the lost family. I was afraid a photo would haunt my dreams as they must Alma's.

I tossed the box, full but not heavy, onto the back seat of the Jeep. Being only a short drive, I knew I could drop her things off at the nursing home and still get to work by eight. I needed to because Donnie had called yesterday evening to tell me he wanted to come to work today. I needed to let him in, and unfortunately, I also had to call my boss with this latest news first thing. I worried that Janice might see the story of the murder in a newspaper this morning before I could call and explain.

Slipping through the front door of Sewanee Nursing Home behind a nurse arriving for her shift, I juggled the box so that I could check the time on my phone. Ten minutes. No problem.

A worker at the front desk directed me down Hall B. I made my way past mop buckets and carts holding medicines and fruit juice boxes. If I'd had a free hand, I would have been tempted to hold my nose.

Nursing homes, I thought, *all smell the same, sickly and dispirited.* I saw the room door hung open, but I rapped my knuckles softly on the panel anyway.

"Ms. Fleck?"

There were two hospital-style beds with only one occupied by a figure with her face turned away from me and the cover pulled up over the ears. Only thin tufts of gray hair showed above the badly pilled blanket.

"Ms. Fleck? It's me, Stella. I'll just leave your things on the chair here." I'd spoken too softly for anyone to hear me, hoping I could be out before I was discovered.

I tiptoed to the chair arranged between the beds for visitors. As I lowered the box, a voice boomed behind me, causing me to clutch my heart.

"Grab my other list before you go—it's on the nightstand—and I need you to move my bed closer to the window. How's a person supposed to live without some sunshine? Can't get the nurses to do a blasted thing for me," Alma said loud enough to wake the dead, but evidently not her roommate, who continued to snore quietly.

I turned to find Alma staring up at me from a wheelchair. I winced. Her bird-like figure seemed shrunken and dwarfed by the large cast boot on her lower leg which was propped straight out.

"List? But I got everything you asked for." I jabbed a finger to indicate the box.

"Stella, don't whine. It's not ladylike." She twisted the chair in an arc like an old pro. "Push the head of the bed about a foot toward the window. You'll have to move the dresser first, and then scoot that little table along too. I need it to stack books on. That's what the second list is. You can run to the library and check them out on your lunch break, right? I have to have something to read."

CHAPTER 7

Donnie rushed toward me. "Let me carry that, Miss Stella. It's too heavy for you." He took the weight of the box from me like it was no more than an empty carton although it was quite heavy. UPS had just dropped off five hundred tourist brochures that I would leave at other businesses around the area for advertising.

"Thanks. Just set it in the corner. I won't have time to take them around for a while." I followed behind him, feeling a twinge of guilt that the handyman had come to work after losing his brother only yesterday. At eight o'clock on the dot a car had stopped in front of the building. From the window I saw Mrs. Clark driving and at the same time pointing a wagging finger at Donnie. The man spilled out of the passenger door looking for all the world like he couldn't get away fast enough.

I'd assumed he would take a few days off, and I'd even thought about hiring someone else, although I didn't know where I'd find the money in the budget. The other local contractors, when I'd first explored my options, all charged far more for their services than Donnie. My mind just kept buzzing with the reminder that I only had two weeks left to get this place cleaned and repaired and put display shelves and cases in place. Those were on order and would arrive on a freight truck shortly.

Then there were the dozens of craft items in boxes in a rented storage area just off the mountain. Those crafts were being provided by the State Office of Tourism, and I hadn't even seen them yet. Janice had told me they'd been donated by the other four Heritage Craft Centers across the state and were just to get me started. That worried me, as they were probably things in bad shape or less interesting to tourists. To finish filling the showroom, I was expected to go out and find antique and modern crafts indigenous to our Cumberland Plateau region. Some money was budgeted to buy items, but mostly I needed to be able to convince the owners to give or loan things to the Center for my displays.

Donnie interrupted my thoughts with a question. "I finished painting the back storage room. You want me to start on this room?"

My mouth fell open. "You're done? How'd you finish so quickly?"

The handyman paused as if he had to think hard about how to answer the question. "The paint isn't too good a quality, but I rolled it thick and did two coats. Guess I just kept at it steady. Now I should be able to get this room done in, say, three days." He sized up the room with a glance. "Bigger."

I felt like I needed to shake the water out of my ears. Just last week Donnie had told me this room, the large front room where the displays and crafts for sale would be, should take him a full week. I'd scheduled the delivery of display cases and more shelving accordingly. My heart surged with the thought that I could move that date up. If I did, I might actually have everything ready in time for the grand opening. That's if Donnie came through for me. With that thought my heart sank, as I knew he wasn't dependable, and I shouldn't count on any of the man's promises.

"But last week …" No, I wasn't going to argue with someone who suddenly seemed to have gotten the lead out of his shoes. "Sure, let's get this done, but I thought you said you'd bought the best paint the hardware store carried."

Donnie hunched his shoulders. "Oh, right. Uh, I did, but they don't sell the real good brand I like to use. I'll get started right now." With those words he left to get the supplies he'd need.

He made quick work of spreading canvas tarps over the old wooden floor to protect it from drips and then carried in cans of paint. His movements were fast and efficient. Next came a paint tray, roller, and a long extension handle, as well as a ladder.

He'd need that extra-long reach, as the walls were twelve feet high. They weren't drywall but the original log walls, round and knotted, and it felt like a sin to be slapping paint on them, but someone in the past had beat me to it. It was either paint them anew, or sandblast which would roughen the wood. A new coat of paint seemed the best option and would brighten the large room. Thankfully, it was the cheaper choice too.

What I loved best about this building was the cathedral ceiling gleaming from above with the original wood still unpainted. There were even three massive ax-hewn beams spanning the width of the room. I planned to have Donnie put several brackets on each and string a thin steel cable so that I could hang many of the quilts. Well, not me personally. It would take a tall ladder for that job, and I planned to stay away from all ladders in the future after Alma's fall.

Thinking of ladders, I watched Donnie carry in an extension ladder that he'd previously left out in back of the building. Now he leaned it against a wall. I knew this was the one Ronnie had used to steal my gutters. If the ex-con had returned the ladder to the roof rack of the van, it would now be sitting in the impound lot at the sheriff's department. Thankfully, Ronnie was as slow in getting things done as his brother and had failed to hide this evidence of his crime.

Gibb had said he'd release the van back to Donnie in a day or two after a forensic expert came down from Nashville to go over it. This county was too poor to hire its own. With that thought, I watched Donnie pour a tray full of paint and scamper up the rungs. The tray attached neatly to the ladder. He backed down and worked his way up again with the roller in hand and a clean brush in one back pocket. Donnie certainly seemed to have gotten spunky since the murder. In the time he'd been working for me, I'd never seen him move so fast.

My thoughts were interrupted when the bell over the front door tinkled with a merry tone and Harley stepped in. He pulled off one of those colorful knit caps that look Peruvian. I happened to know that Mom had just finished knitting that hat, and I wondered why she hadn't said a word to me about giving it to my boyfriend. The static electricity tousled his wavy dark hair, which he wore in a long style that reminded me of a traditional Southern gentleman.

"Hi, Stella." He hurried across the room and gave me a one-armed hug while he hoisted a large leather tote bag for me to see. "I thought you might like a picnic." He grinned ear to ear.

Harley was a handsome man in a dark, rugged way versus Lam's blond, movie-star good looks. His features, definitely masculine with a strong jaw and a bit of a bump on the bridge of his nose, fell more into the outdoorsy cowboy category. He'd been one of Tennessee's most successful criminal trial lawyers for years until he'd jumped out of the rat race right before I'd met him. Somehow, because he seemed like a humble guy, I couldn't picture him pacing in front of a jury, mesmerizing them with a commanding voice, but I occasionally daydreamed about him riding in on a white horse. Now forty, he'd experienced a meteoric rise to success but had developed a bad case of boredom.

Harley proved that you can't buy happiness, although lately he smiled a lot more. I hoped I had something to do with that. I especially wanted that to be true since I not only really liked him, but I still felt guilty about destroying his antique car last month during a car chase with a killer. Then there was the small matter of destroying part of his new home in that same vehicle crash. Oh boy, I owed this guy for not strangling me. Or suing me.

"Hey, back at you," I said, feeling my heart thump at the sight of him. "It's kind of cold out for a picnic, cowboy." I knew he loved my pet name for him. "Is your horse tied up at the hitching post out front?"

"Don't laugh. One day I'll come riding up on my faithful steed and won't you be surprised?" He glanced at Donnie up on the ladder and lowered his voice. "I thought after what you found yesterday you could use some fun."

"I could, but I really don't have time." I took the bag from his hand and opened it, leaning my face close to smell the aroma of fresh baked bread. I could see a Tupperware container and a couple of Snickers bars. My virtue wavered and broke when I saw a wine bottle tucked at the side of the bag. "Of course, a quick break wouldn't hurt."

"Let's go up to your office. We'll spread the blanket out on the floor. It's way too cold outside."

I turned to lead the way, but Harley stopped me with a hand on my arm and then pointed at Donnie. He walked nearer to the ladder. "Mr. Clark, I'm Harley Morgan. I just want to express my sympathy for your loss."

Donnie blushed. "Thank you, sir. Right nice of you."

"I'll be in my office, Donnie, if you need me," I said. We climbed the stairs, and I pushed open the office door still minus its doorknob.

"What happened? You had a knob here last week," Harley asked.

"Oh, long story." I removed the wine bottle, placed it on the desk, and tugged the blanket from the tote bag. Gripping two corners, I snapped it out into the air, letting it settle to the wooden planks.

Harley took a corkscrew, plates, silverware, and real cloth napkins from the bottom of the carryall. I opened the Tupperware and found thick slices of roast beef. Another plastic container held lettuce and slices of tomato that still looked good for this time of year. I gave an appreciative moan when I saw how pretty the loaf of bread was with the top browned and sprinkled with sesame seeds.

His chest puffed out. "I'm learning to cook. Made the roast yesterday."

"Did you bake the bread?" I asked.

"Yes, ma'am." He tipped an imaginary cowboy hat. "This morning."

I laughed, thinking about how much I enjoyed my time with Harley. We'd been on several dates over the last few weeks, and every one of them had been fun. We'd gone for walks, been to the movies, and just sat around his house enjoying the antics of his kitten Smoky. We had even roasted marshmallows in the fireplace.

I found that I wanted to tell him the story of my walk across the porch roof and see his reaction. Sharing my fear of heights, he glanced out the window and whistled.

"I'm impressed, Stella," he said, walking back and settling onto the floor beside me. He leaned forward and kissed me on the tip of my nose. "I'm glad you're in one piece, but I admire that you're so driven to do well with this job."

"Like I keep saying, I'm on probation."

"I know a few people in state government who owe me favors. I could put in a good word for you."

Harley, slicing the bread, didn't see me frown upon hearing his suggestion. I was surprised he didn't know I wanted to earn permanent job status through good work. I forced a smile.

"No. I can do it on my own but thanks." I spread mayonnaise on the slice of bread he offered and stacked up a sandwich. "Good work on your first try at baking," I said around the first bite.

"Wine's a bit sweet. How are you doing after yesterday? That must have been pretty bad finding a body," Harley said, rubbing my arm. "I'm sorry I was out of town. Just for the day, but I wish I'd been here for you."

"That's sweet. I guess I'm okay. I didn't even know the twin Ronnie, but of course, that doesn't really help when you see a body." I swallowed, trying to keep the tears from flowing yet again. They seemed to spring up at odd moments. "Anyway I thought it was Donnie, and boy was that confusing for a while."

"You said Donnie isn't a great handyman, but he seems to be working hard right now."

"He is." I chewed a bite, taking my time. "And he surprised me by wanting to come back to work before the funeral but said it would take his mind off of the loss of his brother. He's been great today. No practical jokes. No riddles. I'm sure he's not in the mood for that now, but he is doing his best work today. He seems changed."

"Shock and grief changes everyone."

"I suppose."

"Does Gibb have any suspects or theories?"

"He thinks Ronnie must have had an accomplice. Maybe one of the other inmates who got out recently or even the same day. Thinks they planned a few jobs for money to get themselves started. I guess stealing the van was pretty safe. Donnie probably wouldn't have turned his brother in for that, and it's probably not worth five hundred. Donnie told Gibb that he didn't know if Ronnie had brought someone else to Sewanee with him or not. Says Ronnie came to visit their house alone."

"Sounds like a reasonable starting point for the investigation."

We finished our sandwiches in silence, and Harley tore the wrappers from the candy bars. He handed me one. "Our favorite."

"Gibb said he's going up to the prison today. He'll be able to check out others recently released and also find out how Ronnie did in prison. Did you hear that he was in jail for robbing a bank in Nashville ten years ago? Shot a bank guard."

"Didn't kill him though."

"What? Oh, I didn't think to ask Donnie."

"I meant the ten-year sentence is too short. If he'd killed the guard, he would have most likely gotten life."

"I hadn't thought about it. Guess you learned a lot being a criminal lawyer."

"A lot about criminals and crime." Harley's words sounded bitter and unlike his usually happy tone.

"I'm sorry. You really didn't have much fun with that career."

"No, but the money was good." Harley poured the last of the wine into our glasses and held his up for a toast. "Here's to more fun in retirement." His smile returned.

"More fun," I agreed.

I drank a sip and took a bite of the sweet candy, thinking that it had been nice of Harley to want to cheer me up today. He might have toasted to more fun, but he wanted to be with me today even though he knew I wouldn't be in the happiest of moods. Just as caring, Lam had called last night to see how I felt. Dating two guys felt sinful, but I wasn't sure if it was sinfully good or bad.

And the guys—both knew that I was going out with the other but neither had complained or even mentioned the subject. Maybe that topic was taboo with men.

It was funny, though, that both he and Lam had wanted to take me on a romantic indoor picnic. For someone who'd gotten back home late yesterday evening, Harley'd certainly gotten up to speed on the news quickly. I wondered who he had talked to, and an image of Mom flashed in my mind.

"I should let you get to work." Harley packed the tote. "But I could stay and help if you'd like." He leaned in and touched his lips first to my cheek and then so lightly to my lips that I only felt a slight flutter. Now that was a nice offer.

"I might take you up on that in a couple of weeks if it looks like I might not meet the deadline."

CHAPTER 8

After a couple of productive hours working, I slid my coat on. "I should be back in an hour. Hour and a half tops," I said to Donnie, wrapping a scarf around my neck, and even squishing a felt hat onto my head. Throughout the day I'd been hearing the wind gusting, growing stronger, flailing its way through the tree branches and beating against the log walls, although to no avail against the sturdy structure. Flurries were forecast for tonight and through to mid-morning but with little accumulation. Winter was here.

Donnie, still working, had completed the first coat of paint over half the room already. "Yes, ma'am. I'll just keep at this while you're gone."

"You can go home early if you like." I walked over to where he kept working steadily. Two of the paint cans were now empty.

"No. I'd just as soon stay and work, plus I need to wait on Debbie to pick me up."

"Guess you'll be happy to get your van back, but thanks, Donnie. I appreciate it. If you keep this pace up, I think I can swing a small bonus at the end." I'd be happy to pay some extra right out of my pocket if he'd help me meet the deadline of the grand opening. With a sigh, I finally recognized the unusual feeling I'd felt today—relief. I liked it.

"That would be nice, Miss Stella," Donnie said, still not looking me in the eye. "I'll do my best to earn it."

I watched his head swing up and down as he moved the paint roller in vertical sweeps. Down, over, and up. Down, over, and up. Then he'd dip the nap into the paint tray again. Suddenly, I realized it wasn't just the hard work that made Donnie seem different to me today. The hat he usually wore, that awful sweat-stained ball cap, was missing. It had been a constant in all the time I'd known him, hiding the bald spot. The hairless dome of his head above the fringe of hair appeared different, but I couldn't quite put my finger on the change.

Suddenly, the answer popped into my head. "Shiny," I said too loudly.

"Sorry. The paint?"

"Uh, no. I was just thinking out loud about, um, something." That was the difference in Donnie. The bald top of his head didn't look as shiny as usual, and it almost looked like some hair was growing in. Maybe he was using some of that special medicated shampoo to regrow hair which I'd seen on TV commercials. Well, it was none of my business. To cover my embarrassment at blurting the word out, I said, "I'm just going to the library and then the nursing home."

Donnie only nodded in response.

I slipped out the back door but almost fell down the steps as I stopped short. Donnie's van, white but spotted with rust, sat in the same spot as it had less than forty-eight hours ago. The vehicle was parked just forward enough that once again, just like the day of the murder, I couldn't see who, if anyone, was behind the wheel. My heart skipped several beats when the driver's side door opened with a grating scream of metal against metal on rusty hinges. I don't know if I expected to see the ghost of Ronnie Clark, but Deputy Mann slid off the seat. Seeing me, she jumped, and I felt better knowing I wasn't the only jittery female around.

"Didn't see you, Ms. Hill."

I decided that since this woman worked for Gibb I should at least try to be friendly even if she'd been gruff to me the first time we'd met under official circumstances.

"Call me Stella," I said, forcing my voice to sound sincere. "The state guys finished with the van quicker than Gibb thought. Did they find any clues?"

"Can't say. Evidence is confidential, Ms. Hill." The deputy heaved her gun belt up an inch or two.

Feeling my smile morph into a grimace, I wondered if her action with the weapon was like a nervous tic. Before I could reply, a Sewanee police car with Gibb behind the wheel came around the corner of the building.

"Hey, Sis. Is Donnie here?" Gibb said, climbing out of the car.

"He's inside painting," I answered.

"Deputy Mann, go on in and give Mr. Clark his keys back. Tell him about the copper." Gibb watched as she climbed the three steps and disappeared into the Center.

I raised my eyebrows.

"I kept the copper guttering since it was stolen goods. I figured that way Donnie can't sell it before we can get it back to the owner." He pointed at me. "I'll help you fill out the paperwork."

"Well, what in the world will I do with all of it bent and twisted into pretzels?"

"Lam said he could get his recycle guy to pick it up, and he'll pay you the value of the metal after he takes it through the weigh station. Should cover the cost of new ones and then some. Metal costs are higher than a meth addict." Gibb hunched his shoulders and zipped up his jacket, turning up the collar against the wind and a few swirling snowflakes.

I smiled. Maybe I'd just found my bonus money for Donnie. "Did you learn anything at the prison? You went today, didn't you?"

"Warden said Ronnie Clark was a model prisoner. All ten years. Said he even earned an Associate's degree in management online while he was in. Didn't cause any trouble and didn't make any friends that have gotten out recently. Said the man never got any mail except official stuff like parole notices, which he didn't get, and never had visitors."

For some reason that last comment brought stinging tears to my eyes. To cover the sudden emotion I paced over to the van and tugged the creaky door open. Leaning in and not hearing any protest from the sheriff, I asked, "Did the tech guy find anything in here?" Hopefully Gibb would be more helpful than his deputy. I felt like I had a right to know. After all, the man who owned the van worked for me, and I'd found the body of his brother. Didn't that earn me the right to be informed?

"Sis, not really and you don't need to worry about all this." His hand rested on my shoulder. "Are you afraid the killer will come back?"

"I hadn't thought about that at all until you just mentioned it, but if he didn't have any friends in prison, then that shoots your theory down."

"It could have been someone he knew from before going in, or the warden might not know the whole story. It doesn't seem too likely that it was just a random killing. I mean not here in Sewanee. Maybe someone from the past has just been waiting for him to get out so he could hit him. That's my next theory to check out. Old high school friends. People he worked with."

With a shiver, I realized I didn't want to talk about killers anymore. "I've got to go, Gibb."

"Where you heading?"

"Just the library." I didn't plan on telling him that Ms. Fleck had roped me into more assistance. "I'll have my own internet connection soon, and then I can finally work out of the office. Can't wait. The library's computers are snails." I dug my car keys out of my bag. When I looked back at Gibb, I saw him grin in that awful way only a little brother can when he has bad news. He obviously planned to enjoy what he was getting ready to dish out.

"Ms. Fleck called me," he said in a sing-song voice. "She's got a phone in her room now, but she didn't know your cell number. Seems I keep taking calls for you."

My mouth fell open. "And did you give her my number?"

"Oh, yeah, but also she said she had expected you over at lunch time. Alma's pretty mad that you're late with her books, but you can make it up to her by bringing some pudding cups. Evidently the nursing home food doesn't measure up. The tapioca is like silly putty."

"Well, of all the nerve." I hopped onto the Jeep seat and gave the door a hard slam.

Gibb, laughing, sauntered over and motioned for me to roll the window down. "Vanilla, not chocolate." He now laughed so hard he snorted.

I bounced the Jeep onto Main Street faster than I intended, causing a pickup to brake hard, and then I went through the yellow light at Sewanee's only traffic signal. It took me only a few minutes to reach the library, where I sat in front of the computer screen for over an hour filling out the forms for the federal grant I'd been eyeing for days. I'd been interrupted by Alma's broken leg the last time I tried to work on it. My justification was sound, and I knew all the buzz words to make my case. I could almost taste the $20,000. Money like that would mean the difference between getting my Heritage Craft Center off to a gangbuster start versus what could be a mediocre opening. It might mean the difference between permanent employment and the director's job slipping from my fingers.

It felt nice to concentrate on something so mundane as typing. It drove all thoughts of killers out of my head. Who would have thought that I'd be more relaxed just sitting in the library than I'd been for days? Of course, Ms. Fleck wasn't here telling everyone to be quiet. In fact, I could hear a conversation off to my right about the merits of canned pumpkin in pies versus fresh and, in the children's corner, it sounded like several preschoolers were fighting over a copy of *Where the Wild Things Are*. I'd swear I heard the cover being torn off.

I tapped the print button so that I could have copies of what I'd sent. There was only one printer, and I knew it was in the librarian's office behind the checkout desk. After a patron paid the nickel-a-sheet fee, the pages were handed over. With my legs stretched in front of me and my fingers laced behind my head, I waited a few more minutes to let the job print out. I watched a middle-aged woman whom I'd never met finish checking out books for a customer. This substitute librarian must not be from Sewanee.

I slipped off my chair and crossed carpeting so worn it was a slick road to the desk. The woman pushed aside a book as I approached. Her name tag read Frances.

"Hi, Frances. I've got a few pages coming over the printer. So you're filling in for Ms. Fleck?"

"No, actually I'm the new Sewanee librarian," she said with a wide, friendly smile. "I did work as the assistant in Manchester, but I got the transfer news and promotion just yesterday. I'm delighted."

"But … but, what do you mean? Isn't Ms. Fleck going to come back when she's better?" The words rasped from my throat.

"No. I'm it," Frances said, looking puzzled.

"Does she know? I mean, did you visit her or maybe call? How did she take the news?"

At this point Frances pulled a stack of books out of the return bin and dropped them on the counter top with a thud. "That wasn't my responsibility. I'm sure the district administrator would have called to inform her. I don't even know Ms. Fleck, except by reputation." She sniffed and turned away again, making it clear she was done dealing with me, except in a few seconds she returned and thrust my copies at me.

I shuffled out of the library in a daze, dragging my tote in one hand and clutching the now-crumpled pages of the grant application tightly in the other. Somehow I managed to drive away and was now pushing a grocery cart around the Piggly Wiggly. My emotions were rolling like a kid racing down a hill in an old tire. Last time I'd done that the adventure hadn't ended well—I'd thrown up. How had I become so involved in someone else's life just by trying to be helpful?

Here I was being blamed for an accident when I had no time to deal with another problem.

If Alma had known this bad news, she hadn't said a word to Gibb when she'd called. He would have told me, and I was sure he wouldn't have found it funny. Was Alma waiting to confront me when I delivered the books on her reading list? The old woman already believed I'd caused her accident. Now she could add to her list of things that were my fault the little matter of being forced into retirement! Good Lordy, it would kill her, and she'd haunt me forever.

I picked up two packages of pudding cups, and then placed a few more into the cart in all the flavors. Farther down the aisle I grabbed a half dozen packages of fancy cookies and as if they were eggs, laid them beside the pudding. On the way to the checkout I had to scoot past the personal grooming products. I selected lilac-scented lotion, a neck-rest pillow, TV ears for the hard-of-hearing, ear plugs for those who aren't, and a teddy bear because I needed a hug.

CHAPTER 9

"Hi. Uh. Hello?" I tiptoed across the scuffed green linoleum of the semi-private room.

Lying in a shaft of sunlight in the bed which I'd moved to its vantage point by the window, Alma snored softly with her back to me. I leaned over the frail figure in the hospital bed and placed my fingers so lightly on her shoulder that I scarcely felt the thin cotton nightgown. "Ms. Fleck, I brought you a few things. Not just the pudding, vanilla, but I thought you might like some cookies and lotion. Do you like lilac scent?"

"I'm allergic," Ms. Fleck's voice barked from the doorway.

Once again I was talking to the sleeping roommate while Ms. Fleck crept up behind me, scaring the daylights out of me.

"Please don't do that again! I don't think I'm strong enough for another fright." I staggered to the chair between the beds and fell back onto the seat to catch my breath. "Your roommate is in your bed."

"I know." Alma tapped her temple. "Unfortunately, Betty isn't all there. Nice though. Doesn't mind sharing but she's not well-read. Speaking of which, did you get my books?"

"Yes. But the latest Lee Child was checked out and there's a waiting list. Maybe I could order you a copy. Hardback. My treat."

The older woman wheeled her chair farther into the room, staring me in the eyes as she rolled closer at a glacial pace. "I heard some news today," she said.

My heartbeat shifted to fifth gear and a cold sweat broke out, causing an instant chill to skitter down my spine. Here it comes. Alma is going to blast me for bringing about her forced retirement which, since she wasn't ready, is probably the same to her as being fired.

I squeezed my eyes shut.

"Are you preparing for some bad news, young lady?" A claw of a hand grasped my arm, nails digging into the skin. "It's very bad news," she said. "The nursing home's cook quit yesterday, and this Mr. Tindal, the owner, still hasn't hired a replacement."

My eyes snapped open. "Well, for Pete's sake, who's doing the cooking? Is he going to let you starve to death?"

"Probably. The nurse's aides are filling in, opening cans. Lunch was watered-down Campbell's soup and a slice of white bread." Alma groaned. "No butter."

"But is that all? That's your bad news?" I asked. The rush of relief over the subject of Alma's complaint felt as if I'd been thrown a life jacket. She must not know about the retirement yet.

"Is that all? What a question. I thought you might care a smidgen."

The room door swung open fast and hard, relieving me of the need to reply, and two of the nursing home's residents scurried into the room. At least I assumed they were living here by their attire and ages. They closed the door behind them after first peeking each way up and down the hall to see if their entry had been observed.

"Jack reporting in from the recon mission." This came from a man standing slightly slumped and saluting. His plaid robe and leather slippers had seen better days.

Standing with him was a whisper of a woman, tall, pale and ethereal, and a true classic beauty. She seemed to be more made of dreams, shifting her image. Now she focused.

"Alma knows who you are, Jack. Don't be so dramatic. Leave that to me," the woman said with a voice that projected and had definitely benefited from diction lessons. She dug an elbow into his side, causing him to drop the quivering hand. "Besides, now is not the time. We can see that Alma has a visitor. I am Annaleigh Boudreaux. And you are, my dear?" She rearranged herself into another pose, tipping her head to the side and lifting the chin.

Watching the pair had fascinated me so that my brain couldn't switch gears fast enough from the show these two put on—it was obvious this woman had actress on her resume—and I replied with a grunt.

"Is she simple, Alma dear?" Annaleigh swirled so that her dressing gown, which looked to be silk in a cerulean color matching her eyes, caught the light with the movement. It assured all attention stayed on her like a floodlight.

Now this was the second time in as many days that someone had asked if I was not all present in the brain department. Mrs. Clark had been the first. I was ticked off, but before I could defend myself, Alma said, "No, she's smart but she's having a rough time lately. Discovered a body yesterday and I'm sure she must still be in shock. Stella can be trusted though." She refocused on Jack by rotating one wheel of the chair so that her leg in its cast pointed directly at the man. "What did you find out, Sergeant?"

He cinched the tie of his robe tighter and made a clicking noise with his mouth. It seemed to be his method of getting ill-fitting dentures into place before speaking.

"Seems like cook didn't quit. Story in her neighborhood is she got fired. Reason unknown," Jack said.

"How did you discover this valuable clue?" Alma asked.

Annaleigh purred, "Jack's nephew lives down the street from Molly, and we called. We borrowed Mrs. Hadley's daughter's phone. As you know, neither Soldier nor I have a private line in our own suites." She cast narrowed eyes to the newly installed phone resting on the bedside table.

Jack said, "If I had some transport, I could go question ol' Molly. See why she got the can."

"That's got canned not got the can." I spoke before I could stop the words.

Jack eyed me up and down. "Bet you got wheels, girlie."

I jumped to my feet. "I've got to go. It's been nice, Ms. Fleck. Take care. I'm sure we'll see each other again soon." I edged toward the door and safety without taking my eyes off the trio.

"Just a minute," Alma barked.

By the time I extracted myself from Alma, I was late and drove faster than I should have to meet Lam.

"So exactly how did the evil Ms. Fleck get you to agree to play detective?"

Lam continued to massage my shoulders as he talked, his thumbs working magic on the tight muscles across my shoulders. I'd realized weeks ago that Lam was just like quicksand—all innocent on the surface, but if a woman didn't realize how sexy he was, well, you were in over your head in seconds. A moan escaped my lips. I'd agreed, when Lam called earlier, to meet him at the house he was thinking about buying. Getting a back rub was an unexpected bonus.

"Just, uh, down a bit, please." I leaned forward so that Lam's hands naturally slipped lower, and then he moved them even farther down. His hands couldn't encircle my waist, but he used the grip to pull me against him and then nuzzled my neck with kisses. For a moment I just let the sweetness wash over me, and then I twisted in his embrace so that I could kiss him.

When Lam pulled away, he said, "That's the first."

"Silly, that was in no way our first kiss."

"Hmm, the first time you kissed me."

I had to replay the last few weeks in my head, searching for the right answer, but Lam had nailed it. I mean, I'd kissed him before but not as passionately as I just had. I'd been letting him take the lead this whole time, which seemed like an important piece of the puzzle to me. Why couldn't I decide which man, Harley or Lam, I liked best? I guess there wasn't any harm in dating two men, but that wasn't what had concerned me lately. I wanted to understand why my thoughts on the subject were like a murky pool. Why was I as nervous as a girl on her first date?

"You're right." I smiled, deciding that I'd gloss over this moment and deal with it later. I would play Scarlett O'Hara yet again.

"The cottage is fantastic," I said. "So much potential. Have you made a decision yet?" I turned to stare out the window of the living room of the cute little house that definitely evoked a fairy tale.

Although the woods beyond the glass were brown this time of the year, I knew that the scruffy bushes in the lower canopy which surrounded the house were broad leaf rhododendron. They kept their leaves through the winter, but the cold weather made them curl into tight, dark sausage rolls, making them look dead. In the spring those dark green banners of life would unfurl, and flowers would blossom and create a cloud of pink so beautiful they would rival any storybook setting.

The inside of the structure was less idyllic, but Lam had a creative sense of flair with decorating. He would modernize and fix up this place with his own hands the same way nature would take care of the forest.

He nodded, looking more serious than usual. "Yes, I'm ready for a place. The townhouse just seems too noisy anymore with all those twenty-somethings moving in. The community has become party city. Say, what did you tell me that cook's name is?"

I'd told Lam about Alma's complaint with the food soon after arriving and now it dawned on me that Lam had brought up the subject first. He asked if I'd had a good visit at the nursing home. How had he known I'd been there this afternoon? For all he knew I'd answered his call from the Center, where I wished I had been. When I'd arrived here at the cottage, he'd already known about my visit with Alma. It had to be Gibb.

"Um, Molly. Molly Simms. It was cute. This old guy, well, he must have been in the army. Alma called him Sergeant and this Annaleigh has nicknamed the guy Soldier, and when he talked about the cook, he said old Molly. Soldier must be pushing mid-eighties so how old is the cook?"

"No telling. I just fixed a Volvo fifty-three footer for a guy named Mark Simms from over at Tracy City. Wonder if there's any relationship there? Why don't I call him tomorrow?" Lam glanced at his watch. "I think it's too late for a follow-up service call now."

"Tracy City! That's where Jack's nephew lives. I bet there is a connection." I couldn't keep the excitement out of my voice and paced into the tiny kitchen. "Let's see, what story could you come up with for needing to know why the cook got fired?" I leaned forward on the Formica countertop, chin in hand.

"How about if I just ask? It's a small town. Doubt he'll mind telling me. He and I got along fine when we were talking engine problems. Plus, I cut him a pretty good deal because he needed some new brake pads too. Those aren't cheap on big rigs."

I grimaced. "Maybe. Worth a try. Say, how did you know I visited Ms. Fleck today?

His signature rogue smile spread across his lips and the blue eyes took on that bedroom glaze. I swear he was sexier than ten Hollywood movie stars.

"I have dark secrets, darlin'." He crossed to my side in a heartbeat. "Do you want to know them?"

CHAPTER 10

"Mom, no. You don't need to wait supper for me." I tried not to sound panicked as I juggled the cell in one hand and the steering wheel with the other.

Normally I didn't use my phone while driving, but there were no cars on the road out of the Mountaintops housing area where Lam's future home was located. Also, I kept the speed down worried that a little critter might try to beat the Jeep as it crossed the asphalt. Furry critters rarely won those races.

I had decided I'd better leave Lam behind for the evening when he'd taken on that serious bedroom look. He was definitely ready to move our relationship to a new level, but I wasn't. I had too much work to do to allow myself to be distracted, and there was one last task I needed to do before I headed home for the evening.

Mom's voice crossed the distance on the airwaves. "But, Stella, I made your favorite. I'll leave a plate in the oven on low. Why in the name of Zen do you need to go back to work this late? It's after seven."

My favorite? My favorite food? I didn't for a second dare hope that Mom had fried chicken for me. Or that there would be any mashed potatoes. Or even the most basic comfort food, a slice of white bread. I frowned, as that made me think of Alma, and I realized I should have had a bit more sympathy for her plight. She was stuck at the nursing home, a captive without a cook, just as I was with Mom and her vegan diet while I lived with her. Well, that made me feel even more guilty, knowing that I planned to stop at the Food Mart and get gas and a Lunchable—maybe a Twinkie—but not so guilty that I'd forgo something good. I'd eat at my desk before heading home, and Mom would never know.

"I've got to pick up the inventory forms," I said. "I forgot them earlier. Tomorrow I'm going out to the rented storage area first thing. I need to go through the display items and see what I've got to work with."

I soothed Mom's concern with the promise to eat what she left for me and to drive carefully and then disconnected the call. I had the feeling that Doodle Dog and Carly were going to like sharing my plate tonight. They'd both put on some extra weight since I'd moved back home. After a quick stop for my supper, the one that I knew I'd enjoy, I parked in front of the Center. The meters were free after six in the evening, and the bright light from the street lamps made me feel safer than I would at the back of the building. I'd never been this skittish before the murder.

In my haste, I fumbled with the door key and then twisted the deadlock back into place behind me once I was inside. I guess the murder and Gibb's comments about killers had affected me more than I wanted to admit. When I took a deep breath and faced the room, the bright new paint dazzled my eyes in the glare of the hanging lights. Unbelievably, Donnie had almost completed the job in one day. For a moment I just twirled around, taking in the big room. How bright and welcoming it looked. I would kiss my handyman if he hadn't already gone home.

Almost trotting, spirits running high, I hurried through

to the back room where I'd set up a dorm-sized refrigerator. It was installed on a long countertop right next to the utility sink. I grabbed a bottle of tea.

Although I hated to think of myself as a scaredy-cat, something caused a shiver to race over my skin, leaving goose bumps in its wake. For reassurance I glanced toward the back door and saw that it was securely locked.

"Come on, chicken," I muttered, but the words came out more like a croak because of my dry throat. I sipped the tea and then climbed the steps to my office.

Since the doorknob was still missing, the door stood half open, and I peeked in before crossing the threshold. I had no more than sat my bag of food down when I heard a thump coming from the storage closet next to the office. Once again, in vain, I scanned the area, hoping that there would be a tool I could use as a weapon. The wooden bear in the corner still smiled his toothy pine grin, and the soft glow of the quilts hanging on the walls warmed the room, but there was nothing with which to protect myself.

I swore that if I lived through tonight I'd dig around in Mom's basement and find Gibb's old baseball bat.

With shaking hands, I tugged off my shoes, thinking that I would tiptoe down the stairs and escape, but when I stepped silently from the office a man's scream rang out. I must have jumped three feet into the air.

"Lord, Miss Stella. You scared the life right out of me," Donnie said, clutching a container of scrubbing cleaner and a roll of paper towels to his chest. High spots of color on his cheeks lit an otherwise pale face.

"I thought the place was empty," I said, stuffing my feet back into my shoes.

"'Course, you figured I'd be gone, but since I had the van back, I called Debbie and told her I'd be late."

"I came in the front or I'd have seen you were here. So my fault and no harm, except I think I lost a year myself," I said, drawing in a deep breath.

"And it's late enough that I thought you weren't coming back. Washing my brushes left a mess in the sink, and I need to clean up. Just getting stuff."

That was odd, because just a few days ago he'd left the utility sink a disaster zone. Left it for me like I was supposed to clean up behind him. By the time I'd discovered what he'd done, the man was long gone for the day. In fact, he'd never once stayed late to finish a task.

"Donnie, are you okay?" The words popped out of my mouth without thought, but certainly not without reason. This post-murder Donnie seemed like a completely different man.

His eyes grew round and what little color he'd had on his face drained away. It even looked as if he might faint. He fumbled for words. "Uh, okay. Yeah. Just. Sure." He drew a deep breath. "Yeah, I'm okay. Just been a rough few weeks, uh, I mean two days. I'd better get home to, umm, the missus."

I reached out and patted his arm and noted with surprise that tears welled in his eyes. It'd been silly of me to not realize how shook up Donnie was and had every right to be. Just a few short days ago he'd been telling me that his brother, in prison for ten years, was returning. I remembered that Donnie had not seemed happy about the event. Next came the murder. Maybe Donnie suffered from guilt that he hadn't welcomed Ronnie's return and now it was too late. Or could he be afraid of his brother's killer returning? I didn't think Donnie would want to discuss the subject with me. I was his employer for a short time, not a friend.

"Thanks for staying late," I said. "I can't even begin to tell you how much I appreciate it, and you've definitely earned that bonus. Even if you did scare me so badly I've probably got some gray hairs now."

For the first time, he smiled and rubbed a hand over the bald top of his head. "You've been right nice to me, Miss Stella. Thank you."

But his happy mood didn't last. Just as quickly, I noticed how the man's shoulders sagged as he started down the stairs. I followed.

"When is the funeral?" I asked.

"Oh, it won't be for a few more days. Your brother said he'd let me know when the body …" His voice trailed off.

"The offer to take time off still stands. You've gotten us ahead of schedule anyway." I didn't have the heart to say that I really hoped he wouldn't take me up on the offer, but he did have the right to.

"No, I'd rather be at work," Donnie said, walking through his newly painted masterpiece and on into the back storage room. He laid the paintbrush out on a paper towel after smoothing the bristles into shape. Then he sprinkled cleaner into the utility sink. He just looked so tired I couldn't stand it.

"I'll get this. You've done enough for today. You look beat." I lifted his jacket off the coat hook and shoved it into his arms, turning him toward the door.

He sighed. "I ain't going to say no. I'll be in tomorrow for sure. Early." Donnie gathered up his hat, a newspaper, and a plastic grocery bag which had held his lunch, and then left.

I listened for a moment and then heard the old van start up and pull away. As I turned to finish the job of cleaning the sink, I saw the edge of an envelope underneath one of the cloth painting tarps. Donnie had folded the ones he no longer needed, since he'd almost completed the job, and stacked them on the floor. I imagined he was waiting to finish with all of the painting, and then he'd put them back into his van.

With a fingernail I scooted the paper from underneath the floor coverings. I just wanted to see if it was mine or something of Donnie's, but as it came free, the contents caught on the edge of the fabric and came partly out. I could see a photograph of myself.

Although the image was of me, it wasn't I who had put it in an envelope and left it here. It also wasn't something I'd posed for. I saw that it had been taken from maybe across the street as I cleaned the windows outside the log building. I remembered that day last week, wanting to finish the task before the weather turned colder as November wore on.

I peeked inside and saw there were more photographs. Fanning them out, the faces of Gibb, Mom, and Lam peered back. All were in candid poses when they obviously didn't know someone was watching. Also, others showed different places around town including the police station, JoAnn's Café, and the hardware store. The name of each person photographed and the location was printed on the back of the paper. The photo of the hardware store also annotated that Charlie Russell was the owner and manager and John worked the paint desk.

I shoved the items roughly into the envelope and then repositioned the lot back exactly as I'd found it. I wondered if, and why, Donnie had done this. It seemed shady, but there was no law against taking photographs around town. Still, I planned to mention what I'd found to Gibb.

CHAPTER 11

The next morning, warmer than it had been for a few days, was capped with a clear blue sky. It seemed as if the night had been very short. Standing outside the Center ready for another day of work, I stifled a yawn. The contents of my tote scattered across the seat of the Jeep when I turned it upside down. Then I dumped each item, one at a time, back into the depths of the cloth bag in my search for the elusive key to the storage unit. The day Janice had hired me she'd given me two sets of keys to the Heritage Craft Center, each set on its own ring. Then she'd handed over a smaller, separate ring with a plastic tag that said Larry's U-Stor. I'd Googled the business and found it located at the base of the Cumberland Plateau and just off of Interstate 24.

In total disbelief that I could have lost the key, I wiped sweat off my brow. Wouldn't I have put the key someplace safe like in my tote or the wallet? I mean, I would have done that, wouldn't I have? I checked each space, digging my finger into the slots for credit cards and rooting around among the pennies in the change compartment. With no luck, I dropped the wallet and the rest of the miscellaneous essentials of life, like lip balm, back where they belonged in my bag.

This couldn't be happening. I was a sane and reasonably competent person. Why was it so difficult for me to hang onto keys? Mom always said it must have something to do with a past life, and Gibb said it was the three-year-old in me.

"Why me?" I wailed.

"I don't know. What's up?" A voice sounded close to my right ear.

I jerked upright, banging my head against the door frame of the Jeep.

"Owwee." Stars twirled in my vision.

"Geez, I'm sorry, Stella. That must have hurt."

Now I recognized Harley's voice. He pried my hand away from the top of my head and gave the throbbing spot a kiss.

"It's okay," I said, resisting the urge to make a smart-alecky retort. "What are you doing here and so early?"

It was only about 8:30 in the morning, but Harley had told me before that he wasn't much of a morning person. He'd joked that he had never seen dawn and didn't care that it was supposedly beautiful.

I'd arrived at work at my normal time to pick up the key to the storage unit. Unbelievably, I'd brought the inventory forms home last night after eating at my desk but had forgotten the key. This trip was wasted time on two counts though. First, I no longer needed to let Donnie in since I'd entrusted him with a building key yesterday. The change in the man had given me confidence that I could trust him. Second, I hadn't so far been able to find the storage unit key in my desk or anywhere else in the building.

Donnie had helped me look, leaving his paintbrush to do so. He had been hard at work when I'd arrived, although he'd surprised me yet again, as he had not driven the van in. Debbie had dropped him off. This morning he was finishing the painting job with the trim work. Then, before I could tell him what else I wanted him to do today, he had rattled off plans that covered my list and then some. I'd shut my mouth.

"Early?" I prompted Harley when he just grinned at me.

Harley looked like a man with a secret. "Just stopped to get some coffee at the café. I'm parked out front. Come around and let me show you something," he said, grabbing my hand and tugging me around to the street.

Although many of the nearby parking spaces were taken, I knew immediately that Harley wanted to show me his new wheels. An antique Dodge truck with a glittering, pearl-blue paint job sat like a vision from the past. It outshone all the other vehicles parked up and down the block and could only belong to Harley Morgan. The chrome alone was blinding and made me wonder just how much the vehicle had cost. Seeing his smile, I knew he considered it worth every penny, and I also knew the man had plenty of pennies.

"Shue, it's gorgeous." I peeked in the window. "Have you named her yet?"

"Him. I named him Trickster. 1951. Not original, but boy does he have some tricks up his sleeve, I mean, under the hood." Harley trailed his hand over the rear fender. He imparted so much love into the gesture that I could almost hear the truck purr.

I already knew that my boyfriend loved antiques, particularly vehicles. That thought stirred the tragic memory that I had destroyed his classic '54 Ford Fairlane only last month. This man had forgiven me, but I wasn't sure I'd ever do the same for myself.

Opening the passenger door, I saw pristine leather seats, a wood-paneled dash, and more shiny chrome.

"Have time for a ride?" Harley sipped his coffee, waiting on my reply.

I bit my lip. "No. Absolutely not. I have to go down to Larry's U-Stor and start figuring out what I've got to put on display before my glass cabinets and the shelves get delivered. It's like Christmas. I'm so excited."

"How 'bout if I drive and then I can help out? Some of the boxes could be heavy and you might need a truck." He grinned. "I'm a truck kind of guy, you know. When I'm not a horse kind of guy."

"Well, I hadn't thought about needing some brawn, and I'll need a box cutter too. Okay. You've talked me into it. But it's probably going to be dusty work." I pointed at Harley's jeans, which were obviously brand new. As a high-priced lawyer he used to dress in expensive suits and silk ties. He'd hardly been retired long enough to break in the denim.

"No sweat." He shrugged.

"Let me find the key then and we're off."

With Harley's suggestion that my missing prize might be in the glove box of the Jeep, we were heading down the mountain within five minutes. I couldn't believe how smooth and comfortable the old truck proved to be. Harley recited all the specifications of the engine and its impressive horsepower as he guided the antique with one hand on the big white plastic steering wheel. I reached over and tapped the horn ring just to hear what I anticipated would be a unique honk. I was right.

Harley smiled ear-to-ear over every mile and then, at the foot of the Sewanee Mountain, he exited the interstate and turned left without needing to ask me for directions. That struck me as odd, especially combined with the fact that Harley had shown up so early this morning acting as if he knew right where I was going to be. That was in spite of the fact that I had intended to be on the road first thing with no stop for the key.

"Have you been to Larry's U-Stor before?" I kept my voice neutral.

"No."

Out of the corner of my eye I saw Harley jump just a fraction.

"But just last week I was thinking I might need to rent some storage space. I looked online for what's available in the area."

I couldn't help but grin. My boyfriend had a sharp mind, but I was pretty sure I had just caught him and Mom in their scheme. She must think I needed more time with Harley, and she had advised him that today offered a chance. Cele must have called him while I was in the shower this morning to let him know where I'd be.

As far as him wanting to rent storage space, there was another storage unit business right outside of Sewanee that would be more convenient for him. Janice had rented one that was closer to Nashville because she wasn't too familiar with the plateau area. It hadn't mattered to her that I would have to waste time hauling the boxes up the mountain.

For right now I would let it slide about their scheme. Maybe in a few days I would bring the topic up with Harley, but only after I'd talked this over with Mom. First, I wanted to know why Cele favored Harley over Lam.

I glanced down at the key in my hand. "Number 313. Whoa, I didn't notice that before," I said, shaking my head.

"Don't tell me you're superstitious," he said, steering down to the third row of the long, low buildings that looked like ugly concrete bunkers from an old war-time movie set.

"I'll overlook that remark. I'm a perfectly rational woman." I crossed my fingers where he couldn't see them.

We knew we'd arrived at the right bay by the spray-painted number on the roll-up door. It couldn't be missed, as the numerals were two-foot high and blood red. Harley had to get down on one knee to manipulate the key in the Yale lock and then had to give the door a sharp jerk to get it started up. Once it was moving, though, it ripped from of his hand and clattered to the ceiling with a crash like rumbling thunder. Dust rained down and sent us both scurrying while flapping at the cloud.

When the dust settled and I got a view of the inside of the room, my hands flew to cover my mouth.

"No, no, this can't be happening. These boxes are in terrible shape." I shuffled in a daze of disappointment over to one stack of four cartons. They leaned drunkenly. "This bottom one is crushed, and this one has split open." I touched the ragged edge of a gaping hole and had to leap backward as the stack toppled over, hitting me. The action shoved me back into Harley's arms.

He helped me regain my balance and then said, "You're right and I just heard something break." He squinted into one of the dark corners of the nine-by-eight-foot room. "There's standing water back here."

That news was the last straw, and my tears flowed in earnest.

I didn't have the heart to go through every box. The damage seemed to get worse as we shifted cartons and worked our way toward the back of the storage unit. The stuffy, damp air caught in my throat and clung to my hair. I finally asked Harley to take me back up the mountain. Maybe a treasure was hidden somewhere in the boxes, but there certainly wasn't enough to fill my display cases and draw in the tourists. Most of this belonged in a dumpster.

When Harley parked beside my Jeep, I thanked him one last time for being so helpful. His idea to document the damage with photographs might just save my job. Or not. I slipped off the truck seat, and with a forced smile, told Harley I'd see him soon. He'd been so wonderful trying to cheer me up on the drive back to Sewanee that I didn't have the heart to tell him how down I felt. Partly it was that I now needed to report yet another problem to my boss, and partly because I didn't know how I was ever going to fill up my Heritage Craft Center with examples of the crafts that made the culture of my beloved Tennessee mountains different from that of every other place in the country.

I let myself in the back door and stopped dead in my tracks. Raised, angry voices coming from the next room assaulted my ears. Recognizing that it was Donnie and Debbie Clark, I turned, intending to slam the back door hard enough to alert them of my presence, but their next words stopped me.

"Tarnation," Donnie hollered. "I didn't expect this. It's scared the life outta me."

"You need to find some backbone. Don't you remember what it was like? Think of the prize not, well, you know," his wife replied, her voice louder than his.

The fear in the man's voice was evident but Debbie's words sounded like those of a bully. Then she changed her tone. "Come on. It's going to be okay. We're too smart for them."

Now I was interested, wondering what they were talking about. I took a step forward, bumping an empty paint can that was on the floor near the counter. The metallic rattle brought silence to the other room. In seconds Debbie charged through the doorway.

"It's your boss, Donnie," she called over her shoulder. "Guess I'd better let you get back to work."

She stopped, fists on her hips, right in front of where I bent to set the can upright. Since it was at my eye-level, I saw the letters l, o, v, and e tattooed across the knuckles of her right hand. The jagged outlines looked as if she had done the work herself while drunk. A quick glance showed the message of *hate* displayed across the other hand. I forced myself to stand and face her.

"Hello, Debbie. Is everything okay?" I tried to smile but couldn't when I saw her frown. She certainly looked like one tough bird. The woman must be about my age, but she seemed older, harder, and on edge.

She said, "Sure, we was just talking about the kid. He got into some trouble at school today. You know how boys can be. Donnie and I have to go and talk to the principal."

"I know this must be a difficult time for you both. Is there anything I can do to help?"

"Donnie and I are doing the best we can given our awful loss. Thank you for asking though, and that bonus you mentioned to Donnie will come in handy. You know we have to pay all the expenses for burying his brother. Of course, not that we mind. Poor Ronnie," she said with a sniffle, "didn't get to enjoy his freedom. A nice send off is the least we can do."

"Did you know Ronnie well?"

Debbie's eyes widened. "Sure. We all knew each other from high school, but Ronnie was never a straight arrow. Know what I mean?" She didn't wait for an answer but hurried out the door with a quick good-bye and a reminder about the bonus.

I shook my head. The woman was brash. I still wondered what they had been arguing about, and whom did she think they were smarter than? I walked on through to the other room and found Donnie sitting on the bottom step of the staircase with his forearms resting on his knees and his head bowed. He looked like a forlorn scarecrow that had been left in the field. When he heard me, he jumped to his feet.

"Sorry about that, Miss Stella. Didn't intend to waste so much time, but uh, Deb was just talking about her mama. She's hard to deal with sometimes."

"Uh, no problem." I almost asked about his child but bit my tongue. Debbie had given one version of their argument and now Donnie another. Obviously neither wanted me to know what was going on. Of course, it was none of my business. "If you need to leave early, it's okay. You've really saved me by not walking out after all you have been through. I couldn't have blamed you."

"Thanks, boss lady. I better get back to this." He waved to indicate the paint can at his feet that was almost empty.

I peered around the room and realized that only a small section of trim around the front door remained unpainted now. A feeling of pure joy shot through me, but just then the bell over the front door tinkled. It stopped me from saying anything to Donnie as my brother stuck his head in the doorway.

"Sis, got a minute?" Gibb called out. "What in the world?"

I realized that I was still wearing a serape which I'd found in one of the stored boxes. The Mexican cape made from a woven blanket had still been folded into a cellophane wrapper, taped shut, and labeled *Made In Mexico City*.

"Oh, this old thing," I said, striking a pose as if I were all dressed up.

"Weird," Gibb said to me and then, "Hello, Donnie. That paint job looks good."

Donnie kept his head ducked between his shoulders, and he didn't turn away from his work as he mumbled a thank you.

Gibb motioned me to join him outside and pulled the door closed behind us before sitting down on the edge of the porch. As I settled beside him he said, "You smell musty." He scooted a few inches away from me.

I held the serape to my nose. "You're right. I'll wash it tonight.'

"It's not your best look, Sis."

"It's a long story. What's up?"

"Two things. I went back to the prison today. I wasn't making any progress around town so I backtracked and interviewed more people. Everybody there liked Ronnie. He was one of those model prisoners they give the responsible jobs to and one guard said he always got his work done better than most and faster too. Another guard said he expected Ronnie would do well once he got out. He didn't think he'd be one of the ones to be back behind bars before the year was out. When I told him Ronnie had been killed, he felt right bad."

"Did you talk to any of the inmates?"

"Yeah, one old guy. He said Ronnie didn't associate much and kept his nose clean. No friends."

"That's sad."

"Don't feel too sorry. The man did shoot a bank guard."

Gibb and I sat in silence as the sun dipped behind thickening cloud cover. I tried to imagine living in a bleak prison with no friends. The vision came to me in many shades of gray, completely devoid of color. In comparison, I realized how full and rich my life had become with the multitude of beautiful quilting fabrics that surrounded me. The hues, bright and bold to soft and pastel, were becoming old friends to me now, and I could always count on them for a smile. I felt sure that Ronnie Clark, hard worker that he had been, had not had much to smile about in those ten years of his life. I dabbed at my eyes, thinking of how he had only had a day of freedom.

I glanced at Gibb. His face, handsome in a way that most would describe as boyish, looked determined, maybe even grim today. Even the multitude of freckles couldn't lighten his image. I hoped that his job—well, his profession—wasn't turning my baby brother into a cynic unable to believe there was good in people or that someone could change.

But Ronnie had not had time to show he'd changed. He'd been murdered. Even as that thought entered my mind, I visualized the remaining twin just inside the Center behind the door at our back. I'd taken an instant dislike to Donnie Clark's insolent behavior and laziness, but I had changed my opinion of him practically overnight—since his brother's murder.

Clearing my throat, I finally said, "Well somebody killed him. Ronnie Clark didn't shoot himself. I mean, he didn't, did he?"

"What? No. Doc says he was shot by someone sitting in the passenger seat. Ronnie was turned slightly toward his killer. Entry wound shows an angle he wouldn't have used." Gibb spoke as he fished a roll of ring-shaped candies out of his shirt pocket. He tore the paper back a bit and frowned when he saw that the top piece of candy was a green one.

I automatically reached over and took it, as Gibb had never liked that flavor. I'd eaten a lot of the green sweets in my life, although I didn't for the life of me know what it was supposed to taste like other than sugar.

"Sounds like he must have known the person if he sat there calmly talking," I said, tucking the ring into my cheek and sucking on it.

"That's probably what it means, but let's not assume anything. Someone could have gotten into the van uninvited and immediately popped Ronnie. Not even given him a chance to speak."

"Oh, right."

"Something odd though." Gibb chewed his candy with a loud crunch. "Ronnie actually got out of prison two weeks earlier than he told Donnie."

"I remember Donnie saying his brother was getting out that day and coming to visit was the first thing he wanted to do." I could practically hear Donnie's words of a few days ago in my ears. "The warden didn't think to mention that fact when you first spoke to him?"

"Well, he wasn't hiding it, Sis. It just didn't come up. When I told the guard Ronnie had been shot, he just happened to say that it was sad. You know, sad that he didn't even get a month of freedom, only two weeks. Look, I've got to go." He stood and started toward the squad car parked at the curb.

"Wait. You said you had two things on your mind. What else did you want to tell me?"

"Oh, yeah. I gave your lawyer boyfriend a speeding ticket."

I sputtered, "What? When?"

"Just a few minutes before I came here. He said he'd just dropped you off." Gibb dipped to the car seat. "Nice wheels though," he said, pulling away.

I spit my candy onto the sidewalk.

CHAPTER 12

Donnie and I worked through the afternoon, mostly in companionable silence, until I made him leave for home and supper. Now that I'd come to like him, he seemed the type to need someone to take care of him. He made me want to be a good boss and a friend. We'd gotten a lot done, and if it had not been for my new problem of needing to find craft items to display, I would have been tired but happy. My thoughts were spinning. News about the grant wouldn't come for weeks, and even if I received an award, the money would not be in my hands for probably two or three months. That left the paltry sum in my budget that already haunted me.

Many people would probably be willing to donate or loan me items, but that would take time—and lots of it—to get the word out. I slid my appointment book across the surface of the desk and flipped through the pages, counting. Only a little over a week left now until the grand opening. My first advertisements would be out in the local, Nashville, and Chattanooga newspapers starting this Sunday. Janice had even sprung for a tiny classified in Southern Living. She'd set the date for this opening on the very day she'd hired me, and even though I'd suggested a delay, she had stubbornly refused.

If there was any hope for me, it was Donnie. Thanks to him the building clean-up was ahead of schedule, and I felt I could leave a lot of what remained to him while I went out begging for crafts. I would just get it done. I had to. I felt the tension in my jaw muscles and forced myself to relax.

With my coat in one hand and tote in the other, I hurried down the stairs. First, I planned to stop by to see Alma and then head home. This evening would be a good time to start calling everyone I knew. What would I say? I would describe all that the Heritage Craft Center could do for Sewanee. There was the tourism it would bring to the entire Cumberland Plateau, dollars for other businesses, new stores, and new restaurants. Well, I'd better not mention that to JoAnn, but she was on my list to call. Her family had been pioneers to the mountain in the mid-1800s. Surely she had some antique cookware or gadgets.

"Oh," I spoke out loud. "Recipes!" I'd bet my lunch money that JoAnn had plenty of recipes for the foods of the past, like ramps, which were popular before French fries, and bear meat, which I'd read was greasy. I'd do a display centered around stories of how the kitchen and feeding the family had changed through the years. Maybe a small pamphlet of the recipe collection would sell.

As I entered the storage room, I saw a note lying on the counter with a nut and bolt on top of it. Thinking that maybe Donnie had left it for me, I picked the slip up and squinted at his small, neat handwriting. It was a shopping list for the hardware store. Probably he intended to run out tomorrow and didn't want to forget. He needed a box of bolts the same size as the one now in my hand along with sand paper and four tubes of caulk.

I lay the paper down but tossed the bolt back and forth from one hand to the other. The note, specifically the even script, had jiggled some memory. I picked the list up again and returned to my office. The work estimate that Donnie prepared weeks ago was filed in the cabinet, and it took only a second to retrieve the pages. A glance told me that the writing style wasn't the same with the estimate showing larger, loopy letters and several misspelled words. Curiosity edged into a tickle of anxiety until I realized that maybe Donnie had gotten some help from his wife. Of course, that had to be the answer. Debbie probably helped him at home with the paperwork. Running a business was hard work.

Dropping the note back in its place, I locked the door on my way out of the Center but slowed as I descended the steps. The driver's door of my Jeep stood open. My first thought, that I was lucky it wasn't raining, quickly evaporated. Obviously even I remembered to close my car doors. Suddenly, I felt watched and rushed forward. All I wanted was to lock myself into the vehicle and race away. As I threw my things across to the passenger seat, the open door slammed into my back, banging my elbow hard enough that I yelped in pain. Regaining my balance, I whirled around but found myself thankfully alone. Had I felt a rough hand on my back? I couldn't be sure.

With jerky motions I climbed onto the seat and started the Jeep, making my way around the building. I braked to a stop before turning right onto Main Street.

Twilight was descending, but there were still a few people on the sidewalk and a trickle of cars moving slowly past in the lanes. No one was running as if they had just scared the life out of me. To my eyes Sewanee appeared normal, but suddenly my life felt changed, the safety of my hometown once again shattered. Only a month ago I'd faced an unbalanced murderer and barely escaped with my life.

Had there been someone there seconds ago? Had they been searching my vehicle when I interrupted them? A person could have easily hidden at the front or back of the Jeep and then popped out when I'd leaned forward to drop my bag on the adjacent seat. An even scarier thought came to mind. What if someone had planned to get into the Jeep, hide in the back, and wait on me? For what purpose? My thoughts whirled like the season's leaves now picked up by the breeze, blown helter-skelter over the asphalt. The strong wind now brought drops of rain hitting hard against the windshield.

Could I have left the door open? Or maybe some kid was looking for cigarettes or money to steal. With that thought, I shrugged my shoulders. The motion brought me back from my worries. I supposed I'd never know and wondered if I should tell Gibb. He might demand that I get him or Lam to drive me to and from work, but I didn't have time for that. I breathed in slowly through my nose and out my mouth as I shifted and finally accelerated. I thought about skipping my planned visit to Alma, but it would give me time to calm myself before going home. Mom could read me like a book, and I didn't want to worry her.

The nursing home looked brighter and more cheerful in the darkness than I'd expected. Light spilled from every window, and the sounds of a TV game show drifted across the parking lot. As I ran across the parking lot, holding my hands over my head since I didn't have an umbrella, I thought it seemed like a party. I pressed the bell by the door and pushed my way in when the buzzer signaled the release of the lock.

It seemed that most of the residents were in the lobby which doubled as a TV lounge. There were two card tables set up and a rousing bingo game competed with the volume of the television. However, it was a quilt frame in the corner that captured my attention. Eight women in straight-backed chairs circled the fabric stretched between the rails. Like a magnet, the colors drew me across the floor.

When I got closer, I could see a Tennessee Waltz quilt. I knew that the two-block pattern had no curved piecing, but the clever arrangement of angles certainly gave that impression. The hues of pink and green with a sharp contrast of navy made me want to run my hands over the taut surface.

I stepped closer and noticed Alma who, in her wheelchair, moved from one woman to another, directing their work.

"Darla, those stitches are too big. Let's tighten up. No more than ten to an inch. Look at Kathy Sue's if you need an example of what I expect. Norma. Norma. You call that a straight line? Those have to come out. Pick. Pick. Pick. Get to it."

A sultry voice whispered near my ear, "Chéri, do you think she was a general in a previous life? Napoleon, perhaps?"

I turned to find the sultry eyes of Annaleigh gazing at me. When I saw the expressive woman trying to hold back laughter, my own spilled over. For a minute we stood giggling together like girls on the schoolyard.

"Where did the quilt frame and quilt come from?" I asked. I was pretty sure it hadn't been there on my previous visits.

"I believe that dear Alma commandeered the contraption from Nurse Ratched, and the quilt is one that a new resident carried to this hopeless land just today. She'd had the forlorn thought of finishing her masterpiece herself in the peace and quiet of this rest home." She sighed with more drama than a teenager.

I blinked and, realizing my mouth hung open from her description, snapped my teeth together. At that moment something bumped the back of my legs. I whirled around to find Alma. She'd practically driven her wheelchair up on my ankles.

"Ouch," I squealed.

"Alma, I do declare you are a danger to us all," Annaleigh purred. "Earlier she bowled down two of our men, and they are in short supply among us ladies."

"Don't be a wimp, Stella. Getting old isn't for sissies and your turn will come all too quickly. Now what did you find out about cook?" Alma asked.

"Uh, well," I stuttered. Alma's eyes narrowed and I realized I had better come up with something fast to satisfy her. "I have someone checking and I'll be talking with him later." Lam was definitely getting a call from me tonight, and I prayed he had gotten some information to help me out of this predicament.

"Stella, this is serious. I thought I had impressed that upon you. The eggs at breakfast had barely felt the heat of a skillet. I don't like runny food." Alma looked back over her shoulder at the quilting group and shouted. "Jane, you've already used your allotted breaks. Sit back down and get to work."

Annaleigh sighed. "Alma you might well work them to death, and then where will you be?"

Alma chose to ignore the actress and directed her next jab at me. "I have an idea for that Heritage Center of yours, Stella. You are going to love it. Come with me and meet my crew."

The old woman grasped my elbow with her claws and tugged me forward a step. "My chair. You push."

I gripped the handles on the back of her wheelchair and moved us toward the quilting circle. From her seat, and with her foot still held straight out in front of her in its cast boot, Alma told me to move her clockwise around the frame.

She tapped each woman on the shoulder and announced their name as we passed.

I couldn't help but fall instantly in love with the quirky group. There was the sweet Martha who must have been in her late nineties. She looked as if a breath meant for blowing out candles on a cake would topple her over, but I noticed her stitches across the quilt top ran tiny and even. Next to her a stout and fairly strong-looking woman made, I kindly thought, dynamic stitches fit for basting. This must be Norma, as she picked out her work with a smile on her face. The tall and willowy Jane sat beside her looking as if she were having the time of her life. When she gazed up at me upon her introduction, I could tell that the only wrinkles her face would ever see would be smile lines. Kathy Sue nodded at me with a quick jerk of her chin and gave Alma a glare. Here, I knew, was the champion for the others. This Kathy Sue wouldn't let Alma go too far. Penny, Rhea, Anne, and Theresa rounded out the crafters.

"So that's the crew, Stella," Alma crowed. "Are you getting the picture?"

"Picture? I don't understand," I said.

I felt Annaleigh's hand on my arm. She whispered seemingly in my ear but somehow her words carried throughout the room, "Be careful, Chéri, it may be a trap." She looked over her shoulder.

Alma huffed. "Annaleigh, I believe Soldier is trying to get your attention."

When Alma motioned, Annaleigh and I both looked to see him sitting at one of the tables, studying his bingo card and oblivious to what was going on across the room. The caller drew a tile from the wire cage and yelled B3. Soldier jumped to his feet. "Yippeee. Bingo. Bingo."

"Wow, you'd think they were playing for money," I said.

Both Alma and Annaleigh gave me a withering stare. "Of course they are, sweet, innocent child." The actress tossed the words over her shoulder, making an exit worthy of Elizabeth Taylor.

"She has to get her cut before he spends it all buying black market cookies," Alma said. "So, Stella, doesn't this give you some idea." Her liver-spotted hand gestured our attention back to the quilting bee. "Quilting, your Heritage Craft Center. Quilting. Craft."

"Oh, oh. Oh my!" My heart seemed to leap into my throat. "They're perfect. Shue, just perfect."

"I knew you'd get it," she said, adding under her breath, "with a lot of prompting."

"I heard that."

"Well, now let's begin the negotiations." Alma rubbed her hands together and the dry papery sound brought to mind the skeletal hands of death.

Now my heart sank from my throat all the way to my toes.

CHAPTER 13

"So Alma is abusing you?" Gibb laughed so hard he began coughing until Lam finally got up from where he was sitting beside the fireplace and pounded him between the shoulder blades.

"It's not funny," Mom said. She moved from where she sat on the fireplace hearth to stand behind me, rubbing my back like she did when I was a child and upset. She'd been a wonderful mother. "At least she thought of you, Stella. It is an amazing idea. I mean a living history display, a quilting bee, right in the Center during the grand opening. I think it will be fantastic."

"Should sell a lot of quilts," Harley said.

"Yes, but I had to make a trade for it. I'm cooking breakfast at the home tomorrow morning. Well, ummm, Saturday and Sunday." I hated to reveal how Alma had bested me in our negotiations, but Mom would know and then Gibb. He'd be sure to tell Lam and on and on. It was best to get it over with. Just rip the Band-Aid off.

"I hope you don't have to buy the groceries," Gibb said.

"No. Alma promised that there's still plenty of food in the pantry."

"Honey, did you tell Alma you aren't, uh, Sewanee's best cook?" Mom asked.

"Mom! Really. I can handle eggs and toast. But I think seventy some residents are there. Maybe they won't all show in the dining room." I called Doodle Dog to jump onto my lap and gave him a big scratch behind both ears. Carly, giving a jealous whine, jumped up to settle on the couch between Esther and me for her share.

"I'm sorry, Stella, I'd help but I have to drive over to Memphis for the weekend," Harley said.

"I'd offer but I'm driving to Knoxville to help out an old friend with an engine overhaul," Lam added.

I just nodded. Somehow I'd muddle through without poisoning anyone, and it would be worth the work to have the quilting bee display for the whole week. I was just still amazed at this meeting I'd come home to.

Lam and Harley were both here—sitting as far from each other as possible—as well as Esther, our old family friend. The last attendee, Frank Coffee, had been a friend of Mom's since the first grade. Tonight I noticed for the first time that Frank, a widow of almost twenty years, seemed interested in Mom. That might be a new development, which I intended to watch over. Frank had won my heart last month with his efforts to help Mom through the ordeal of being accused of murder.

As soon as Harley had told Mom about the sorry state of my donations, she'd called everyone and asked them to come over in the evening. They were all excited, and I had to admit hope had caught up with me again.

Esther shifted the crutch she'd used following polio as a child and said, "Lordy, Stella, I didn't realize this new job of yours involved so much work. I'm proud of you."

"Thanks, Esther, but I'm on probation for a few months. Let's wait and see if I can get hired on permanently before anyone congratulates me." I watched as Mom picked up a tray of some kind of greenish-gray, doughy lumps.

She held the plate out to me. "This will cheer you up. Tofu stuffed okra."

Behind Mom's back Esther drew her finger across her neck.

"I couldn't, Mom. Truly, I'm stuffed." My stomach chose that moment to growl. I clutched my middle. "See, it's complaining that I ate too much lunch."

Esther jumped into the conversation to save me and said, "I've got some little carved animals and toys that my pa did up for me and my brothers. I remember Pawpaw sitting on the porch in the evenings whittlin' till it got dark. No television. For that matter, no indoor plumbin' either. Me, I'm right fond of progress." She laughed, causing her double chin to jiggle. "I'd be happy to see them in your store, Stella."

Esther was eighty-five so that had to make the toys from around the thirties.

Frank said, "My mama made dried apple-head dolls and corn shuck dolls. She sold them at the flea market to help feed us eleven kids." He dropped his head at the memory, shaking it slowly back and forth.

"I'll take good care of them, Frank. Keep them in one of the glass cases. Do you have some pictures of her that I could put in with the dolls?" I asked.

The evening, full of reminiscence of days gone past, went on for another hour. Everyone promised to call others and make my case. When Harley said he needed to get home to feed Smoky, I offered to walk him out to his truck. I tried not to look at Lam as I crossed the room but I felt like I was betraying him. It seemed as if dating two men preyed on my mind more than it brought fun to my social life.

As Harley shut the front door behind us, he slipped his arm around my shoulders and pulled me to him. "I was hoping to get a moment alone with you."

"Harley, I'm sorry about—"

Before I could finish my sentence about the speeding ticket, he shushed my words with a kiss. When he raised his head, he said, "Don't worry. I'm not. Gibb will come 'round." Then, with a confident grin, he strode over to his truck, disappearing down the drive.

I leaned against a porch post and stared into the darkness of the forest as it swallowed the glow of Trickster's tail lights. Sometimes I did wish I lived in a simpler time where the steep climb to the top of the Cumberland Plateau had isolated our community. As a child I'd read many stories of the pioneers who settled here. They were hardy souls who'd treasured their privacy, shunning the cities. Making do meant success, and the lazy moved back to civilization or died.

It wasn't all work, though. My thoughts wandered to the square dances that were still a common form of entertainment around Sewanee. I remembered hearing Wailin' Willy and the Four Plucked Angels play at a square dance just last month. Their music, one hundred percent American bluegrass, was a perfect reminder of what made this mountain sing. I knew they had cut a CD, and I could play it in the store. Maybe Willy would have an antique banjo and fiddle he would loan to the Center. In addition to the music, video of a dance would be fun. I could just hear the notes twanging throughout the big ol' log cabin as the tourists browsed the craft items—ones made long ago for show and new ones for sale.

That brought my thoughts to the moonshine still that I wanted for a display. I felt sure that tonight would be a good time to ask—no, demand—that Gibb find me one. After all, he had given Harley a speeding ticket, and I felt he owed me one. Just thinking about it again made me mad. Little brother wasn't the only one full of tricks. A sneaky thought had been dancing around in the back of my mind all evening. I had a long-time girl buddy whom I planned to introduce to Gibb. This boy had a date coming up that he was never going to forget. I giggled and decided I'd make the call tomorrow.

CHAPTER 14

When I opened my eyes Monday morning, my body groaned in sympathy for my pounding head and aching lower back. I was sure I owed the pain to hours spent standing over a hot stove in the nursing home kitchen for the last two mornings. Once I'd gotten the temperature adjusted, after turning a dozen eggs into crispy disks that a dog couldn't have eaten, I did okay. Or at least no one complained except Alma, but even she'd said thanks as I'd washed up the last dish.

Headaches this bad only struck me maybe once a year and this one was a doozy, but I didn't have time to be sick. At least that's what I told myself as I crawled out of bed and into the shower. I completed my morning preparations with a pair of baggy sweatpants, a sweater that had a hole at the neckline and a half unraveled cuff, and no makeup. *Now I look like I feel*, I thought, standing in front of the mirror, twisting damp hair into a knot and snapping a large clip over the messy mass.

I shuffled downstairs and found that, fortunately, Mom had already left for shopping at the farmer's market. Now I wouldn't need to force down the oatmeal she always made for me, but I did eat two spoonfuls of sugar, telling myself it was good medicine for a headache. I tossed Mom's note into the kitchen trash can, the one meant for composting, and headed out the door.

First on my list was something to eat and not anything nutritious. Hopefully, the gas station would have some of those raspberry glazed donuts left, as well as a fresh pot of coffee.

Fifteen minutes later I'd chomped my way through two donuts and slurped down a coffee so strong that I could have run the rest of the way to work faster than I drove. Maybe I even felt human at this point, until I stepped into the door of the Center. A shrill whine filled the air of the showroom as if the building had been invaded by every bee in the county. The noise penetrated my hands after I slapped them over my ears and it assaulted my brain. The headache roared back, a runaway train inside my skull.

Weaving around several bags of trash ready to be put out for pickup, I made my way into the main room to see it crowded with display cases scattered willy-nilly along with at least five wooden crates in the center of the room. I could hardly believe it. The freight truck must have come very early this morning instead of around noon as I'd been told to plan for.

I found Donnie wrestling with a super duty drill and a drill bit that looked something like a paddle.

"Donnie, Donnie," I screamed. I don't believe my handyman heard me but instead must have reached the intended depth of that hole. When he shut off the tool, he noticed me.

"Oh hey, boss lady." Donnie tugged sound-deadening ear muffs off his head, leaving his ears looking as red as if they'd been boxed by a champion. The ears also looked too big for his head. The smile, so genuine that his eyes crinkled, made me realize we'd become friends over these last days following his tragedy.

Donnie had become a different man and not just his personality. I noticed his ears stood out more because the face was thinner. When had the jowls disappeared and his belly shrunk? The thought flashed quickly through my mind, and then I turned back to the new furniture and ran my hands over the case nearest me. It was just a frame minus the glass.

"Glass is in them crates," he answered the question before I could ask.

"Donnie, I can't believe it. When did the truck arrive?"

"Oh, 'bout six. Glad I was here. Made sure everything was in good shape too before I signed for it. Hope that's all right with you, Miss Stella." Donnie placed the drill on the floor and dusted wood chips off his overalls.

"It's fine. Perfect."

Now I felt badly that I was thirty minutes late, but that still wouldn't have gotten me here in time for the delivery. I was so glad that I'd thought about Donnie when I stopped for breakfast. "I brought you something to eat." I held the bag and cup up. "What are the holes for?"

He took the bag and pulled out an egg and bacon biscuit. After curling the paper wrapper back, he took a big bite. "Right nice of you," he said, after a few seconds chewing. "These tall cases have to be anchored to the wall. Wouldn't want them to fall on some kid if he takes a notion to climb the thing." He held up a long bolt. "Read the instructions and these came along with the cases."

"So you're going to be at this for a while?" I asked, rubbing my temples and remembering the awful whine.

"Got several holes to drill. Say, you look a bit green."

"Just a headache but I think I'm going to leave you alone while you get this job finished. How about if you call me when you're ready, and I'll come back and help you put the cases into place?"

"I don't mean to speak out of my place, but you're a mite small for wrestling something so heavy. I'm going to call a cousin of mine. He'll help for twenty bucks."

"That's thoughtful of you, Donnie." I dug through my wallet and pulled out a bill. I didn't expect him to pay for help from his own pocket. When he took it, I placed my hand on his arm. "Thanks, and I mean that."

I left him with instructions to call if he needed anything and said I'd be back in a few hours regardless. Now, already on the road, I realized that I really hadn't thought about how I could use this time except I wanted, and needed, a quiet spot. That wouldn't be at Mom's, as I knew she had several friends coming over after their trip to the farmer's market. They planned to do a winter's worth of canning while enjoying talk time. Then for several days she'd be at each of their houses in turn doing the same. I guess the mountain had been blessed with a bumper crop of okra.

The library should be restful, especially in the small microfiche room which was the size of a closet. I doubted that the Nashville newspapers from over a decade ago were online, and my curiosity about the bank robbery had finally boiled over.

Frances gave me a sour look as I walked in, telling her I'd be in the back for a while. With my pounding head I didn't feel like trying to make amends to her, although on my way out, if I felt better, maybe I'd talk for a minute. I closed the door of the viewing room behind me and found that even the jarring scraping noise of the chair legs against the floor made me cringe. Fifteen minutes and two pills later, though,

I finally felt better, and with the close air in the room, my eyes were at half-staff. When I saw what I was looking for, it brought me back fully awake.

The headline read BANK GUARD SEES DOUBLE. The first sentence of the story told how Virgil Muller, forty-year veteran as a bank guard, had been drunk at work when the Nashville Guaranty Savings was robbed.

The reporter continued with a quote by the bank president. "Seeing double! Preposterous! Mr. Muller, you are fired!"

The reporter now gave the facts of how, at five minutes before closing, a man with a ski cap covering his face rushed into the lobby brandishing a pistol. The teller handed over close to $15,000 while everyone else was made to lie face down on the floor under threat of being shot. As the robber made his daring escape, Mr. Muller gave chase. The guard reported that the man stopped just outside the door and looked both ways. Then, according to the guard, he cussed a blue streak. At this point the guard grabbed him from behind. The robber twisted away, shooting the older man in the side. The robber then ran through a narrow passage between the bank and the store next to it.

Halfway down that path the criminal pulled his mask off, while turning to see if the guard was near. Mr. Muller, now feeling the effects of blood loss, was no longer able to follow but said he got a good look as the robber took a step or two toward him before running off. "I felt for sure he was going to come back and finish me off with another bullet."

Mr. Muller staggered back to the sidewalk, where he said a car screeched to a stop at the curb. In fact, the guard reported that the robber was at the wheel even though he had just seconds before seen the man running away in the opposite direction. The reporter added that, thanks to the guard's description of the older model car, the police were able to find it quickly. The vehicle was discovered abandoned and had been stolen earlier the same day.

The guard stated he had not been drinking but suffered from a summer cold and had taken over-the-counter medicine.

A fuzzy photo showed an older man lying on a sidewalk with a cop leaning over him. The caption stated 'Policeman offers aid while waiting on the ambulance.'

My thoughts were a jumble with the details of the story. It seemed so odd to read the story from the perspective of knowing who that robber had been. I'd never met Ronnie Clark, but I could picture his face easily since it was certainly a familiar one to me.

Donnie had told me that his brother had gone to court admitting guilt and asked for mercy in sentencing. Ronnie did claim that he had shot the guard accidentally, and that he was coming back to the guard to help and not to kill him. He said, under oath, that he ran because he heard shouts from the front of the bank.

The microfiche machine fan hummed steadily and the heat from the light bulb was enough to put me in a trance as my mind explored that time a decade in the past. Then, staring at the green wall of the booth, I remembered how I had stood next to Donnie's work van mistakenly thinking that my handyman was dead. The face of Ronnie had looked exactly like the man I'd hired. It seemed to me that years in prison would have changed the face that had been created so identical to another that I couldn't tell them apart.

Then I wondered about the guard, the older man Mr. Muller, stating that he'd seen the robber reappear again in just seconds. How could Ronnie be two places at once or, rather, so quickly? One answer had already formed in my mind. In fact, it had been playing on the fringes yesterday.

I scrolled the microfiche film down to the next day's newspaper hoping for more information. A follow-up article appeared. This one was accompanied by another grainy photo of Mr. Muller now lying in a hospital bed. He stated that he didn't believe it was right that he'd been fired from his job. The reporter asked if he had been fit to work that day since he'd obviously not been able to capture the robber or even to be a reliable witness to the events.

"I must have blacked out for a few seconds. I was hurting something fierce with that bullet in my side. That's the only explanation," Virgil told this reporter. "I never missed a day of work in my life, and I wasn't going to start because of a little cold."

I moved through four more issues of newspapers before finding another mention of the robbery. This one answered my last question about how Ronnie had been captured. He had been seen by at least two people when he stole the get-away car, and one had recognized him. Tough luck for him but good work by the police.

I snapped the machine's light off and rolled the film into a loop small enough to slip into its storage box. Now there was only one unanswered question. Where was the money? The article mentioned that the take was close to $15,000. It had never been recovered, and in court Ronnie said it had been lost in his haste to escape capture. No one believed that story. It wasn't a huge amount of money but certainly enough to drive some to murder even a decade later.

By the time I left the library, the headache had receded to a vague nagging pain that I could deal with. I'd even managed to apply some blush and comb out my hair in the library restroom so that I didn't look like a zombie anymore.

When I saw that a gentle rain was falling, I stood still under the overhang outside the door. I waited for a moment, although I knew it was one of those all-day-water-the-plants kind of rains. It settled things down though by wrapping the treetops in low-hanging clouds and damping the normal noises. The birds sat quiet, all fluffed out, on branches. It was a nice moment, and I tried to stop the questions from echoing constantly in my mind and just enjoy the solitude.

My thoughts continued to twist on the subjects of murder and robbery like brightly colored clothes going round and round in the dryer, flashes of hues with no hint of which was a shirt and which a skirt. I made myself mentally switch off. Sometimes when I didn't know all the answers to a problem, I tucked the puzzle pieces to the back of my mind. I let them jostle around on their own, hoping they'd sort themselves together into a pretty picture.

When I got into the Jeep, I flipped through the contact list in my phone and pulled up the number for my friend Arcadia D'Rocca. She owed me a big favor. I knew the kind of women Gibb liked to date and Arcadia did not fit the bill. He liked them sweet and demure. Wild, strong women had been his kryptonite ever since the incident in high school when he fell for the class bad girl and had gotten into trouble. Now operation Put-Little-Brother-in-His-Place was about to begin. After talking to Arcadia, as I jabbed the end-call icon and started the Jeep, I grinned like an opossum.

CHAPTER 15

When I walked through the door of the Center, the scene that met my eyes was amazing. All the cases were in place in the room with the glass and shelves fitted into them. Every inch of glass sparkled and I saw why. Mom was busy cleaning with her green method of old newspapers and vinegar-laced water. She must have given up her morning of canning for me.

Then I noticed that there were even a few items already on display. With his back to me, Harley arranged pieces of face-jug pottery. Three that I could see. I almost squealed with joy, as they were my favorite type of handmade clayware. I loved how the creative potters fashioned detailed human faces, from comical to downright scary, on the outside of mugs and jugs. There were jug-handle ears, scheming squinty eyes, and chiclet teeth. In other words, they were adorable.

I noticed Lam rooting around in a box. He stood, shaking out a yellowing wedding dress and then a baby's christening gown. They were beautiful in their simple elegance, and I hoped they were hand-stitched.

"Miss Stella," Donnie, the first to notice me, said hurrying over. "What do you think? It's starting to come together, ain't it? Your mama—what a sweet lady—stopped by, and then she called in the others. Cousin Dwight's worked right hard. I'm proud of him."

In my excitement, I grabbed his arm. "Oh, Donnie, thank you, thank you. I can't believe my eyes." I was ready to dance the man across the room when I noticed his cheeks were now glowing like birthday candles, and I let go. "Is that your cousin?" I pointed to a young guy now stuffing the mounds of shipping wrap used to protect the glass into empty boxes. "I want to thank him."

"Yep. That's Dwight." He walked me over to a wiry young guy. No one else had noticed yet that I'd returned because someone had brought a radio in, and it was blaring country music.

As I thanked Dwight for helping Donnie, the sounds of Lam and Harley talking became clear over the noise of the radio. Except really they were yelling. I turned to see what they were upset about. My boyfriends were arguing over which one of them was helping me more.

"It's just a moonshine jug. Now, this says something important about my people." Lam's voice was a rumble.

I glanced over my shoulder to see Harley scrutinize the dresses Lam held. "Where'd you find these? You know Stella said this pottery was her favorite." His tone sounded more in control than Lam's.

Then, just as Harley reached out and fingered the fabric, Lam shoved him, his hand giving Harley's shoulder a quick, hard push. I had just a second to register the surprised look on Lam's face at his own action and saw him start to say something. I could see that he'd instantly regretted what he had done. The unexpected motion caused Harley to drop the jug, and it shattered on the floor.

His expression, if possible, showed even more surprise than my old friend's, but if Lam had already gotten control of his emotions, it was too late now. Harley swung his fist and caught him on the side of the head. Harley bent double, cradling one hand and yowling with the pain he'd inflicted on himself.

Harley turned away from Lam, and when he straightened, it was easy to see that the discomfort he felt had given him back his self-control. He looked ready to face Lam calmly. That's when Lam tackled Harley, and they fell. Locked in an unhappy embrace, the pair rolled across the floor, both shouting insults.

Mom was the first to react, rushing to try and pull them apart but having to dodge so that they didn't sweep her off her feet.

The last fight I had witnessed was over the swing set at the elementary school playground. I realized that I was paralyzed with shock just as I had been long ago, standing with my hands covering my mouth. What could only have been seconds felt like long minutes.

I turned to Donnie and a single word squeaked from my lips, "Help."

He motioned for Dwight to assist, and together they dived into the fight. Still, it seemed like some game with the two men rolling first one direction for a few feet and then reversing, legs flailing. They were bumping into everything, including a solid kick to the glass of one of my cases. Mom, Donnie, and Dwight hopped around in the effort to stay on their feet while trying to grab ahold of something—an arm, a leg, a shirt—to use to pry the brawlers apart.

That's when I noticed my boss Janice standing in the doorway of the Center. I hadn't heard the bell over the grunts and groans of the fight. Her mouth, compressed into a stern straight line, managed to say it all. My previous joy at seeing my beautiful display cases evaporated in the face of this disaster. I wasn't sure she would let me keep my job another five minutes, much less grant me permanent job status.

I sprinted toward her just as a figure filled the doorway behind where she stood. Whoever it was looked huge. He was a mountain of a man and looked even bigger because he was carrying something, some large metal object, although he would loom over most others anyway. Not being able to see Janice because his vision was blocked, he bumped into her back, forcing the woman forward a few staggering steps. Fortunately, she didn't fall.

"Ms. Price," I said, clutching her arm, helping to steady her. "Are you alright?" I had to raise my voice to be heard over the fight and the attempts to break it up. It sounded like Mom had gotten the upper hand by yelling.

"What is going on, Stella?" Janice asked. "There had better be a good answer for this spectacle."

I reached out and attempted to brush her hair back from where it had fallen across her face from the forward motion. She slapped my hands away.

At that moment the man standing just inside the door dropped the large metal object he'd been carrying. The clang as it struck the floor reverberated through the room assaulting the ears. At least it served to stop the fight. A glance showed me—if I knew my mountain history—part of a still. Then, in a booming voice, the man asked, "Where do you want the still, lady?"

That's when I noticed the reek of alcohol. It wafted through the room and brought tears to my eyes as the clear liquid leaked from the still onto my wooden floor.

This had to be the worst moment of my life, and I spoke without thinking. "Well, it can't get any worse."

The big mountain man gazed at Janice and said, "You ain't from these parts are you, pretty lady? I got some 'shine in my pickup if you'd like a drinkie."

Janice gave a humph and shouldered past the man and out the door. In seconds I heard the screech of tires from a fast departure.

"Oh, shue. This can't be happening." I pinched myself hard on the arm, hoping that I'd wake and discover that this had all been a nightmare. It wasn't.

The man who had delivered my still said, "Well, she was kinda snooty, weren't she? You must be the sheriff's sister. Where do you want it, lady?" He had to dip his head so that he was eye-to-eye with me and that gave me a whiff of his breath. It was one hundred proof—he'd already had a drink or two or twenty—and I felt my stomach protest with a lurch.

I backed up a step so that I could get some fresher air into my lungs. "I'm sorry. I'm not ready for it yet. I need to build a stand in front of this window. Why don't you just leave all the pieces out back? I have a small shed. We, I mean someone here, can put it together," I said, waving in the general direction of everyone standing behind me.

The bunch of them were a pitiful spectacle. Lam rubbed his cheek, which was turning shades of purple and blue. Harley cradled his hand while Mom wouldn't look at me. She seemed, all of a sudden, to find the ceiling fascinating. Donnie had gone to help Dwight finish the task of preparing the packing material for the trash.

"Here," I said to the mountain man as I felt the tears building behind my eyes, "follow me and I'll open the shed for you."

"Sure thing, lady." He heaved the still back up onto his shoulder.

As I walked past Mom, Lam, and Harley, I poked the air in front of them with my finger. "You three stay put. I'll be right back to deal with you." I speared them with a teary-eyed glare. I needed a few minutes to cool off so that I didn't say anything I'd really regret. Harley started to say something, but I held both hands out.

It took at least fifteen minutes for the man, whose name was Earnest Carter, to transfer all the parts from his truck to my shed. The parts included the copper coils and several Mason jars. One was suspiciously full of a clear liquid. I decided not to ask questions after Ernest was nice enough to offer to return to reassemble the still. I gratefully agreed to call in a few days for his help, as the contraption turned out to be much more complicated than I had ever imagined.

Earnest surprised me by asking dozens of questions about the Heritage Craft Center and left with the promise to bring me a plow handmade by his great grandfather. The man turned plumb pink when I asked if I could record him explaining how moonshine was made and any stories he had about revenue men.

After that I felt I could face Mom and the boyfriends without exploding—at least if I didn't think about the look on Janice's face when she'd stomped out. I would have to call her and beg to keep my job. The three had the good grace to look sheepish when I faced them. They stood in a rag-tag line looking the worse for wear like wayward sailors after a bad port-of-call.

First, I said, "Okay, Mom, you can go home. I'll talk to you later, and thanks for helping today." I knew that this—not letting her hear what I said to Lam and Harley—would be the worst punishment I could dish out.

She opened and closed her mouth. Then stepped close and hugged me. "I love you, honey. Don't forget that I breast-fed you for a year," she whispered in my ear before leaving.

I turned my attention to the two men in my life. Lam's flannel shirt, missing a button, was twisted askew. Harley cradled his right hand, and I could see that the pinkie finger was swollen and already purple.

"Lam, why did you hit Harley?" I asked.

"That wedding dress was my grannie's. Her mama made it. The christening gown was worn by every one of her eight children."

Harley dipped his head. "I'm sorry, Lam. I apologize."

Lam had to consider only a second before he said, "I accept your apology, and I owe you one right back. I'll replace that jug." He reached out, offering Harley his hand to shake.

Harley looked plenty relieved to put the fight behind them, but when he stuck his hand out, we all could see that it would hurt too much to shake hands. Lam thumped him on the back instead.

Lam said, "Hope that finger isn't broken."

Harley said, pointing, "Looks like you got cut on the broken pottery. You're bleeding pretty good."

Lam raised his forearm to see how severe the cut was.

"Oh, Lam," I cried out. Seeing them both hurt drove my anger away.

"I think you might need a stitch or two." Harley offered Lam his handkerchief and even helped tie it around the arm with his good hand.

"You probably need an X-ray," Lam added.

"Come on, you two. I'll drive you to the hospital. Let me get Harley an ice pack first."

CHAPTER 16

"Mom. Mom," I called. I wanted to get Mom's attention before she had a chance to start asking me questions about Harley and Lam. I had to get Mom to do something for me and do it quickly. I glanced at the clock on the kitchen stove as I shoved the back door closed behind me and called again more loudly. "Mom." I tossed my keys and tote onto the table, and that's when I noticed the casserole dish containing stuffed cabbage rolls on the counter alongside a salad bowl filled with several kinds of greens and peppers cut into chunks.

Mom barreled into the kitchen. "What are you yelling about? Are the guys okay? I've been worried sick, Stella."

"I'll tell all in a minute, Mom. Just do me one little favor without asking any questions." Before she could speak, I held my hand out to stop her protests and continued. "Give Gibb a call and ask him to come over. Don't, I repeat, do not say anything about staying for supper, but just tell him that you need a quick favor and then he's free to take off."

I needed Gibb to come over, but I didn't want Mom to scare him off by trying to push any of her cooking off on him.

"Now what on earth do I need to do that for?"

"Because if you don't, you won't get to hear how things turned out with Harley. You remember Harley, the guy you've been rooting for these last few weeks? The guy you were passing inside information to?"

Mom gave me that stare that only mothers can master, but she saw that I wasn't, for once, going to budge.

"Okay, okay." She snatched up the phone and punched the numbers to dial her son. I wondered if she was the only person in Tennessee who still had a phone with a cord connected to the wall.

I listened to the beginning of the conversation—enough to hear that Gibb would come by soon—but then dashed up the stairs to my room to change.

I wasn't really going out, but I needed by the time Gibb showed up, to look like I was ready to head out for a girl's night on the town with Arcadia. She would be here any second, setting my plan in motion. I pumped my fist into the air, but mostly I was just trying to cheer myself up. I was still smarting from this afternoon's events.

I'd only been able to reach Janice's assistant when I had phoned to apologize and explain. Janice had been in a meeting all afternoon and then, the assistant said, she had a press conference and cocktail party to attend. My boss had asked the assistant to tell me to come to Nashville tomorrow sometime around lunch for us to have a long talk. My stomach twisted into a knot and tightened. I wasn't sure I could even eat a bite of supper, not even out of my cracker, Slim Jim, and cookie stash. The fear of being fired from a job I already loved made me sick.

As bad as that was, I now felt responsible for getting both Lam and Harley injured. I wasn't at all sure about what to do to fix things. The guys had helped each other into my Jeep and talked about cars all the way to the urgent care clinic. It hadn't taken long to get an X-ray for Harley and three stitches for Lam. Harley had a clean break in the little finger and would need to wear a splint for a few weeks. The doctor had admonished the guys, saying they were too old to be fighting like boys.

On the drive home I'd hardly been able to get a word in, as they'd been laughing over what already seemed like a good yarn to tell their friends.

I shook my head at the memory as I stepped into a skirt, tugged on cowboy boots, and pulled a sweater over my head, causing my hair to crackle with static electricity. Jewelry topped off the outfit, and my makeup only took a couple of minutes. I swiped a ton of blush across my cheeks and then some on my eyelids to convince Gibb that I planned to go to the Honky Tonk with Arcadia for a drink and dancing. Little did my brother know that he was in for the evening of his life.

When I returned to the kitchen, I was in luck to find Mom wasn't in the room. Knowing she would insist that I eat some supper before leaving, I took the smallest cabbage roll and plopped it onto a plate, pale green and stringy. The smell that assaulted my nose made my already tense stomach turn. It was a relief to set the plate on the floor, giving myself some distance. I looked at Carly curled on the braided rug under the kitchen table. I only needed for Mom to think I'd eaten. If she had a garbage disposal, I wouldn't have to keep torturing the dogs.

"Carly. Come here, sweetheart. I know you want something to eat. Yummy," I said, clapping my hands together to call the little dog. Carly edged closer but clearly wasn't excited by the smell. Now where was Doodle Dog? He was much more the chow hound and more reliable for getting rid of Mom's food. "Here, baby. Yum. Yum," I said, pushing the plate closer to the dog. Carly stopped and rolled to her back, whining. The smart little pooch was begging for mercy.

I heard Mom coming back through the dining room toward the kitchen. I barely had time to snatch the plate from the floor and stand up. When Mom walked in, I was holding the dish but didn't have a fork.

Mom took in the situation and went to the silverware drawer. Handing me the utensil, she said, "Well, at least you're going to eat something good for you. I'm surprised." Her mouth turned down at the corners as she took in my appearance from head to toe. "Obviously you're going out tonight. Do you have a date?"

"An old friend. Girlfriend."

"Oh," she said, sounding disappointed that I hadn't mentioned Harley. "Aren't you going to eat that?" Mom pointed at the plate. "Sit down. I'll get you some water."

But Mom didn't turn away. She continued to watch me holding the plate and fork. I speared a piece of the cabbage and brought the bite close to my mouth. I was just going to have to eat the whole thing. I could fit this into my plan though and make it more realistic. After Arcadia arrived and Gibb was here, I was going to suddenly claim that my stomach was too upset to go out.

Then I would talk Gibb into taking my friend to the Honky Tonk, Sewanee's only bar. Arcadia's job as a restaurant and bar reviewer for the Nashville area gave me the perfect reason that she had to go. I'd claim that, with the bar located down a couple of our switch-back roads, Arcadia would need a guide and escort, as sometimes it got rather lively. Gibb knew that. He regularly got called out to stop bar fights.

I scraped the bite off the fork with my teeth, wishing I could swallow without tasting. It definitely wasn't fried chicken, or gravy, or anything that normal people considered edible, but I had no choice. One bite after another had almost cleaned the plate as Mom sat across the table from me. Her smile made the awful meal almost worth it.

A knock on the kitchen door caused Mom to jerk around. "Must be your friend. Anyone else would come on in." She waved me back to my seat. "I'll get it. You finish that. You finally seem like you're enjoying something that I've cooked."

I knew the arrival had to be Arcadia, as I'd told her to come to the back door.

"Welcome," Mom said, swinging the door wide and stepping back to let my friend enter. I breathed a sigh of relief that Arcadia hadn't changed one bit since I'd last seen her about three months ago.

I jumped to my feet and rushed to hug my friend, embracing her thin figure wrapped in clothing that could only be described as interesting, if I wanted to remain polite. Over Arcadia's shoulder I could see Mom eyeing her up and down from the hair, purple today, to the platform boots and, in between, the tattoos—full sleeves down both arms with an inked ribbon around her throat. All these were beautiful, colorful images professionally done.

My friend still smelled like mint because she loved to chew the leaves. It brought a rush of memories of all my friends back in Nashville and almost made me cry. I loved my new life here, but I did miss my girlfriends. Our group of five had gotten together at least twice a month for the last several years to eat out or have a drink at whatever was the newest trendy place about the city.

That was how we had met Arcadia. At that time she'd been a reviewer for the big-city newspaper. Now she worked for herself blogging her reviews. She happened to be sitting at the table next to ours and listened as we grumbled that the restaurant wasn't any good. She'd rushed over, pulled out a chair, and made herself at home with us as she took notes on our comments.

Now I leaned back and touched her cheek with a finger. "You got a new tat. I love it." A vivid yellow and black bumble bee graced her ivory skin.

She laughed her usual throaty chuckle filling the kitchen. "I got two new ones, but you'll never guess where the other is. Believe me, you don't want to know." She whirled around and hugged Mom. "You must be Cele, and I've heard you are absolutely the world's best Mom."

"Well, that's nice to hear." Mom's smile widened. "Sit. Sit. I want to hear how you met Stella. And what do you do?" She slid away from the table as Arcadia took the chair.

"Wait." Arcadia sniffed the air. "What is it you made for dinner? I know that wasn't our girl Stella cooking. I haven't eaten all day, and it smells wonderful."

"Really?" I asked before I could stop myself.

Mom gave me a sharp look and replied, "It's cabbage rolls stuffed with beans, cauliflower, and sunflower seeds."

I studied the last bite of my meal on the plate. I would have never guessed that the rolled cabbage leaves contained those ingredients, but it sounded much better than it had tasted. I looked back at Mom, and if she had been charmed before, she was now enchanted with my friend.

"Would you like some? I made plenty," Mom said.

"Yes, please. I'm a vegan so it's not often that I can get a real meal at anyone's house. Sometimes they eat their hamburgers in front of me while all I get is potato chips." Arcadia gave me a pointed stare.

"But it's all I had," I wailed.

"See?" Arcadia accepted the plate Mom offered and immediately popped a fork full into her mouth. "Um, um." For the next several minutes she continued to eat while Mom promised to write down the recipe and also to give her several jars of canned vegetables to take home.

"Oww, sweet deal, but you're making me feel guilty. I came empty-handed tonight. Wait." Arcadia snapped her fingers and pulled her bag closer. "Here," she said, thrusting what looked like a baggie half full of marijuana toward Mom.

That's the moment Gibb slipped in the back door. I could see his glance take in Arcadia and how totally different she was from the Sewanee crowd. Then his gaze caught on the baggie, and he crossed to the table and picked up the bag before Mom could take it.

I knew my friend well enough to know she didn't do drugs. She was an avowed health nut, but my brother didn't know that. The look on his face was worth everything I was going to hear from him once he realized he had been conned. I had known that Arcadia was the perfect one to put Gibb in his place, and she did owe me that huge favor. That's how I'd gotten her to agree to this. The mint had been an accident, I was sure.

"Gibb, this is my friend Arcadia D'Rocca," I said, as I watched him open the bag and sniff. His face glowed red as he sealed the bag and handed it back to Mom.

"Mint," he said.

I stuffed the last cold bite of supper into my mouth to stifle my laughter.

CHAPTER 17

My Jeep sailed down the mountain toward Nashville, slicing through a light, early morning fog. I yawned. I hadn't been able to sleep much last night between wondering how Gibb and Arcadia had done together and my dread of meeting with my boss.

My appointment with Janice—and possible firing—wasn't until noon so I'd decided to do something that I'd been wanting to do since my trip to the library. I needed to talk to both the bank president and the guard who had been shot. I had a theory, and they were, supposedly, the only people who could help me figure it out.

So far, as he'd admitted, Gibb had made no progress in solving the murder of Ronnie Clark. It wasn't that I wanted to interfere, but I was involved, and the more I got to know Donnie, the more I liked the man. He was a decent human being. Well, that led to another crazy theory of mine that I needed to prove. It hadn't been hard to figure out that something was wrong with Donnie. He certainly was a changed man from the handyman I'd hired a couple of weeks ago. I now believed Donnie was dead and Ronnie had taken his place. The new Donnie didn't look quite right, and he was a hardworking and efficient handyman. Donnie had never been a good worker, but I couldn't just hand this over to Gibb without being more sure of my theory.

First, I was thinking that obviously Debbie had to know. No one could mistake another man for her husband of many years. The question then had to be if Debbie was involved or was she being forced to go along with the deception? I didn't know the woman well, but I would bet on her involvement. With that thought, though, and because I couldn't know for sure, I didn't want to do anything that might jeopardize her safety. And there was a child to consider.

I wondered that I wasn't afraid for my own safety, but I'd never had any feeling that this Ronnie, the fake Donnie, even though he was a convicted criminal, would hurt me. There was the incident outside the back of the Center when I'd been shoved, but somehow Ronnie always seemed benign, safe, passive. I shook my head. Was I being naive? Someone had shoved me, but maybe it had been a kid out doing something he shouldn't have.

I would gather some evidence before I took this to Gibb in a few days. Thinking about my brother made me giggle again, and I'd been doing that at odd moments all morning. I wished I'd had a camera when he'd thought Arcadia was giving Mom a bag of marijuana. Probably walking into the Honky Tonk with her on his arm, so to speak, had him crawling under the table. I laughed outright. Oh, to have been a fly on the wall.

I'd been surprised when my brother hadn't brought Arcadia back to the house to pick up her car until sometime after midnight. They must have returned during one of my fitful periods of sleep even though I'd been listening for the unmistakable rumble of his old Mustang. Now I'd have to wait until later today to find out how the date went. It had been easy enough to pretend to be sick after eating Mom's casserole. Arcadia played along, saying she'd be fine finding this place and sitting there alone for a few hours. She'd even given a little shiver when she said those words.

After that I hadn't needed to suggest that Gibb escort my friend and stay while Arcadia got everything she needed to write the review. Mom had done the dirty work for me. So much the better.

After the pair left, Mom and I had spent an hour talking, so I'd gotten her up to speed on the condition of our two boys after their brawl. Then I'd asked her why she was pushing Harley at me.

The answer came on a long sigh. "It's just, well, Lam is like my son. I know, I know," she said, flapping her hands in the air. "I'm finished meddling. I promise, and I think after tonight Gibb is too." She'd grinned and told me she had sewing to do.

Her business was still going strong, and I knew she was finishing up five quilts for a gallery showing in Japan. Mom and I both were surprised at the price her work brought in that country. I loved seeing her take on this challenge and expand her business, and although she didn't have time to make more quilts, she was designing some patterns and kits. I was trying to help as much as I could around getting the Center ready.

Before she headed to her studio, Mom bent and kissed me on the forehead. "I just want you to be happy, sweetie. Follow your heart, and I'll be right there behind you, supporting you, waiting on some grandkids." She tossed the last words over her shoulder on her way out of the room.

A honking horn brought me out of my reverie, and I slowed to let an antsy driver pass. Then, I exited the highway. A couple of miles later I was in the Ridgeway section of

Nashville, where I'd discovered on the internet that the now-retired bank president Mr. Doan lived. The houses here were all older and small but sitting on huge, manicured lots that must cause developers and real estate agents to drool.

The house number was prominent, and I swung the Jeep up the driveway as Mr. Doan had instructed when I'd called last night to see if he'd mind me stopping by with some questions. The man had sounded eager for company.

"Come on in, young lady. Come in. You're right on time, and the brownies are ready to come out of the oven in about—" The sharp peal of a kitchen timer sounded. "Well, right about now. Ice cream? Or are you a purist?" He led the way through a living room with too many pieces of furniture scattered haphazardly and stacks of books everywhere.

The kitchen was stuffed also but with every kitchen gadget ever invented.

As I watched him remove the brownie pan from the oven and test it with a toothpick, I answered, "Oh, ice cream. Vanilla or chocolate. Either makes me happy."

He laughed. "Or both? We'll be twice as happy. Now where is that ice cream scoop?"

He continued to search through drawers, scattering other items like a potato masher, garlic press, and a boiled egg slicer across the Formica counter before the scoop surfaced. As he pulled two cartons of ice cream out of the freezer, he asked in a muffled voice, "What got you interested in that old robbery? If I might ask."

I didn't think I had any right to hide anything from the elderly man who was being so friendly, so I laid the facts out quickly. When I'd finished speaking, he pressed a bowl containing a beautiful brownie sundae into my hands.

"Dead, huh? Well, that's sad." Mr. Doan carefully cut a piece of brownie and balanced the bite with the chocolate and vanilla toppings.

I watched quietly while he savored the sweet taste, as I could see he was thinking things through.

He swallowed. "Young lady, you said you read the newspaper accounts. What did you expect me to be like? What kind of man did you expect to find this morning?"

I sputtered, not wanting to answer the question. Everything I had read led me to believe Mr. Doan would be a pompous person, someone full of himself.

"I'll bet that the word pompous rolled through your head." He pointed at me and laughed. "And you're right. At least in the past. Not a year after the robbery, after I'd fired poor Virgil, I was fired also when my little bank was gobbled up by a larger one in a merger. Losing everything, or almost everything," he reached over and patted the kitchen wall to indicate the house, "opens your eyes. But I really can't tell you much about the robbery. I was sitting in my office on the phone. I didn't realize my bank was being robbed until it was practically over. Shouting alerted me, and then my big contribution was to fire the man who had acted so heroically."

My throat tightened as I watched Mr. Doan staring into space. I hated that I'd revived sad memories for him.

"Who you need to talk to is Virgil." He tapped the end of his spoon on the tabletop like it were a drum. "Definitely."

"I tried to find him on the internet but couldn't."

"Pull your phone out, Stella."

"Really? You've got his phone number?" I felt like hugging the man and dancing him around the room.

Twenty minutes later I headed the Jeep through the heavy downtown traffic toward Janice's office in the state building, but not before I'd spoken with the former bank guard. I had found out that he traveled with his job, and Virgil said that sometime this week he would be coming near Sewanee. He promised to stop and talk with me. I couldn't do any better than that, so I found a parking garage with an empty slot and tried to soothe myself with the thought that I'd been halfway successful today.

Now if I could only keep my job, I'd be one happy woman!

CHAPTER 18

The drive back to Sewanee was like a vacation now that I'd been given a second chance by Janice. I'd groveled plenty, and then, once I'd started to tell her about my ideas for the Center, Janice had warmed to me. She even liked that I'd been resourceful enough to find a still, although she didn't know I had inside help with my brother being the sheriff. Permission to keep it came with the condition that the smell could be eliminated. I had been happy to agree to her terms, but when I walked into the Center, the aroma of good ol' mountain corn mash assaulted me. The pungent odor of one-hundred-proof brought tears to my eyes.

"Ain't it awful?" Donnie asked. "I tried scrubbing, even bleaching them spots, but it don't smell no better to me. I'm not a drinking man myself. Can't understand how anyone can pour that stuff down their throat." Donnie had a young boy with him, and his hand rested protectively around his slight shoulders. "Miss Stella, this is my son Jay. He's the best kid in the Volunteer State." With those words Donnie ruffled the boy's hair.

"Dad," Jay whispered his embarrassment.

"Well, it's true. He's in the top of his class, all his teachers can't say enough good stuff about him, and the coaches are always fighting over him. Jay's good at all the sports."

"Jay, it is very nice to meet you." I automatically reached out my hand to shake his.

The young boy hesitated and his gaze focused on the floor. I hadn't meant to put him in a tough spot, but I realized the boy was shy when his hand in mine shook. So this was the boy whom Debbie said had gotten himself into trouble at school the other day. She'd even said that she and Donnie were going to have to talk with the principal.

"Well, your dad is right to be proud of you," I said. "I bet that you've never seen the inside of the principal's office, have you?"

Jay's head jerked up. "No, ma'am. I've never been in detention either. Plus I've got perfect attendance." He smiled and then stared again at his shoes.

"Well, I got my share of hours after school," I said.

"Me, too." Donnie laughed, and it was obvious that being around Jay made the man happy. "He got out of school early today and walked over, so if you don't mind I thought I'd take him across the street to get a bite to eat."

"No problem. How about you take the rest of the afternoon off? I'll bet you can find something fun to do," I said.

At this point I really wanted to confront Donnie, but I still needed to hear Virgil Muller's story. I wondered again that I wasn't afraid of the handyman, but somehow I wasn't. I would wait a day or two when I had more evidence that this was really Ronnie. But somehow I did not think he'd murdered his own brother.

I followed them through to the back room, where Donnie slipped into his coat while Jay did the same. I watched as the father grabbed the knit stocking cap that I'd seen him wearing these last cold days off the hook. He pulled it over Jay's head, tugging the hat all the way over the boy's eyes.

"Dad," Jay protested but sounded happy as he did. He pushed it back so that he could see and preceded Donnie out the door.

Donnie turned back at the last second. "I fixed the light switch here. Noticed you had it covered in tape so I figured it was shorted out." He flipped the switch up and light blazed in the room from the overhead fixture.

In mid-step, hearing the words, I stumbled but caught myself on the edge of the counter. My breath rushed out in a whoosh and that gave me an excuse not to answer right away.

"Are you okay, Miss Stella?"

"Fine, uh, just tripped, and thanks for fixing that. Go have a good time." I waved him out the door. Now that was what I called proof! Maybe not something that would stand up in court, but it was good enough for me. The real Donnie hadn't learned to be an electric man, as he'd called an electrician, over his last few days, and he certainly would not have forgotten getting shocked. Now I'd have to confront this man tomorrow. Still, I wasn't afraid of him. Someone had murdered Donnie, but I just didn't think Ronnie had done it.

"Sis, where are you? Where have you been all morning? Get down here." The sound of Gibb's voice boomed from the front of the Center, and then I heard him stomping up the stairs. He was on a rampage and going to check my office first. Oh, boy, was he mad! I still had my coat on, so I scooted out the back door and ran around the building. I leaned up against the wall, still giggling at having pulled a fast one on my little brother.

It had been a very productive day, but I needed somewhere to hide out until Gibb gave up the search. Surely he'd have to head back to work soon. I scurried around the police car parked in front and across the street toward JoAnn's. Then I decided that I didn't want Donnie, uh, Ronnie to think that he needed to ask me to sit with him and his son. Closing the gate behind myself, I veered toward the back door of the café, racing down a path of flat stones sunk into the ground by years of use.

I hoped she wouldn't mind me hanging out in the kitchen for a few minutes. JoAnn and I had become good friends over the last few weeks. Either that or she was just being extra nice to one of her best customers. This would be the perfect opportunity, if she wasn't too busy, to ask about the recipes and cookware. I tapped on the back door and peered in, but the four people I saw were too busy to hear.

Once I'd entered, I stood quietly watching the controlled pandemonium as JoAnn looked over some paperwork that a delivery man was showing her. Boxes labelled The South's Best Quality were stacked five deep, and JoAnn did a fast inventory checking off her count on the page with a pencil. Then she turned to see if she'd gotten all of the flour sacks she'd ordered. That task complete, she tucked the stub into her bouffant hair and signed the man's electronic tablet. When she turned to watch him leave, she finally noticed me.

"Stella?"

"Sorry, JoAnn. I came to ask a question, but I see I've caught you when you're busy."

She turned to glance at the room with a questioning look on her face.

In the far corner an older man had his arms up to the elbows in hot, sudsy water. I could see the steam rise as he swished coffee mugs with a kitchen sponge and dropped each with a clatter into the other side of the sink, waiting to be rinsed. A precarious stack of white plates was next in line to be washed.

Across the kitchen, in front of a massive stainless steel bowl of greens, a young woman prepared salads. JoAnn hurried to the stove and jostled a skillet on a red-hot burner. It appeared to be her way of stirring the contents. She shifted with barely a pause to grab a spatula and flipped over several sandwiches on the griddle. Next, the cook jerked open one of the oven doors and, with efficiency, removed a pan of biscuits and tipped them to slide onto a warmer set to the side. The golden tops glowed, and the aroma filled the room.

"Busy? Lord, no, honey. This ain't busy. What did you need?"

"I wanted to ask if you have any recipes that have been passed down through your family? You know, antiques? I guess recipes can be antiques." I edged closer to the bread, wondering if I could have a biscuit hot from the oven. They smelled heavenly, and I could imagine the butter melting and then the jam glowing on top.

"Your mama already called me yesterday, and I'm so excited. I sat up late last night going through my recipe boxes and picked out some I think you'll find real interesting."

"Boxes? You have more than one?"

"Five. Cooking runs in my family." Her smile grew ear-to-ear. "They've come down to me." She slipped two plates off a stack and loaded them with grilled sandwiches and the café's specialty of homemade sweet potato chips. "Order up," JoAnn yelled so loud that I jumped. "Oops, Katie's busy," she said with a glance at the young woman who was now slicing tomatoes. "Let me take these out and then I'll show you." JoAnn gathered the bottom corners of her apron, one in each hand, and picked up the plates. She hurried through the swinging door.

I moved across the kitchen and peeked through the small round porthole window of the door. JoAnn sat the plates in front of the man I now knew was Ronnie and his nephew Jay. She stood a minute talking to them and patted the boy on the shoulder before going to the side board to grab a bottle of ketchup for Jay.

As JoAnn moved around the room checking on other customers, I watched Ronnie and the boy. They looked a lot alike, which wasn't unexpected, but what surprised me was how they also had similar movements and habits. Each carefully checked under the bread of their sandwiches and moved the tomatoes around to their liking and then added a spoonful of chow-chow from a jar on the table. As I continued to observe, they both took small bites and washed them down with their drink between each mouthful … coffee for the man and milk for Jay.

It wasn't that Jay was copying him either. He didn't watch the man. I wondered if there might be something else going on. I clucked my tongue as I thought about how obviously happy Ronnie had been with Jay by his side. I'd bet my bottom dollar that the pride had been genuine. Would an uncle be that concerned for the boy? I didn't know. Maybe.

I jumped out of the way as JoAnn pushed back into the kitchen.

"Where was I now?" She dusted her hands together. "Ah, the recipes. Grab a seat here at the table but get some biscuits if you want. I got lots to show you," she said, moving to a desk crammed in the far corner and gathering boxes and a couple of thin books into her arms.

140

I'd be willing to stay for hours if I got fed. I slid out a stool that was tucked under a large, high table that looked as if it were used for food preparation. JoAnn's young assistant held out a plate with three biscuits. For a second she hovered.

"Jam?"

"You bet. Strawberry?"

The canning jar followed, and soon I was happily munching on the bread while JoAnn went through recipe after recipe. I kept my hands off them for fear of smearing the paper with butter.

Within minutes my thoughts jumped from one idea to another with instructions on how to make your own lard and recipes that included opossum meat, which I didn't even want to think about. That had to be worse than tofu.

"JoAnn, these are fantastic. I feel like the luckiest gal in the world that you're going to loan me some of these."

"Well, all of them. Just take them and sort through the lot. I reckon you can just make copies?"

"Copies will be fine."

"Maybe I should make some copies myself and put the originals in a lock box," JoAnn said. "The older I get the more valuable these hand-me-downs are to me." I watched her fingers linger over the spidery handwriting on a yellowed page.

"I'll take good care of them and get them all back to you as soon as possible," I said. I chewed my lip with the thought of losing any of these pages. Last month I'd lost part of Mom's quilt pattern for a retreat, but that wasn't valuable. She could reproduce it in her sleep. These pages were priceless, at least to JoAnn. "Maybe I shouldn't," I said, lifting my head quickly to look her in the eye. "JoAnn, I'd just die if anything happened to your stuff."

"Don't worry. Everything will be fine." JoAnn sorted the pages back into order and replaced them in a flour sack. "I trust you."

The salad-maker called out, "I heard the front door. You want me to get it."

"Nope." JoAnn stood. "We're done. Right?"

I nodded as I wiped my hands clean on a napkin and folded the end of the cloth bag over. I cradled the bundle in my arms. Tomorrow I'd drive to the nearest copy center and make the duplicates so that I could return JoAnn's precious recipes as quickly as possible.

She had already gone into the dining room, and I followed as far as the door. I wanted to let her know that I'd be back tomorrow, but through the window I glimpsed Gibb pulling out a chair. Maybe he'd hoped to catch me here since it was too early for him to want supper. JoAnn took his order, and then she got the coffee pot from the sideboard. After setting him up, she made another circuit of the customers. I watched Gibb and noticed that he had his gaze locked steady on the man I now knew to be Ronnie. A frown turned Gibb's expression serious.

CHAPTER 19

Lam stepped in the door of the Center just before six to pick me up for our date.

"Hey, no fair. You're early and I'm not ready." I yanked off the work shirt that protected my blouse and gathered the cleaning cloth and bucket of warm, soapy water I had been using and started toward the back door.

Lam followed. "The guys finished the last repair, and I sent them home. No use having them standing around, smoking and telling jokes, and for once I didn't have any paperwork. Sometimes I think I liked it better when I was the mechanic."

"Well, you always were good with your hands." I spoke without thought. "Could you get the door for me, please?"

Lam moved close but didn't open the back door. While my hands were full, he took my face between his palms and kissed me.

"I could show you how good I am with my hands." His voice had that deep quality that came with the dreamy gaze.

A sigh was my only response as he took the bucket from me and tossed the dirty water onto the gravel of the parking lot. I stuffed the paper towels in the trash can and washed my hands at the sink.

"How's the cut?" I asked, pointing at his arm.

Lam blushed with the memory of the fight. "Fine. Itches some. Hey, I heard back from Mr. Simms, and the nursing home cook is his wife. Says she was fired and she's plenty mad about it. The story, according to her, is that some guy, Mr. Tindal, bought the nursing home just less than a year ago. Ms. Simms claims this guy is super cheap and is cutting costs everywhere and it's hurting the residents. She said he ordered her to use less butter and to buy the cheapest cuts of meat."

I placed my hand on Lam's arm. "Where do you want to go tonight? Could we make a quick stop to talk to Alma?"

"Sure. There's nothing on at the theater so we've got time. Thought we'd just get something to eat." He laughed. "You just want me to protect you from Ms. Fleck?"

I rolled my eyes. "Don't laugh and don't underestimate that, uh, older woman."

He smiled with what seemed like a touch of indulgence. I squashed down the irritation I felt.

Lam asked, "You ready then?" He helped me into my coat, and within fifteen minutes we were walking across the lobby of the nursing home.

Today the home was oddly quiet, and the quilting frame sat lonely in the corner with the chairs willy-nilly around it. We went down the hall, skirting a food cart as we approached the door to Alma's room, and I heard Lam sniff the stale air. It carried the odor of bland food, dirty mops, and even urine.

I pinched my nose closed for a second's relief. "Boy, this gets worse every time I come here," I said in nasal tones.

"I visited my aunt here about a year ago, and it wasn't bad. She stayed four months recovering from pneumonia. I remember she was happy with the care." He stopped and scrubbed his toe against the floor. "This is just downright dirty." Lam walked over to a mop bucket and leaned over the water, which looked filthy.

"What are you doing?"

He sniffed. "There's no cleaner in here. It's just plain water. That's no good."

I scooted into Alma's room and heard Lam follow. It was empty.

"They are all down in the sunroom," a voice called out from the hallway.

As usual, I jumped a mile, startled by the abrupt sound.

"Thanks," I replied even as the aide continued on carrying her bundle of soiled sheets.

"Come on. I think that's just down here." I motioned to Lam.

Lam reached the closed door to a sunroom a step ahead of me but found the door locked. He peered through the glass, and I leaned around him to do the same. At first none of the fifty or so people crowded into the space noticed the knocking.

It looked like a rousing argument in progress with Alma at center stage. She whirled around and around in her chair. Her finger pointed to different people to give them the right to speak but mostly she seemed to be preaching. Her voice reached us but was too muffled to make out the words.

Finally, sweet Martha saw us and began to wave wildly. Alma, her attention captured, directed Soldier to let us in and Annaleigh joined him. She bee-lined to Lam first and completely ignored me. Her perfume swirled in a cloud as a dressing gown in an emerald-colored patterned silk created the illusion that she floated like a ballerina.

She paused in front of Lam for dramatic effect. "I do declare," she said, words dripping with a Deep South accent. "We have not met before unless we were special companions in a prior life. Do you feel the beating of my heart, my love?" The actress grasped my boyfriend's hand and pressed his palm to where he could supposedly feel that beating.

I'd swear she somehow made her bust quiver. How'd she do that, I wondered?

For once, around a female, Lam was speechless. He tugged his hand away but continued to stare at Annaleigh as if he could not tear his gaze away. She held him under some spell.

"How do you do that?" I directed my question to her.

"Raw talent, dear girl, raw talent." She shifted her voice so that each time she uttered the phrase it implied a different meaning.

"Uh, we uh, need to …" Lam's words stuttered to a halt.

"We need to talk to Alma." I completed Lam's sentence and then stepped on his foot as I moved away toward Alma.

"Oww. You did that on purpose," Lam said. The pain enabled him to break away from the actress, and he joined me in the center of the room.

"Whatever you do, don't look her in the eye again," I whispered in Lam's ear.

"Well, as I live and breathe," Alma spoke, gazing up at Lam. "It's Mr. Wythe, whom I have not seen in many years. Do you not read anymore, young man, since leaving our august educational system of which the libraries are the backbone?"

"Hello, Ms. Fleck. No, I mean, yes, of course I read, but I've got a device. That's why I haven't visited the library," he said.

"Oh, you mean one of those newfangled electronic gadgets. It's not the same." She huffed. "There is nothing that can surpass the feel of pages, the knowledge of ages, the imagination of creative talent, there at your fingertips. And what do you read?"

"What?" he asked, disbelief and a trace of fear, in his voice.

I was surprised to see how flustered he was with Alma's question.

"It is not a hard question, young man. What types of reading do you enjoy? Fiction? What genre?"

"Well, uh, fiction. Yes. Adventure and I like to, uh, occasionally read romance."

I couldn't help but erupt with a sharp bark of laughter. It wasn't because my boyfriend was admitting to being a man who enjoyed a romance, but that he was getting grilled by the evil old woman. This would give him a taste of what I'd been going through.

I leaned over and, on tiptoe, whispered in his ear, "See? Now you know what my life has been like, and there's nothing wrong with romance."

Alma twisted and gave me a hard, squinty stare. "It is not polite to whisper in front of others, Stella. Now please share your comment with the rest of us."

"Oh, I cannot tell a lie. I asked if he liked historical romance or modern." I gave Lam a grin that must have looked like the dog who ate the Thanksgiving turkey while I crossed my fingers behind my back. I heard a twitter of giggles from those who were standing around in the room and able to see what I had done.

Lam's head snapped toward me. "Stella! Wha—"

"Lam, go ahead and tell Alma what you discovered," I said.

"Ah, do we finally have news of cook?" Alma asked.

Lam seemed reluctant to let me off the hook, and I could see his emotions warring in his mind. Then, making his decision, he turned politely back to Alma. "Yes, ma'am. I spoke with Ms. Simms' husband this afternoon. He confirmed that the cook was fired because she refused to participate in the cost-saving measures being put into place by the nursing home's new owner."

"So Mr. Tindal is the enemy!" Alma's voice boomed through the room and several of the residents jumped. One woman, maybe Alma's roommate, had been snoring softly, slumped in a chair. She jumped to her feet.

Alma continued. "Watery soup. Bread without butter. No jam with breakfast. Only one cookie for dessert. Are we going to stand for this?"

A few of the gathered residents answered with a no, but the response was pretty quiet and unenthusiastic.

Alma tried another tactic. "Lukewarm showers, threadbare blankets. Winter is here and my toes froze last night."

The noise was louder this time.

"No coffee!" she bellowed.

"Alma's right," the old soldier yelled as loud as he was capable. "What can we do, Alma?"

The room became quiet, deathly quiet, as all eyes turned to Alma. She looked hardly bigger than a child in her wheelchair; however, her face showed the determination to equal any task. I had no doubt that the old librarian would come up with a solution to the problem.

I'd already decided that I should make a call to this Mr. Tindal, although he certainly was under no obligation to speak to me. Maybe I should also call some of the family members of the residents. Surely Mr. Tindal would care if they became unhappy and threatened to move their loved ones to another nursing home. At least I could make that threat.

Alma rubbed her chin, deep in thought, and then said, "Strike."

"What?" Annaleigh asked. "We don't do any work, Alma, dear."

"Details, Annaleigh. Mere details."

CHAPTER 20

"You look happy, sweetie," Mom said as she dished up oatmeal for me from a cast iron kettle on the stove, a pot that had probably seen more birthdays than Mom. "Happiness. That's all I've ever wanted for you and Gibb."

I dumped two spoonfuls of sugar on top after she set the bowl on the table in front of me, and then she countered with a quarter cup scoop of frozen organic blueberries. I knew they were organic because she grew them all around the cabin at the edge of the woods. She gathered them and froze batches for use through the winter.

"I know, Mom, and I am happy. Mostly." I added the latter, thinking about my dilemma of dating two men. Last night Lam had made even a trip to the nursing home fun, and Harley was taking me to the movies tonight. He always planned something special for afterward.

For the most part my life did feel perfect. I loved being back on Sewanee Mountain. I adored my job, although not the worry of whether I'd get to keep it. Most of all I was happy back here in the cabin living with Mom in the place where I'd grown up. Even the vegan food couldn't spoil it. I knew being an adult living with my mother wouldn't be what I'd want forever, but it had turned into a special time. For both of us, I was sure.

I reached down and gave Baby a scratch behind the ears. She purred, twisting in and out around my legs. Sleepy, curled on top of Doodle Dog sleeping on the braided rug, raised his head to see if I was giving out something to eat. When the cat saw I wasn't, he dropped his head back to his furry pillow.

"Oh," Mom said, "the Lynch sisters are going to stop by today, I mean, at the Center, and drop off the straw brooms and the tatted doilies. They called yesterday." She dropped into the chair across the kitchen table from me with her own bowl of oats and berries minus any sweetener.

"Have you seen or heard from Ellis Wells?" I asked. "He promised me a keg of handmade nails and some of his forged horseshoes. I think they'll sell well."

Mom, mouth full, looked quizzical while shaking her head to indicate she hadn't heard from the man.

"You know. Good luck horseshoes. Over the door." I waved vaguely, pointing over the back door, and like magic, Gibb pushed it open at that moment.

"Oops," Mom said, placing her fingers in front of her mouth and talking around a bite of the oatmeal. "I forgot to tell you that Gibb was planning to stop by this morning before you left for work," Mom said, scooping up her bowl and glass of milk. She hurried out of the kitchen.

"Well, I guess I can't blame her for running," I said. "She did call when I asked and got you over here, unwittingly aiding me in my evil plan." What started as a giggle escalated to uncontrollable laughter with snorts as I watched Gibb's frown deepen. It gave him a more kid-like appearance.

He stood with knotted fists on his hips and a sullen expression that could have wilted a steel beam if I hadn't been his sister and immune to it by virtue of practice.

"What were you thinking?" he sputtered. "Arcadia—what kind of name is that—is wild. She drank and danced all night. Half the time by herself."

Gibb's tone implied that dancing without a partner was an obvious sign of being completely, flat-out crazy. However, I knew Brother well enough to understand that he really meant dancing by oneself in front of others who would think the woman in question was his date. I hoped that lots of his friends had been at the Honky Tonk to see the spectacle.

"You could become a monk," I said, hooting with new vigor. "You know, live a solitary life of reflection. No dating." I almost swept my oatmeal bowl off the table with a wild gesture and had to grab it as it clattered toward the edge of the table.

"I have a reputation to keep up." He tapped his badge.

"I think your job record can stand one wild date." I wiped tears off my cheeks with the hem of my sweatshirt. "Oh, shue, I would have liked to be a fly on the wall. With a beer to enjoy along with the entertainment."

"How'd you get Arcadia to do it?"

"Oh, easy. She's been my friend for years, she owed me a huge one, and she is a fantastic person. Oddly, when I called, she required me to send her your picture. I guess she has high standards." I put my empty bowl in the sink and washed it quickly.

"Really?" Gibb looked pleased as well as surprised.

"You know, it was fun staying one step ahead of you yesterday. It reminded me of when we used to play hide-and-seek." I pulled my coat on. "Now I have to get to work."

For a second I thought that I really should tell Gibb what I had learned over the last few days about my handyman. He should be the one confronting and questioning Ronnie instead of me. But somehow the expression on my brother's face in JoAnn's Café yesterday, as he watched the man he thought was Donnie, made me cautious about telling him. Gibb was a good man and a fair sheriff. He would give Ronnie the benefit of investigating anything the former convict revealed to him. I was sure though that Ronnie would sit in jail while Gibb did so.

I wanted to talk with Ronnie first and see if he had any idea who had killed Donnie. I could honestly see many more people wanting to do away with that twin versus Ronnie. I just did not think he'd done it. My stomach twisted though. Was I being naive? Gibb and my friends regularly told me that I was, but could I be so wrong? I had grown to like Ronnie and watching him with Jay had sealed the deal for me. I had to talk with him first and give the man an opportunity. He'd spent ten years in jail, and Donnie had been in on the robbery with him. I felt sure of that. Maybe there was even a third man involved ten years ago. Someone had killed Donnie. I planned to find out who.

Maybe, since I was about to do something that Gibb would be opposed to, I shouldn't gloat so much. I might need his help, and I certainly didn't want to get too far on his bad side. I giggled again. My plan had been fun but now was the time to make up.

"I'm done, Gibb. Just leave my love life to me and I'll leave you alone. No more schemes, no more pushing Lam, and no more traffic tickets." I wagged my finger in his face.

"Okay, okay. But Lam is a good guy. I don't want to see you hurt him."

"I don't want to hurt him either. I love Lam. I'm just not sure how I love him. I'll figure it out."

"Huh, one thing, Sis." Gibb's face brightened again. "Could you give me Arcadia's phone number?"

Well, didn't that beat all, I thought, as I cranked the Jeep. I waved for Gibb to pull out ahead of me and then rummaged through my tote searching for my phone. As the Mustang roared down the driveway, I punched in Arcadia's number. The call rolled right to voice mail, but that was okay. I just felt an obligation to let her know that Gibb would be calling, and I assumed he planned to ask her out. Either that or apologize, but I told her to call me with all the details.

I made the quick trip to work, but as I approached the Center, I noticed a man getting out of an older model car and starting toward the door. I stopped in the driving lane and rolled down my window. His age made me guess that this might be Mr. Muller, the former bank guard.

"Hello," I called out. "I'm Stella Hill. Are you Mr. Muller?"

The man turned, his movements stiff and slow. "I am. I'm sorry I didn't call ahead as I promised, but it was so early I didn't know when you might be up and at work. I was going to come by later if I didn't find you here." Now he was close to the Jeep, and I saw that this was a man who showed every one of his years on his wrinkle-sculpted face. Between the age of the car and his clothes, I knew immediately that he wasn't rich.

"I'm glad I caught you then." I made sure my smile and voice told him that I appreciated his going out of his way to visit me.

"How about if we meet over at that café?" I pointed across the street. "I could use some breakfast, and I'd like to treat you to say thanks."

Mr. Muller considered in silence just long enough that I feared he would turn me down, but he nodded.

"I'll go around and park and be right there."

JoAnn already had two coffee mugs filled and a basket of biscuits on the table when I trotted in.

"Hey, JoAnn. I'll have the Mountain Man special. Mr. Muller, I promise you won't regret ordering the same."

He nodded again and murmured a thank you. JoAnn headed into the kitchen after asking how he wanted his eggs. She already knew how I liked mine and that I chose ham over sausage.

"So you met Albert Doan? Good man, and please call me Virgil."

"He was very nice. I wasn't able to find you, but he offered to give me your number. I hope I'm not intruding into your life, bringing up bad memories."

"No, no, I'm okay with it. When it first happened, getting shot, and then fired, it was the worst time of my life. Wasn't sure for a few weeks if I'd make it out the other side, but I did, and I'm the stronger for it."

I asked, "How did you and Albert get to be friends?"

"Peculiar, ain't it? Albert came to me not long after and asked for my forgiveness."

"That was very kind of you to forget his past mistake."

Virgil gave a wary smile. "I wish I'd been so loving to my fellow man, but I didn't give away any forgiveness that first time he asked. I reckon it took about a half-dozen tries on his part."

I sat straighter in my chair, leaning forward in my eagerness to understand. "I'm surprised."

"People get to most destinations by way of a journey. Life's a crooked path. I'm a preacher now, traveling, and I reckon that Albert was helping me get there by way of me turning him down. You know, the fact he felt I was worth asking and over and over. I didn't feel I had any worth till somebody needed me that bad." He held a piece of toast in his hand but had completely forgotten it. He stared at the plate in front of him as if his whole past were visible there.

"Do you mind telling me the whole story again? You must have gotten tired of it, and I did read the newspaper articles."

Virgil told me pretty much the same thing I'd read. He spoke as if this was an account he'd memorized long ago, and I was surprised that there was no emotion with the words. I felt that if the same thing had happened to me, I wouldn't get over being shot and fired in only ten years' time.

"Do you think you saw twins?" I asked and held my breath.

"Couldn't have been anything else. I was pretty muddled at first, pain and then surgery. I was happy to be vindicated with the arrest and the police finding out pretty quick that Ronnie had a twin. That didn't last long. The wife, meaning the brother's wife, and her mother said right away that the other one, Donnie, had been at home. Albert's statement that I must have been drunk had already fixed everybody's mind against me. Even I'd started doubting myself 'cause of how woozy I got from blood loss."

He continued. "I went to the courtroom every day, not just when I had to testify. When I did testify, I told my story like I knew it happened, but by that time I don't think I sounded too convincin'. Trial didn't last but two days. The jury was back in an hour."

A wave of sadness washed over me at the thought of Ronnie being handcuffed in the courtroom and taken directly to prison, but he had robbed the bank and maybe he'd been the one to shoot Virgil. Or, as I hoped, maybe he'd been the get-away driver.

Virgil watched me with calm patience.

I sipped the last of my coffee. "Do you want to know why I'm so interested?"

"No. You seem like you got a good head on your shoulders. I'll trust you to do right with whatever is going on." He wiped his mouth on a napkin and stood. "I'd best be getting on my way."

We crossed the street together, and as we walked the short distance, I told him about the Heritage Craft Center.

"Could I take a peek inside?" he asked.

"Sure. I've only got a few items on display, but maybe you'll be able to stop again some time when I have everything just right." I swung the door open and led him inside.

Virgil crossed to the middle of the room and turned in a circle, taking it all in. Then he looked up at the ceiling and said, "It's a right handsome building. I was born in a log cabin so I'm partial to them."

I smiled. "Like I said, only a few items on display." The guard walked in his slow, stiff way over to the case with the face jugs.

A motion off to my right caught my attention. Ronnie was coming down the stairs, and when he glanced down over the railing and saw Virgil, he missed a step and nearly fell. The things he had been carrying flew from his hands and bounced downward. He caught himself, ending up splayed on his back on the stairs with a look of total shock on his face.

With the noise, Virgil whirled around, but Ronnie was already twisting onto his knees and racing up the stairs, trying to get to his feet as he went but not wasting time to do so. He looked like a crab. Then finally from upstairs, in an oddly deep voice, Ronnie called out, "Just slipped. Be right down in a minute, Miss Stella."

"Think everything is okay?" Virgil asked.

"I, I think so," I stuttered, amazed at the effect Virgil had on Ronnie.

"I'd better be going so you can check on that fellow."

I walked the elderly man to the door and thanked him again. With a twist of the dead bolt I made sure that my upcoming conversation with Ronnie wasn't going to be interrupted. The action gave me a second's pause. Was I trapping myself? Or could it be that my handyman was going out the second floor window at this very moment, but I didn't believe he would run from me. When I turned, I found Ronnie standing only a few feet behind me. He held a hammer in his hand, and my heart felt as if it had just blasted off on a trip to the moon.

CHAPTER 21

For long seconds neither of us spoke and I could not tear my gaze from his eyes, which held more pleading than Doodle Dog looking for a handout. Finally, unable to speak, I pointed to the hammer.

Ronnie brought his hand up to where he could see the object he clutched, but it took several long seconds for comprehension to dawn.

"No, no," he gasped and threw the tool to the floor so hard that the claw dug into the wood. "I would never. Not anyone. Not you, Miss Stella." Now he calmed, taking a deep breath before he added, sounding more like the man I had come to know, "I'd never hurt you. You have been so nice to me. I already had the hammer in my hand. Just forgot."

I wiped sweat off my forehead and continued the motion to push my hair back from my face. "I know. Or, well, honestly, I hoped." My breathing evened out.

"You can call your brother now, Miss Stella. I'm ready."

Ronnie's shoulders slumped, and as I watched, he turned a sickly grey color. I worried that he might be having a heart attack, but it seemed more like his body was preparing to go back to prison.

"I'm not calling Gibb. Let's go up to my office where we can sit and talk this out. You want a cup of hot tea?" I touched his arm, hoping he would accept. He needed to relax, and the tea might help him return to normal. I'd call 911 if he seemed to worsen.

"Yes," he licked his lips. "Yeah."

I suggested he go on upstairs, but he said he'd help me and then followed me to the back. Probably he wanted to make sure I wasn't going to make that call behind his back. Who could blame him? As I made two mugs of hot tea, we remained silent. Ronnie immediately took a gulp of his and then sucked in cool air over his probably burnt tongue.

In my office I sat behind my desk and pulled out a legal pad and pen to take notes. Ronnie more or less collapsed into the ladder-back chair opposite me.

He said, "I wanted to tell you as soon as I got to know you some. Weren't right not to. You have to believe me." He choked on the words.

If I'd expected, or feared, that he would start with excuses, that wasn't the one I had anticipated. His first concern seemed to be for me while I'd thought he would first deny killing Donnie. "Ronnie, I do believe you. You are Ronnie and not Donnie, right?"

"Yes, I haven't done a very good job of playing my brother."

"This was premeditated, wasn't it? I mean, this ruse of pretending to be your twin. Gibb learned that you got out of jail two weeks before you told Donnie you would be out."

Ronnie wiped the back of his hand over his eyes. "Lord, yes, but not planned by me. It's Deb. I swear she's got me trussed up in this mess like a turkey. I never saw it coming."

"Why haven't you run?" I figured I knew the answer, but I wanted to hear it all from him.

"Jay," he sobbed. "Deb says he's mine and I believe her. It could be true." He blushed.

"Also you want it to be true. I could tell right away."

Ronnie sighed and reflected before answering. "You're right. I do. I would like to know for sure, but it wouldn't make any difference 'cause I still love him. Do you know if there is any way to find out?"

"There's DNA testing." I chewed the end of my pen for a moment. "I don't know though if it would work with identical twins. Let me do some research. Well, you know what? I can do that right now."

Yesterday my internet connection had been hooked up, and I'd managed to forget since I'd been without one for so long. I'd been trying to do everything on my smartphone and at the library. It hadn't been nearly as convenient. I flipped open my laptop and tapped away for a few minutes, trying to keep my face neutral after skimming the first few articles. Then I read through a few more but really just to delay giving the bad news.

"I can see it in your face. It doesn't matter. It really doesn't." Ronnie pounded his thigh with a fist. "In fact, I'm glad I'll never know for sure because Jay feels like my son, and that's all that I care about."

"I think that's the right way to think of it, Ronnie. Jay needs a daddy. There's no one better than you for that job." The enthusiasm rang in my voice.

"You mean that, don't you, Miss Stella? I'm nothing but a convicted bank robber. An ex-con, yet you've treated me well."

"But you didn't rob that bank alone, did you? Tell me what really happened."

He bowed his head and studied the floor for several minutes. When he looked back at me, I thought he had transformed into a new man. He sat up straighter.

"I don't think you should get involved. Just being nice to me is way more than I deserve right now."

I wanted to help Ronnie, but I didn't know if I'd be able to convince him to let me try. At the least I wanted to hear the whole story and felt he owed me that much. I told him so.

"You're right. Let's start with the fact that my brother was a good-for-nothing no-account, well, let me just say that he never seemed like my brother. Deb was the perfect wife for him except she was way smarter than Donnie. Probably me, too. If I remember right, the bank job was her idea. We were sitting around playing cards one night when she mentioned it. Deb was really unhappy with how they was living and convinced Donnie that it would be easy. He seemed to take to the idea and tried to get me to go along. I refused for weeks."

I realized I was sitting on the edge of my seat. "What changed your mind, Ronnie?"

"Oh, being young and stupid, I guess. Grew up poor and couldn't stop thinking about the money Deb talked about. I'm not without fault in all this, Miss Stella. Donnie claimed all I had to do was drive the car and that we wouldn't get caught. He shot that poor man, and then when the police showed up, he claimed it was all me. After I was in jail, he came and talked to me. Told me Deb was pregnant and would I go it alone? Begged me and said he'd save all the money for me. He claimed we got more than they were letting on in the papers, sixty thousand."

Ronnie stood and moved across the room to look out the window. "Donnie got me a lawyer who said I'd probably get about five years. I was already in jail, and I was guilty, so it didn't seem to make much difference."

"Oh, Ronnie, that's the most awful story I've ever heard." I sniffed hard and then grabbed a tissue and blew my nose. "Wait," I said, and then more loudly, "Wait. How did Deb get you into this mess? Now, I mean."

With the sound of a car out front Ronnie suddenly crouched beneath the window ledge. "It's the sheriff. It's Gibb," he hissed, as if my brother could hear him from the street.

I jumped to my feet, but I only got as far as the center of the room before I realized that I didn't know what to do. Spinning in circles wasn't going to help us.

"Calm down, Ronnie. He's probably not here for you. He hasn't said anything to me about being suspicious."

He moaned. "Maybe that just means he doesn't trust you anymore." Ronnie crawled from under the window but kept his back plastered to the wall.

Physically pulling and shoving, I managed to get him to his feet and into the hall. With a quick shove I pushed him into the utility closet. "Just be quiet."

Gibb's voice boomed from downstairs as I heard the front door of the Center open. "Sis, get down here. All hell's broken out at the nursing home. Is this your doing?"

Ronnie and I both cringed as Gibb's boots stomped against each stair tread. "See, it's something else altogether. Ronnie, please don't leave town. Let me help you. If you run, it will look like you're guilty of murdering Donnie."

"I, I don't know what's best," he whispered, and his eyes still looked wild. His basic instincts screamed for him to run.

"You might never see Jay again if you do. I'll probably have to leave with Gibb but please calm down. When I get back, let's come up with a plan to help you."

I whirled around and leaned against the door, shutting it by leaning against the panel. With the final click of the latch Gibb loomed over me.

"What did you tell Ms. Fleck? That it was okay to protest?"

"I don't know what you are talking about. Come downstairs. Calm down." I raised my voice to cover the noise from the closet. I could hear Ronnie's shaking causing a clatter of something, maybe a broom or mop, to beat a rhythm again the wall.

Making sure I drowned out any chance of Gibb discovering Ronnie, I hurried him down the steps, gibbering the whole way.

"What do you want to do about this? And what are you talking about?" I asked. We were far enough away now for me to draw a breath and hope that Ronnie would calm down. I hoped he wouldn't do anything stupid. Once I dealt with whatever this problem was, I could help the poor man who was right now huddled in a closet.

"Alma has corralled all the nursing home residents into the kitchen and dining room and barricaded the doors." Gibb swiped his hand through his hair. "Sis, I've got all those old people protesting the bad conditions at the home. Some, make that most of them, need medicine and special care. We can't have them getting sick or hurt because of Alma."

"I sort of knew about this, but Lam did too!"

"Alma said you were helping her." Gibb shoved his hat back on his head. "Get your coat. We've got to get over there. I've got Deputy Mann there by herself now."

"When and how did you talk to Alma?" I asked, slipping my arms into my coat.

After we'd climbed into the police car, Gibb answered my question. "We were shouting through the dining room door. They have tables and the ice cream cooler shoved against it to keep everyone out. I could break it down, but I'm afraid I might hurt one of them. Old fools." Gibb flipped on the siren and flashing lights as he stepped on the gas.

"Gibb, I'm ashamed of you. They are not fools." I had to raise my voice to be heard, but I knew he had when he blushed.

"Sorry," he mumbled.

"They'll come out when they run out of ice cream anyway."

"Sis, that's what I'm worried about. Some of them might try and hold out, but they need medicine. What if one of them keels over?"

"Or overdoses on ice cream," I said with a giggle, thinking that wouldn't be the worse way to go out.

Gibb groaned. "The head nurse told me she called this Mr. Tindal and supposedly he's driving up the mountain from Chattanooga as soon as he can. I need you to fill me in on what's going on with this guy." Gibb swung the car off the road into the parking lot of the Sewanee Nursing Home. The car rocked to a stop.

Things looked normal, a quiet red brick building, long and low, nothing fancy, sitting in the middle of a lawn with a few bird feeders scattered about and a patio with a dozen or so webbed folding chairs. Only nine cars were in the parking lot, but one was the other Sewanee police car. I remembered Gibb saying that his deputy was on watch alone. At this time of the day the other cars probably belonged to staff, as the few visitors usually wouldn't show until after lunch.

What struck me was that eight staff members, assuming they all drove to work separately, for seventy-eight residents didn't seem like enough help. Surely some, maybe two or three, were cleaning staff and some were aides versus nurses. Could there be as few as one or two skilled nurses?

I told Gibb what little I knew and stressed that Alma was right that the living conditions weren't what they should be. Many times over the last couple of weeks I'd thought about what it would be like to be living in the home. Residents shouldn't feel like it was a sentence to be served in prison. Shouldn't they expect security, a comfortable bed, good food, and respect? Oh, and hopefully some fun.

Darn right, I thought. I didn't have any trouble deciding whose side I was on.

"Gibb, I'd like to speak with this Mr. Tindal when he shows up."

My brother twisted in his seat to look at me. I tried to look innocent, even twisting a lock of hair around my finger, but I don't think I succeeded.

"I think I'd better talk to him first," he said, glaring. "Let's get to this. I don't have all day, and I still have a murder to solve."

I jumped at his remark but covered my nervousness by opening the car door and sliding out. In seconds he was halfway to the front door with his longer stride leaving me to hurry behind. Motion off to the right caught my attention, and I saw Annaleigh wave at me from the window of what must be the dining room. Veering off, I hoped Gibb wouldn't notice that I wasn't with him anymore.

"Stella, sweet girl, how nice of you to visit," the actress purred when I reached the side of the building. I side-stepped between some yew bushes in a mulched bed.

"Where's Alma? Are you okay? Is everyone okay?" I threw my hands into the air. "We're all worried." I peered through the glass, searching for the librarian. I'd expected her to be front and center, maybe with a bullhorn.

"We are not incompetent or children," she sniffed as her chin tipped a bit upward. "We have found great stores of food, and we are taking good advantage of most of it. Not the canned prunes though. Why, Norma has shown that she is an expert chocolate chip cookie chef. We are on our third batch. I believe they are the world's best, and I've toured extensively."

"Chocolate chip? Umm, those are my favorite." I leaned in the window, believing that I could smell the sweet treat. "World's best, you said?"

"Oh, to die for, my child."

"Do you think you could get me one?"

"Why don't you come in, and you can have all you want."

Some subtle shift in Annaleigh's tone made me think of the witch in the Grimm's fairy tale of Hansel and Gretel. I think she saw my hesitation because she said, "It would be very easy, my dear. Just hop onto the window sill and swing your legs over." Her accompanying gestures were extravagant.

"I'll just come in the back door."

"Impossible. It is, at the moment, blocked by the old upright piano. This is your only way in, my child, if you want some cookies."

"Uh, maybe I'd better not."

"You could also have some cookies to take home with you."

I thought I smelled the aroma of a fresh batch being pulled from the oven. I turned my back to the window and positioned my hands to help me boost my butt to the sill. It really was easy. I swung my legs over and dropped the couple of inches to the linoleum floor.

"Really I can only stay a few minutes."

As I said the words, someone threw a sheet over my head, and I could feel a rope being wrapped around and around my body. Although it wasn't very tight, my arms were pinned neatly to my sides.

CHAPTER 22

"Hey, what's going on?" I screamed. "Arrrggg. This sheet smells bad, and it's really scratchy."

"Yes. That's right." Alma voice sounded from in front of me. "And that's part of what we're protesting. I like my sheets to smell like the great outdoors. Don't you?"

"Well, of course. Mom usually dries her sheets outdoors, and I use this nice-smelling brand of dryer sheets," I huffed, trying to breathe through the fabric, which was making me hot. "That's not important." I raised my voice and struggled so hard that I overbalanced and fell to the floor. "Ouch. Now look what you guys have done. I'm hurt."

"What hurts?" Alma asked.

"My elbow. I think I broke my arm."

"Alma, I don't think this is necessary," Annaleigh's voice oozed concern. "Stella has been very nice to you. To all of us, really."

"Nice? She broke my leg," Alma said.

"I did not," I mumbled.

"I heard that, young lady." It sounded as if Alma had moved closer.

"Maybe this could be illegal. Kidnapping, you know." Soldier's voice entered the conversation from off to my right.

"Stella, we need some help," Alma said. "If you do as we say, we'll let you go without anyone getting hurt."

"Anyone? Anyone! I'm already hurt." My voice had risen another octave.

"I'll get you a whole batch of cookies." Annaleigh said.

"Is it a big batch or a little batch?" I asked.

"Pretty big. Probably sixteen cookies," Soldier replied for his friend. "They're really great. I wish we could have them every day. All we want 'cause I can eat a lot of cookies."

"I'll make that a negotiating point," Alma said. "So, Stella, first we want your cell phone. You do have it with you, don't you?"

"Of course. It's in my back pocket. You'll have to set me free to get it, and hopefully I didn't break it in the fall."

"Okay. Second, we want you to talk to your brother." Alma barked a laugh. "His deputy, while she was alone here, decided to arrest us all. Deputy Mann, I believe her name is, even read us our Miranda rights through the barricaded door."

"You're kidding. That sounds serious. Get me out of here so I can fix this." I tried struggling to my knees but couldn't get any traction of the slick waxed flooring.

"Okay, free the prisoner," Alma shouted.

Hands reached out and began to unwind the rope and then to untangle me from the rough cloth. As the sheet was lifted off my face, I gasped, drawing in a deep, satisfying breath.

Annaleigh, although she was much too frail to be effective, helped me to my feet and whispered in my ear. "My dear, I'm so sorry. I'll get you the recipe also."

Alma snapped her fingers. "The phone, girl. We don't have all day before we are handcuffed and shipped off to prison. I hope you have unlimited minutes."

"How many calls do you have to make?" I asked, patting my hair down. Of course I had unlimited minutes, but I wasn't sure I wanted to be too involved in this scheme of hers. Could Deputy Mann really arrest them all like that, and for what? Besides, talking about getting arrested had reminded me that I had to get back to poor Ronnie as quickly as possible. He truly had seemed to be at the end of his rope. Maybe I was thinking too highly of myself, but I thought that I was the only one in a position to help the man. He had earned my respect, and if I didn't succeed, I had to know that I had given it my best try.

Alma jerked the phone from my fingers and thrust it at Annaleigh. "Now call your sister. See if she knows anyone in government or someone who works with the news or even someone in entertainment." She swiveled her chair as Annaleigh began punching the numbers. "Jack, I believe you said your great grandson is a bag boy at Piggly Wiggly. Ask him to start talking to everyone he helps. Have him tell them that we're protesting and don't forget about the police brutality."

"Police brutality." I could barely believe my ears. "All you're doing is sitting around eating cookies."

Jack smiled. "And brownies. And peaches."

"It's the principle, Stella," Alma said.

I watched as Annaleigh finished her phone call, and an idea came to mind. I needed to get out of the nursing home and back to the Center, and I knew who would be the perfect person to replace me as Alma's spokesperson. I really thought I could accomplish two good deeds with one plan. It was obvious that Alma had blossomed, in her own ornery way, by having people around. The woman had begun to form friendships, but I wasn't sure she realized they were friendships. She needed to be pushed toward the next step. The old librarian needed someone to be her friend whom she could not boss around.

Alma was now instructing Annaleigh to pass the phone to Norma, but I snatched it from the actress's manicured hand.

"It's your turn, Alma. So whom do you want to call?" I held the phone up as if I'd dial the number for her.

Watching the older woman's face fall almost made me relent, but I stood waiting. I knew—Annaleigh certainly knew—that Alma believed she had no friends, and I now knew that she didn't have any family left. I said, "Friend? Former library patron? Whom should I call for you?" I pretended not to notice that the old woman now appeared very distressed. Her head had dropped until her chin touched the sunken chest and the claw-like hands twisted together.

Annaleigh stepped forward, as if to try and take the phone. "Stella, this isn't funny."

For the first time I heard Annaleigh's real voice without any showmanship. The raw emotion she felt for Alma made the words come out rough and unattractive.

"Can't think of anyone, Mrs. Fleck? Well, I'll select for you," I said, punching Mom's number into the phone. When she answered, I breathed a quick sigh of relief that Cele was home and then said, "I know you are up to your elbows canning okra, but you need to leave that to the other ladies and get over to the nursing home. Now! Talk to Alma. Oh, and Mom, don't come in the front door. You need to climb in the dining room window."

I thrust the phone at the tiny figure in the wheelchair. "This is your third good friend." I turned on my heel and then spun back around to find Alma staring at the phone as if she'd never seen one before. "Oh, and me. I'm your friend. Talk to Cele." I made motions for her to put the phone to her ear, and I marched away. Behind me, as I climbed out the window, I heard Alma begin a conversation with my mother.

I marched down the driveway, hoping that neither Gibb nor his deputy would see me, and when I reached the road, for the first time in my life I stuck my thumb out to hitchhike. Several cars zipped by without slowing, and I felt offended that they didn't pick me up. Didn't I look like a person in need and not some crazy serial killer? With quick steps backward I made sure I wasn't going to be run down on the asphalt, but I kept my thumb hooked. I needed to make my way back to the Center. Gibb had driven us to the nursing home, and I suspected he wouldn't be happy with me taking off without helping, although what power he thought I might have over Mrs. Alma Fleck I had no idea. I wasn't a magician.

Fifteen minutes slipped away without a car passing, making me even more edgy to continue my conversation with Ronnie. If I couldn't come up with some way to help him, one that included keeping Jay in his life, disaster might be right around the corner. I needed to find out who had killed Donnie before Gibb became privy to the facts I had. As sheriff, he would arrest Ronnie first and ask questions later. I knew Ronnie had the answers, and I wanted to get them first. If only Gibb hadn't interrupted me earlier. Finally a car approached and stopped beside me.

"Well, as I live and breathe child," Esther hooted. "What are you doing out here thumbing for a ride? Cele might give you the first whupping of your little life if she happens to catch you."

"Oh, no! I forgot about Mom. She'll be riding this way any minute." I jerked open the back door of my old friend's car and dived onto the seat.

"Talk of the devil," in her excitement, Esther shouted. "Here comes your mama's truck, and she's slowing down to talk to me.

I grabbed a folded quilt lying on the seat beside me and scrambled onto the floor, shaking the fabric out and pulling it over me as I hid. Something hard poked my hip, but I dared not move for fear Mom would see me. I was afraid she would demand I return to the nursing home with her.

The sound of her old truck stopping in the other lane was followed by Mom's voice. "Esther, you need any help? Why are you stopped in the middle of the road?"

"Uh, a deer. One 'bout ran into me. Whew, it was close, and I needed to catch my breath."

"They're out trying to fatten up for winter. You wouldn't believe what Stella did. She's got me headed to the nursing home to help Ms. Fleck. The residents are having a sit-in. Can you believe that? I haven't been to one in ages."

Guilt stabbed its way into my thoughts. Getting Mom involved hadn't been very kind of me, but there was nothing she liked better than a protest for a good cause. However, Mom should have a choice whether or not she wanted to get involved. I would apologize tonight.

Mom continued. "Esther, I'm so proud of my girl between how she's fixing up the Heritage Center and now helping people. Why, I almost broke the speed limit getting over here!"

I felt like jumping up from my hiding spot and yelling, "Yipeee" or maybe running around to the truck to give Mom a hug. She'd never been too happy with my previous career choice, which she had always called my cubicle desk job. Since I'd returned home, Mom had seemed to believe I was going in the right direction with more creativity in my life.

I stayed hidden, only twisting a bit to relive pain from what, I could now tell by feel, was a galosh. I needed to get back to help Ronnie. Mom could handle Alma. I hoped.

I heard Esther say she needed to get down the road, and the car started forward. I threw the quilt off and drew in a deep breath.

"That was mighty nice to overhear," Esther said.

"Yes it was." I climbed over to the front seat and snapped my seat belt on. "I think Mom can handle Alma better than I could ever hope to, and I believe Gibb is going to need an ally in the lions' den."

Esther patted my hand. "Alma's sure a tough ol' bird. Never let anyone get close to her since her tragic loss. Guess she didn't want to hurt that bad ever again. 'Course she never did take to Cele, her being a hippie and all. Do you think you did the right thing throwing those two together in a room?"

I gazed at the trees zipping past. Esther believed in going a tad over the speed limit and riding with her could be an adventure. Now that I didn't have to fight Nashville traffic, and after a close call with an opossum when he decided to play dead in the middle of the road, I'd given up speeding. He survived.

I said, "I do. I mean, I think so. Now that I've gotten to know Alma a little bit, I see some similarities in the two of them."

Esther laughed. "No offense, sweetie, but you are an optimist." She whipped the car to a stop in front of the Center.

Hopping out, I turned back to her. "Well, keep your fingers crossed for me."

I stepped up onto the porch and grasped the knob expecting the door to open, but it was locked. Rather than pull out my key, I hurried around the building. The back door was also locked. Disappointment hit hard with the knowledge that Ronnie had left work. I really hoped that he hadn't left the state or country. If he'd done that, and taken Jay with him, he would certainly be a fugitive. Nothing I could do would protect him from going back to prison, this time for kidnapping.

Debbie did not strike me as the forgiving type.

Working the key in the door, I wondered if I'd find a note from Ronnie. Since I'd left my phone with Alma so she could continue her campaign work, I wasn't sure what time it was, but I knew it wasn't after five. Normally my handyman would be here, hard at work. I dumped my coat and tote on the counter, looking for a note. I shifted some tools and newspapers around but didn't find one.

Maybe Ronnie had been concerned that Gibb might return with me and had left a note in a more hidden spot. After all, his fear of the sheriff was real. A message would be someplace where Ronnie knew I would see it but not Gibb. Without having to think, I opened the refrigerator and was immediately rewarded.

I scanned the piece of paper quickly and then read it over again. For a moment I just stared into space. Ronnie wanted me to drive out to his house, or rather Debbie's house, now that Donnie was dead. An address was included. He said I had to wait until six when Debbie would be home. I was to leave my car parked out on the road and walk down the dark driveway. He said I must not use any kind of light. He instructed me to hide at the edge of the woods, where I could watch the house and barn.

I flipped the note over. Blank. No explanation. What was I supposed to watch for? Now, even though the room was chilly, I felt sweat on my brow. Was I crazy enough to follow Ronnie's instructions? With a sigh, I realized that I was. I trusted Ronnie.

Mom had taught me and Gibb growing up to be not just respectful of people but to pay attention to them. She said many times it wasn't what a person said nearly as much as how they moved their mouths and what they were looking at when they spoke that would reveal their thoughts and character. I'd taken many of her lessons to heart and felt a swell of pride.

I'd watched Donnie for the short time I'd known him and had not liked him a speck. The best that could be said of him was that he was shallow and dishonest. I'd been in close quarters with Ronnie and knew—but maybe imagined—that he was a good man. I suppose he hadn't always been good, as he had helped rob the bank. He had driven Donnie off to safety as the get-away driver. There was plenty of bad there then, but the prison guard's and the warden's testaments seemed to agree with me that Ronnie had changed. Prison had probably taught him the value of his life and how easily all could be lost with one bad decision.

Would honoring his request tonight be a bad decision? Surely if I walked carefully and neither Ronnie nor Debbie would actually know where I was, I'd be safe. I wouldn't walk down the driveway but would instead enter the forest several feet away and remain hidden.

The first thing I needed to do was check out the address online. I wanted to study the driveway and chart my walk through the woods, which would be dark at that time in November. Walking in the forest at night didn't bother Mom, but I was sometimes a bit more jittery. Knowing the layout would give me more confidence.

I spent close to an hour on the computer, studying the map and then clearing up work and personal emails. When my stomach signaled that it would wait no longer, I made my way to JoAnn's and ordered apple pie with a strong coffee. It was heaven with a flaky crust. I chased the last crumbs around the plate with my fork and then leaned back in the chair, feeling as if I was ready to tackle any problem.

There were still two hours to wait, but I planned to go back to the Center and catalog quilts. They were coming in fast and furious from donors now that Mom had gotten the word out. Most were old, glorious antiques with a few newer ones mixed into the lot. I had taken a quick peek at each one and found that several, to my delight, came with a provenance. Even without paperwork though, most were signed by the artist quilter. In a few months, when things slowed down, I planned to research the names and make bio cards for the displays. To me the person behind the art was an important part of the heritage.

As I was sitting at a window seat, my thoughts had been spinning around quilts while I stared out the window. Finally, my brain screamed out for me to pay attention. Glancing up and down the street, I finally picked up Debbie storming down the sidewalk with Jay in tow. In fact, she was practically dragging her son by the arm. Twice she stopped and whirled around to shout at him. I could tell by the boy's hunched shoulders that he was embarrassed by the spectacle she was making out of him. I could only imagine how bad it was when you could hear Debbie as well as see her actions.

I shook my head in disbelief when, arriving at their car, she jerked open the back door and shoved him inside. In seconds she sped by the café, and even though I knew there was no chance she could see me, I ducked. There had barely been a second to see the forlorn figure slumped in the back seat. The sight made me realize that while I'd been sitting here enjoying my pie, I had been trying to decide whether or not to go tonight. Now my mind was made up. I felt like I had a mission to help Ronnie and Jay.

CHAPTER 23

When I knelt down, I lost my balance and had to put my hand out to catch myself. In the deep layer of fallen leaves, something soft squashed between my fingers, and I prayed it was nothing worse than a mushroom. With a Kleenex, I swiped at my skin, but it was dark enough that I could barely see the white tissue, much less anything else. That was proof that my hiding spot in the branches of an old twisty rhododendron should keep me safe.

I swept a branch with its deep green curled leaves aside to peek again at the Clark house. So far, in the fifteen or so minutes I'd been here, there were just lights but no noise and no one had come outside. It must be at least 6:30 since I had arrived late, although I had no idea. My phone was still a hostage of Alma's, or maybe Mom had brought it home with her. She had probably returned to the cabin by now.

From here I could see that the Clark house was older, probably built in the forties, with that basic plan of two or three tiny bedrooms and one bathroom. There was no garage unless it was separate from the house and located in the back. There probably wasn't one though, as Debbie's old sedan was parked near the front porch. The work van was close by, and it wasn't until I saw it that I realized that Ronnie had not been driving it every day. For some reason Debbie had been dropping him off and picking him up in the evening.

A wooden barn sat off at the edge of a lawn that was a patchwork of grass and weeds. The structure probably wasn't used much, as it didn't look as if it had been maintained over the years. One corner of the roof sagged, and I had to wonder if it could weather many more winters. I hoped so because I was enchanted with a quilt block someone had painted high on the front wall long ago. In the glow of a security light mounted on the roof of the house, I saw a faded but still recognizable Carpenter's Wheel block. I knew that design wasn't popular because of its high degree of difficulty with many pieces and Y-seams.

Someone in the family must have liked it, though, to go to the trouble to paint that particular block high on the barn wall. The harsh lighting from the security fixture made the colors look odd, but I guessed they were shades of blue, probably pleasing against the barn red, but I couldn't be sure. I knew that I'd like to see it in the daylight and take a picture, but that might not be possible. I definitely didn't want to get to know Debbie any better.

The front door of the house opened, and I instinctively leaned back farther into my cover until my back bumped against the gnarled trunks of the rhododendron. Even though I knew no one could look out and see me, I still felt nervous. Ronnie stepped onto the porch but didn't seem in a hurry to go anywhere. For a moment he stood still, just staring down. Then he looked toward the driveway and gave a thumb's up sign.

While I decided whether or not to give a whistling bird call to let him know I'd seen his sign, Debbie came out, pulling the door closed behind her. At the last second she opened the door a few inches and yelled back in to her son, telling him to stay in his room. Then she slammed the door hard enough that I heard the house windows rattle.

With a poke, she shoved Ronnie, and he plodded forward to disappear into the barn while she walked in aimless circles around the yard. By the time he returned carrying a shovel and a lantern, she seemed to have picked a spot, although I couldn't see how or why she chose that particular patch of grass. She stood near and watched as Ronnie dug a hole. It appeared to be hard going at first in the frozen top layer of ground but went faster as he got past the turf.

After about a half an hour, Debbie directed him to start another hole a few feet away. The result was the same and repeated two more times. I was getting pretty cold from sitting on the ground and felt like clapping when Debbie threw her hands up and stomped off to the house. I continued to sit while Ronnie filled in the holes.

When he finished the task, he glanced over his shoulder and then shuffled toward the driveway. I whistled through my teeth two short blasts to let him know that I was several feet off to his right. He edged closer, and I imagined he tried to appear nonchalant in case Debbie might be peeking out a window.

"Miss Stella," he hissed.

"Ronnie." I hoped I kept the edge of irritation out of my voice brought about by frozen fingers and toes. Did he think there would be someone else hiding in a bush, invited to watch two grown-ups dig holes on a cold evening?

"Did you see?"

"Yes, but what are you trying to find?"

"The money. Donnie always swore that there was way more than the newspapers reported. He never let Debbie see a cent of it. I've got to talk to you. Tomorrow at work."

I opened my mouth to ask another question, but Debbie stuck her head out the door and called for Ronnie to hurry. He only took time to return the shovel and lantern before he ran to the porch and disappeared into the house without another word.

Walking with my arms thrust in front of me to prevent running into trees in the pitch dark, I worked my way over to the driveway. I figured I might as well take the easy route back to my Jeep. With a little movement I began to regain some feeling in my fingers, and my feet quickly returned to normal. As usual, my brain felt like a tilt-a-whirl ride at the state fair.

How had Donnie managed to keep the money from Debbie all those years? I guess when he wouldn't share the take with her, it had become a bone of contention between them over the years. Obviously Donnie had told his wife he had buried the take from the robbery. Knowing how lazy Donnie had been, I doubted he would have gone to that much trouble.

I pulled the Jeep door closed behind me and cranked the heater to high. After locking the door, I leaned my head back on the seat and let some of the tension from a hectic day fade away. Tomorrow I was sure I'd hear the rest of the story, but for right now I was left to speculate. It still seemed like Ronnie was not a killer. My money was on Debbie.

I would love to talk to someone right now, and my thoughts turned to Harley. A quick visit to his house would be nice, and talking to him always settled my thoughts. He was one of the most reasonable people—his fight with Lam aside—that I'd ever met. I supposed that was a characteristic of a good lawyer. A quick call to see if he was at home and I'd be there in minutes. I fished in my tote for my phone before remembering that I didn't have it. I'd forgotten yet again that it was no longer in my possession, and until today I had not realized how dependent I was on the technology. Surely Harley and I knew each other well enough for me to drop by unannounced. It probably wasn't even eight o'clock yet.

When I turned into Harley's driveway, I could hardly wait to grab a beer from his refrigerator and then snuggle onto his comfy couch with his little cat Smoky. I flirted briefly with thoughts of how I'd met Harley, and how the kitten, a scrawny but scrappy feline, had brought us together. Of course, Harley saving my life, maybe twice, had gone a long way toward endearing him to me.

I jammed the brakes on just as I entered the clearing in the trees where the lawn started. Was I dating Harley just because I felt I owed him my life? That thought seemed like a punch in the stomach. The air in my lungs seemed colder by many degrees than it had seconds ago, and it took force to draw in and out, so much so that spots now danced before my eyes. Maybe the reaction from a busy and bizarre day had finally struck.

Another much bigger problem had been creeping in the back of my mind over the last hour. In the morning Ronnie was very likely going to confirm my suspicions that his fake wife Debbie had murdered Donnie. Once I had that knowledge, beyond my own weak musings, I should immediately call Gibb. I had a citizen's obligation to inform the authorities. I wasn't going to do that though. Maybe I should be the one to skip the state.

I guessed there was only so much room in my brain for problems, and I shoved the bigger one to the back. Since I was sitting in my Jeep in Harley's driveway, I'd concentrate on the problem of my love life for now. More and more I felt uncomfortable dating two men. Movement through the window of the house caught my attention, and I watched as a woman joined Harley where he was framed in view. He wrapped his arms around her and kissed her on the forehead. They continued to share a hug for what seemed like forever, and it certainly didn't look like their first-ever embrace.

Tears ran down my cheeks, which surprised me. I reached to shift into reverse but ground the gears and then killed the engine. Curse words seldom passed my lips, but a few slipped out when I saw Harley step out onto the porch and escort the woman down the steps toward her car. He stopped when he spied my vehicle. I'd been caught. After a quick pause he opened her car door.

Since he'd seen me, and there would be no way he wouldn't recognize the Jeep, I finally moved forward just as his guest's BMW disappeared as it headed out to the highway.

"Stella," Harley said with a smile. He was obviously happy to see me.

"Hi." I sniffed and leaned away as if to get my tote as I dried my cheeks with the back of my hand. "Can I come in for a few minutes?"

"Of course. There's no one I'd enjoy a visit from more."

As we walked up to the door, I hoped Harley would tell me who his guest was, but he didn't. He pushed the door open, and the warmth of the cozy living room enveloped me. A fire in flagstone fireplace crackled and lit the room with what a woman could only describe as a romantic glow. I noticed two almost empty wine glasses on the coffee table.

Smoky's welcome distracted me. He loved to rush across the wooden floors, all skittery, gaining speed, and then crash into your legs. He weighed about four pounds and was all fluff. I gathered him into my arms and nuzzled the sweet baby against my cheek for what I'm sure was too long.

When I finally placed Smoky on the back of the couch, I turned to find Harley staring at me. There was a slight frown on his lips, and I had the urge to kiss it away. Then I remembered him hugging the other woman. It made me feel too shy to step forward and touch him. Maybe he wouldn't want me to know about the hug. He knew I'd seen her here with him, but he didn't know that I'd seen the hug.

"Too many knows, you know?" I said, meaning for it to be in my head but then realizing I'd spoken aloud.

Harley pointed his index finger at me. "That's it," he said a bit too loudly. "That's exactly my favorite thing about you, Stella."

"What? What are you talking about?"

"Just that. I don't always know what you're talking about. You're smart and sweet, and I swear, just two steps ahead of me all the time." He closed the distance between us, grasping my hands. "I told Connie all about you."

For once I kept my mouth shut, but it wasn't because I was being smart but rather that I was stunned.

"Connie?"

"Constance. My cousin Connie. I would have asked her to stay to meet you, but she only stopped for a minute to talk business. She drove down to Atlanta for a few days of negotiations, uh, that's boring stuff. She's afraid of flying." He walked away into the kitchen and was quickly back with two beers. He held one up in silent question as to whether or not I wanted it.

Not trusting my voice—I might yell with happiness over the discovery that the woman was related to Harley—I nodded.

Harley let me sit where I wanted. I always chose the middle of the couch. Sometimes he'd go to his favorite reading chair, but tonight he sat beside me close enough that his thigh pressed against mine and draped his arm across my shoulders. The warmth was welcome after being outside in the cold so long.

"Connie took over the management of the firm when I retired. I know she's capable of handling it, but she gets frustrated."

"So you kept the firm?" Seeing his eyes light up with business talk for the first time, I wondered if he missed working as a lawyer. I asked him.

"Lord, no, Stella. I'm so happy here. Every morning when I wake up I just lay in bed relaxing, and then I get up and have coffee on the porch. Yesterday I tried making this egg casserole." His face fell with the last words.

"Oh, it didn't turn out?"

"No, but that's okay. I'll just try again." He twisted on the couch to look at me better. "My life here in Sewanee is great. I'm only missing one thing."

Harley took the beer from my hand and placed it on the coffee table. He kissed me, the touch of his lips so gentle at first that I could have been dreaming. When I leaned closer to him, I felt his instant response. Breaking free, Harley buried his face against my neck.

"I know you're too busy right now, Stella. I respect that you're creating a career and a new life for yourself."

I wasn't sure how to respond. This really had to end soon with some decision on my part. For this moment, though, I wanted to change the subject.

"Harley, you don't know the half of it. Say, if you were

my lawyer, is it true that everything I say to you is privileged information?"

"Yes but what—"

"How much? How much do you, I mean, did you charge?"

Harley's face colored with a bright blush. "Well, honestly, a thousand an hour."

I choked on my sip of beer. "I cannot believe that."

"Corporations have deep pockets, and believe me they are not people. Almost every person has some shred of decency in them."

I dug into my pocket and pulled out a quarter. "I want to hire you," I said, slapping the coin down on the coffee table.

CHAPTER 24

Mom had not been home when I'd gotten back to the cabin late yesterday evening. My night had been restless waiting on her to return. She didn't. On the way to work I swung by the nursing home and was surprised to see her truck still parked in the lot. I thought about stopping to investigate, but I knew I had to meet with Ronnie first.

He was already at the Center when I arrived, and there were now six quilts hanging from the ceiling in the manner we'd devised to display them. The right way to say that, though, was that Ronnie had known how to do it. The day we'd discussed it, I'd mostly talked about wanting some of the quilts to be hanging above everyone's heads where they could get a good look at both sides. These, of course, weren't for sale, and none of the antique quilts would be shown like that either. That would cause stress on old seams because thread and fabric both weaken over time.

For a moment I watched in silence as he worked to get another quilt up while standing dangerously high on an A-frame ladder. Looking around the room, I could see my planning coming to life in living color. I was very proud of the bed display I'd placed in the center of the room. The bright brass of the headboard gleamed with polish from many hours of work. That had been my contribution while Ronnie had strung the steel cable across the room from the large beams. The older quilts and more fragile coverings would be shown here on the bed where the fabric wouldn't be stretched.

Mom worried about grubby hands touching the antiques, but I assured her that the area was going to have a red rope around it, just like at a museum, and only serious visitors would be allowed to touch while wearing white gloves.

The quilts meant for sale would be folded and arranged on a couple of large tables where they were readily available for people to touch. I would encourage them to spread the quilts open so they could choose their favorite and buy it.

"Morning," I shouted to Ronnie.

My handyman jumped in reaction to the noise, and then clung to the ladder which rocked back and forth, swaying so that for a moment it balanced on two legs before dropping safely back to four. I stood with my hand over my mouth, suppressing the scream that wanted to jump out.

"Oh boy, I'm sorry, Ronnie. Are you all right?"

He backed down the ladder and wiped sweat off his brow with a handkerchief. "Just, uh, just jumpy." He patted his chest. "Beating a mile a minute."

"I know what you mean. Let me lock the front door, and let's fix some coffee and sit down to talk. I don't want to be interrupted by Gibb today."

Ronnie moved to the front door for the one task and I hurried to turn on the coffee pot. After a sip of the fresh brew I settled back in my desk chair like a kid in bed waiting on a bedtime story.

"Okay, Ronnie."

The man looked at the ceiling, maybe deciding where to start, but I was impatient.

"Ronnie, did Debbie kill her husband?"

"Yep, she did." He still seemed distracted.

"But how did you get involved in that?"

"That's what I want to tell you. I didn't know, Miss Stella," he placed one hand over his heart, "not before she did it. Truly I didn't. I was shocked just as much as anybody would have been. Here's what happened. She sent me a letter right before I got out of prison saying she'd pick me up 'cause Donnie and her wanted to help me."

"Did Donnie know? I can't believe that he did."

"Me neither now, but then I did. I figured I'd need some help so I was grateful."

"Here's the part I hate to tell. Debbie was sitting out front of the prison that day. She took me straight to a hotel." The color of flames flashed across his face. "Well, it'd been a long time, and she didn't have to work hard to have me completely twisted around her little finger. She told me that Jay was my son."

I sat my mug down on the desktop with a thump. Again the man jumped.

"She had me stay there at the little hotel for two weeks, and she visited every day. We went to a tanning salon. And my hair needed to grow out. This fringe is 'cause I had my hair cut shorter than Donnie's. I've been shaving the top 'cause I'm not bald." He grinned while rubbing his hand over the crown of his head. "Plus, she fattened me up."

"I noticed the skin on top of your head isn't shiny the way Donnie's was. What was Debbie's plan?"

"Deb told me that she wanted to divorce my brother, but that she deserved to keep the business and the house. She said she wanted to run no-good Donnie off and for me to take his place so we'd still have money coming in. You know, live happily ever after. Her, me, and my son." He choked on the last word.

"Did you want that?"

"I weren't sure. At least about her, but the son part sounded real nice. I wanted to talk to Donnie, but really I didn't think any of it would work. That evening I was supposed to show up, Deb had a friend of hers pick me up from the hotel and drop me off at the house. I don't think I said ten words that night. It was clear from the git-go that Donnie wanted me gone. He planned to give me a free supper and then drive me to the bus station in Manchester. Said he'd pay for a ticket to Atlanta."

"How did you end up here at the Center stealing the copper?"

"Well, I didn't. I think Deb put something in my food, and I ended up asleep on the couch. It was the middle of the night when I woke, and there was Deb sitting in a chair staring at me. Her eyes ..." Ronnie collapsed forward to cradle his head in his hands as his voice broke, but he sat straight to begin the story again. "She looked pure evil. Told me she'd shot and killed Donnie. I was slow to come to my senses, but that's when I realized I was holding a gun. My Lord, Stella, a gun." His hands shook with the memory. "I'm an ex-con."

"So she had you in a trap once your prints were on the gun." I stood and crossed to Ronnie, placing a hand on his shoulder.

He said, "It's not just that. The rest is worse."

"Worse. What could be worse than that?" I moved to where I was facing Ronnie, to look him in the eyes.

"She's hanging on to Jay like, like she's kidnapped her own kid."

"How'd he get here the other day? You had lunch."

"Up until then Deb let him go to school, but he got out early that day and she didn't know it was going to happen. Jay'd forgot to give Deb the note beforehand that told parents it was a teacher's meeting in the afternoon. Usually she was dropping him off and picking him up. Had him on a short leash. She ain't letting him go to classes now. He's at home in his room, and he's real torn up 'cause he had perfect attendance. That was important to the kid."

"Isn't she worried you'd take the van and get him?"

"Deb messed up the engine. Don't know what, but it wouldn't matter if I did 'cause she keeps the car keys with her every second."

"Do you think she'd hurt Jay?"

"I don't know. Lord, I don't know. She doesn't think she'll be caught for killing Donnie, but I don't know. She won't do anything for right now 'cause she still thinks the money is out there."

"She's waited all this time," I said, shaking my head in wonder. "Why does she think it's buried around the house?"

"Oh, the riddle. I forgot I didn't tell you about that. Donnie used to tease her with it whenever she'd argue that they should spend the money."

"Riddle? Yes, Donnie did like riddles. He was always bothering me with riddles. How does it go?" I sat down and pulled a sheet of paper toward me.

Ronnie cleared his throat. "Who builds a wheel without working with wood? Look beneath the wheel." He threw his hands up to indicate that he had no clue as to the solution.

I wrote it down, although I thought I'd remember. He had given me a lot of information, and I was anxious to sit quietly and work out a solution to help Ronnie. It was obvious that the man was so distraught over Jay and the thought of going back to jail for a crime he didn't commit, that he wouldn't be able to help me.

Also, I was not going tell Ronnie that I had spilled the story to Harley last night. My boyfriend was bound by the rules of his profession to keep quiet, although he'd been very concerned. He had warned me several times that once I knew who the killer was, I not only needed to tell Gibb but that I was in mortal danger. He said things have a way of getting out of hand. He'd told me, wagging his finger under my nose, to call Gibb for him. I felt that he was right, and I promised myself that at most I would wait one day.

"Listen, Ronnie, I want to help you. Please let me. Don't run and please, please whatever you do, don't take Jay from his mother."

The way that he hunched his shoulders, ducking his head, told me he had already thought of that option. I wouldn't have much time on any front.

"Let me think this through for a few hours, and we'll talk about how to handle it. We can get you out of this," I said. I held one hand up as if to make some kind of pledge to him while the other hand was behind my back with my fingers crossed.

I said, "Listen, I think you are as safe here at the Center as anywhere. You stay put. I do my best thinking with a slice of pie in front of me so I'm going to go over to the café. Want me to bring you something back?"

"No, ma'am. I'm just worried sick. I've hardly been able to eat a bite for days." With that comment Ronnie got to his feet and swayed, but then he shook off what must have been some dizziness. He left the room shuffling as if he'd aged decades.

I had already noticed that the work overalls he'd been wearing were getting looser and looser. To anyone who was at all observant, it was rapidly becoming more obvious that this was not Donnie. The original had been a robust man without many cares in the world, perhaps because he hadn't taken time to care about his family or customers. Ronnie impersonating Donnie wore a worried expression all the time.

Stepping out the door, I immediately realized that I'd forgotten my coat. The air was a cold blanket with more humidity than normal. That told me the mountain was probably in for its first snow of the season soon. Just a quick dash and I'd be in the welcoming warmth of the café, but as I crossed Main Street, I stopped dead in my tracks in the middle of one lane. A Sewanee police car was parked in front of JoAnn's, and I assumed Gibb was inside.

I knew I had to face Gibb sooner or later, and it would be better to do that away from the Center with Ronnie there. I'd half expected Gibb to track me down this morning already. If I could keep him away, I could delay his finding out what I was up to—whatever that was.

A horn sounded, causing me to jump. Larry Hargrove, an old friend from high school, sat behind the steering wheel laughing like crazy. His wife Tina slapped him on the arm a couple of times while her mouth worked a mile a minute. I figured she was giving him a hard time for scaring me. It was okay since I was the idiot in the middle of the road. I waved and smiled big as I walked off to let them know I didn't mind Larry's sense of humor. He gave a second tap on the horn, and this time I could hear him laughing even with their car windows up.

Before I entered the restaurant, I sucked in a deep breath to steel myself. I needed to act normal, but Gibb knew me well. A career in law enforcement needed keen observation skills, and he had those in spades.

Gibb sat with his back to me, and to my surprise, Arcadia

was seated beside him. She saw me first, waved, and then caught me in a rib-busting bear hug before I could sit down.

"Stella, I was coming to see you in a few minutes. I'm just driving through on my way up from Chattanooga. Had to review a great new club there last night." She grinned ear-to-ear. "Hot stuff."

"You look like you partied all night." The words blurted from my mouth before I could stop them. "I'm sorry, Arcadia. You know me, and you look wonderful." I gave her another hug to let her know I meant it.

Today her outfit was all black. She wore skin-tight knit pants with a crop top sweater. Jewelry, lots of it, complemented the high-heeled boots so tall that they would put most women on the ground with a broken ankle.

"Did you dance in those?" I pointed.

Arcadia just laughed and nodded.

"Sis, you're awful sometimes." Gibb shook his head. "You know I want to talk to you."

He pointed his index finger at me, and I couldn't have felt more nervous than if it had been his gun. The fact that Arcadia was here was very surprising, since she'd obviously called my brother and not me, but I was glad she had distracted Gibb. I prayed that she was going to stay all day.

"Well, I don't know whether to be offended or not that you didn't call me," I said to Arcadia, ignoring my brother.

"Oh, I did. I tried like a zillion times. Anyway, Alma said to tell you that she expects you to be over there sometime this afternoon." Arcadia began to rummage in a gigantic carry-all bag. "Said to bring ingredients for brownies 'cause they're tired of chocolate chip cookies. Here's the list." She handed over a shopping list written out on the back of a cocktail napkin.

I rolled my eyes and then scanned the items. "Fifteen pounds of butter. And she's still got my phone." My voice cracked. "Fifteen pounds! Are they feeding an army?"

"Practically," Gibb said. "Their numbers have grown. I suppose you noticed that our mother didn't return home last night. Right?"

"Uh, yeah and I saw the truck at the nursing home this morning as I came into town."

Thankfully JoAnn came then to take my order—chocolate silk pie—giving me a moment to think.

"Gibb, you saw how rundown the home is getting. Lam said so, and Mom staying isn't really a big deal," I mumbled. "Shue, just one more."

"Oh, she's not the only one, Sis. There's most of the congregation of the First Baptist Church, the local quilt guild, and a news truck from Chattanooga."

"We have a local guild?" I couldn't help but smile until I saw his anger stoke up another notch by my excitement. "Uh, when did Sewanee get a quilt guild?"

"When Alma organized one and named herself the president."

"Uh, I'm not to blame, Gibb." I tried for a reasonable tone.

"You broke Alma's leg," he said.

Arcadia said, "You broke someone's leg, Stella? An old woman's?"

"Sure she did," Gibb said, giving me the evil little brother grin.

I sighed and said to Arcadia, "I'll tell you the whole story someday. When it's finished."

Arcadia stood. "Sure. I can't wait. However, right now I have to go home and get my review written and posted.

Then sleep. Glad I got to see you." She gave me a peck on the cheek.

I gave a rather anemic wave, but Gibb jumped to his feet so fast he had to grab the back of his chair to prevent it from turning over. He took her coat, held it for her, and then walked out of the restaurant with his hand protectively on her back.

I began on my pie, wondering if Gibb would come back to harass me about the nursing home protest. It just wasn't fair that I was taking the blame. Oh well, I'd drown my sorrows in chocolate and happy thoughts that I now had a quilt guild to join. Hmmm. Quilt guild. That stirred some memory. Quilts. Quilt patterns. Quilt blocks. Where had I seen a different kind of block recently?

"Oh, oh, I know the answer." I jumped to my feet without thinking and did a few dance steps. All the other patrons stared at me and no wonder, as I was still holding my fork, but this was important. I knew the answer to the riddle, and it had been so easy.

I plopped back into my seat. The memory of the Clark's barn quilt shone brightly in my mind. The answer was a quilter. A quilter can build a wheel—at least a carpenter's wheel—without wood. I supposed the cash was buried against the barn wall beneath the quilt block. I still needed to come up with some kind of plan, though, that would use this new knowledge.

First, Ronnie and I needed to get Jay somewhere safe without kidnapping him.

Second, we needed for Debbie to confess in front of a witness that she had murdered her husband, or we needed proof that would stand up in court.

Third, I needed another piece of pie if I was going to come up with a plan that could accomplish all of that.

CHAPTER 25

"JoAnn, can I borrow your phone, please?" I stuck my head around the swinging door to the café's kitchen. The noise forced me to repeat my question as JoAnn hurried past to serve customers.

"On the table, honey." She tossed her head toward her shoulder to indicate a direction.

I shuffled some invoices on her desk until I found the phone and tapped in Albert Doan's number, which I was proud of myself for remembering. I first thanked him for helping me get in touch with Virgil and suggested that if the two of them ever wanted to come to Sewanee, I would give them a tour of the Heritage Craft Center and treat them to lunch in the state's best restaurant.

"Why you've got a date, young lady," the older man said.

I pictured his smile and was glad I'd extended the offer. Then I asked him how much money was stolen from the bank.

"Just a few dollars short of fifteen thousand."

"Someone suggested to me that the newspaper reported a low number."

"No. The police didn't ask or advise me to do that. I just told the truth when interviewed for the article. Virgil called me yesterday and said he'd talked to you. He said you asked if he wanted to know why you were interested."

"Do you want to know?"

"If Virgil can wait, then so can I." His voice sounded as if he wasn't as patient a man as Mr. Muller though.

"I promise to tell all when you come to visit me."

We said our good-byes, and then I left out the back door. In an open field behind the restaurant there was an old tire swing hanging from an ancient oak. I wandered over and slipped my legs through the opening. With the cold air and no jacket, it wasn't nearly as much fun as I'd imagined it would be.

I forced myself to think about Debbie and how to get her to leave Jay somewhere unattended. Ronnie and I would need to make her uncomfortable. She had to be worried that her plan would fall apart if she didn't drop everything and hurry to … what?

I used my feet to turn the tire round and round, twisting the rope. When I could feel the resistance, I lifted my feet and the spinning began. It went faster and faster, sending me in a dizzying circle. When the rope had straightened, it went a couple of lazy turns in the opposite direction. My stomach, after chocolate silk pie, began to protest and I dropped my feet to the solid ground. The scenery seemed to continue moving for a moment but then settled.

An out of control swing is what my life had felt like lately. Everything was spinning faster, and I didn't have a good handle on any of it. I was still ridiculously happy having moved back to the mountain and being near Mom, Gibb, and all my friends, but there was a lot to get done. I needed to turn this employee probation into a permanent career. I'd never wanted anything more, but now I had the chance to help another human being straighten his life out. I did not want to see Ronnie go back to prison for a crime he had not committed. If that interfered with getting the job, I supposed I would just have to find something else. I couldn't abandon Ronnie and Jay.

I climbed out of the tire swing and hugged myself against the cold. The answer to the dilemma had not magically deposited itself into my brain, so I decided that I would get my trip to the nursing home over with before going back to the Center and Ronnie. I had a jacket in the Jeep so I'd be okay. A quick trip to Piggly Wiggly with the shopping list in hand set me back $87. I wasn't expecting to be reimbursed, but I could trade the groceries for my phone.

Pulling into the parking lot, I slammed on the brakes. A news truck sat near the building like an alien spaceship with the menacing satellite dish sprouting from the roof. There were at least two dozen people milling about, and I spied one, a nicely dressed young woman, who carried a microphone. Two police cars rounded out the reasons why I wasn't going to walk through that gauntlet.

I backed the Jeep out to the road, hoping no one had seen me. A long walk with three sacks of groceries wasn't my game plan, so I parked near the driveway but in a spot shielded by a stand of trees. Thankfully I had on short boots instead of athletic shoes today.

Circling around to the back of the building through the woods was a quick and pleasant hike. I wouldn't be able to go in the usual window because it could be seen from the parking lot. Luckily, the dining room of the nursing home jutted out from the rest of the building so that three sides of the large area had windows. One wall, probably the kitchen, wasn't a good way in. Two of the windows had large fans mounted into the openings, and the other three were painted over with white paint.

I would still be able to make it unseen if I could catch someone's attention to unlatch the frame of the next nearest window. With a Kleenex I wiped the dirt away from the glass and cupped my hands around my face to better see inside. Shue, they were playing bingo. Alma had the token cage sitting down where she could reach into it from her chair. She screamed the pick so loudly the people in the parking lot could have played if they'd had a card.

Mom came in from the kitchen carrying something in a bowl. She went around the room trying to interest each resident in whatever it was. She had no takers. When she came close to the window, I pounded on the glass. She set the bowl down on a nearby chair seat and fumbled with the latch. It took effort, but she finally was able to push the sticky frame open.

"Stella, I'm glad you could join us."

I wasn't sure if I detected sarcasm in her voice or not, and for the first time in her life, Mom looked her age. Her hair, flat and lifeless, showed the gray more when she hadn't washed it with saved rainwater. Although she never wore makeup, she did use moisturizer. Now her skin appeared dry and dull enough that a surge of worry for her health seized me.

"What's going on, Mom? Are you feeling okay?" I hugged her. "I never expected this, uh, protest to last so long. Don't a lot of these folks need medicine?"

"Of course, but I bargained with Gibb to allow the nurses in to administer and to check out anyone who wasn't feeling well." She shoved wayward strands of hair off her face. "And I'm all right. Just tired. Alma can really keep a body hopping. I thought I was in better shape."

"What did Gibb get out of the deal?"

"Gibb? Nothing. Oh, I see." She smiled. "I guess a son shouldn't negotiate with his mother." She picked up the bowl and sat back down on the chair, stretching her legs out.

"What's that?" I pointed at small, round pellets in the bowl that looked more like pebbles than a snack.

"Oven-dehydrated okra slices. They've all had more brownies and cookies than they should have." She sniffed. "What's in the bags?" She pointed at the grocery sacks that I'd hauled in the window.

"Uh, butter."

"Oh, boy, and sugar I'll bet. Most of these people were up half the night on a sugar high, and the ones that weren't were up all night!"

"What are their demands?" I asked.

"Well, all honorable and you have to give Alma a lot of credit in being brave enough to tackle this. They want the place cleaned up and more heat. That's important with old bodies. Plus better food. I guess they had a pretty good cook before, but this Mr. Tindal fired her."

"What did the owner say when he saw all this?"

"As far as I know, he hasn't said anything. Didn't show up yesterday after he'd said he would. Gibb called the sheriff in Chattanooga and asked if he could go out and explain the situation to him. Maybe scare him into taking care of this situation."

"If I know Alma, she's having way too good a time." My gaze wandered across the room to the wheelchair-bound figure.

"They all are," Mom said, waving her hand at what looked like any roaring party. There was a table of card players, a couple of the residents were sitting in front of a TV, and, of course, the bingo game was going strong.

Mom poked me. "You'd better go and talk to your brother."

"Okay but let me get my phone back first." I started to walk away when Mom mumbled something I didn't hear.

"What?" I asked.

"Oh, just said good luck."

I glanced over my shoulder at her but then turned to face Alma as I hurried across the floor. I needed to be strong and insist that she give back my phone.

"Alma, Alma." I tapped the old woman on her thin shoulder.

"B4," she yelled.

I rubbed my ear. "Alma, I really need to talk to you."

Alma punched the woman sitting next to her in the arm and instructed her to take over the bingo calling. Then with a frightful squeak of the rubber tire on the floor, she turned to gaze up at me. Displeasure was written in the wrinkles along with her history of hard years.

"Well, Stella, took you long enough. Did you bring our provisions? Reinforcements?" She looked around, seemingly disappointed when she didn't find a platoon of Navy Seals backing me up.

Alma whined, "That girl, that one with the funny name, who called sounded right nice. Couldn't you have at least brought her along? I'll bet she's plucky."

"What? I'm not plucky enough for you?" Even with all my years of being raised right by my mother, I could not keep the irritation out of my voice. "I need my phone back, Alma. I've done everything you've asked of me. I've shopped and run errands and investigated cooks and been, well, uh, been supportive. There's nothing more I can do, and I really need my phone. I need it for my job." I slapped my hands over my mouth, remembering that Alma no longer had a job. Her presence would no longer haunt, I mean, grace the Sewanee Public Library. I still did not know if she knew, and I wasn't going to be the one to bring it up. Surely she would blame me.

Alma smiled a grin that lit her whole face and yet somehow reminded me of Gibb when he was into some mischief. "Job. Hmmm, for your job. I'm sympathetic, I truly am, but I don't have your phone anymore, Stella. Someone borrowed it, and I can't seem to remember who." She glanced around the room but then tapped the side of her head. "Maybe you could go and talk to your brother while I think on it for a spell."

My shoulders sagged. How could this woman of advanced years and very few pounds always get the best of me?

"All right. All right. What do you want me to tell him?"

"Josie! Josie," Alma yelled while wheeling the chair over toward the door of the dining room. "Let Stella out so she can talk to the sheriff." To me, she added, "You just make sure the copper knows that our first demand is to get the cook back. We won't negotiate on that."

Josie, a heavy-set woman in a green robe and scuffed sneakers, worked a key in the lock and slid a chair back that had been jammed under the door knob. As she cracked open the door a couple of inches, she slipped a broom handle out which had a pair of white undies tied to it. "Peace," she called out. "Sheriff, don't shoot. We've got one coming out."

I had to blow my breath out to squeeze through the slight opening which Josie allowed me. My entry into the rest of the nursing home was anticlimactic, to say the least. The few members of the staff seemed to all be gathered in the lobby. Some were reading and a couple of them slept. Only one nurse manned the front desk. Gibb and Deputy Mann were edged over in a corner talking. I marched up and interrupted their conversation.

"Gibb, what are you doing about this situation, and who has my phone?"

My brother turned slowly to stare down at me. "And hello to you too, Sis. What's this about your phone?"

"Alma borrowed it yesterday. Shue, was that only yesterday?" I sucked in a huge lungful of air and snorted it out through my nose, sounding like an ol' mule. "Seems impossible. Anyway, now she doesn't seem to remember who has it."

Hearing some slight noise behind me, I twisted to see what the source was. A figure in a wheelchair—thankfully not Alma—had rolled quietly to within a couple of feet of us. It was Soldier but looking quite different than the last time I'd seen him. He slumped forward in the chair and a string of drool made a slow drip toward a blanket spread across his lap. The man's feet were bare on the extensions of the chair meant to protect toes from the wheels. In all, he looked pitiful.

"Soldier, I mean Jack, are you okay?" I leaned down and peered into a blank face.

"Sis, the old guy can't hear you. He's deaf as a doornail, and I don't think he's got much left on the top floor."

"Huh?" Something here was fishy for sure. I knew Soldier could hear perfectly well, and just yesterday he'd hog-tied me on Alma's orders. There was nothing wrong with the old soldier's mind.

I was still leaning over Jack when he winked at me. So Soldier was now a spy behind enemy lines.

I straightened. "So what are you and Deputy Mann planning?" I asked, thinking I could help Jack get the information quicker.

"Sis, I've got to end this before someone gets sick or hurt. One of the residents could die. We're going to pull the circuit breakers for the dining room and kitchen. From what I hear, they're having too much fun anyway. They'll still have heat and water, but the stove, microwave, refrigerator, and lights will be out."

"Well, what's wrong with them having a good time? Mom's in there, and she'll help. She'll let you know if anybody seems sick." I felt my anger boil over. "It's this Mr. Tindal you should be pulling the plug on. Have you done a background check on the yahoo?"

I watched Gibb's face go from anger to confusion. "No, I haven't and you're right. He didn't show up like he said he would so I've got every right to check up on him. Deputy Mann, I'm heading back to the station. When the electrician gets here, have him search for the breaker box but don't do anything until I get back." He turned without a word to me but then said over his shoulder, "I don't know who has your phone and thanks for the suggestion."

I was left staring at Deputy Mann. She frowned at me and hitched up her gun belt.

CHAPTER 26

I still didn't have a phone, but more importantly, I finally had thought of a way to try to trick Debbie into some action. It seemed to me that we were all stuck waiting on the money. Once Debbie had the money, or knew it didn't exist, then she would be free to make a move. I didn't believe she was going to want to keep playing house with Ronnie, not while he was the only one who knew—or so she thought—that she had killed her husband. Ronnie wasn't safe around that black widow!

I was becoming more and more frightened that once the money issue was settled that Debbie might turn deadly again. Ronnie might be standing between prison and a bullet.

It wouldn't be right of me to dictate any plan to him, as it was his life in danger and not mine. He and I needed to talk, and I planned to advise him to go straight to Gibb. My one-day limit on withholding information was about over anyway. If he refused, then I would offer my idea to give Debbie a shove to resolve this standoff she'd created with Jay as the hostage.

I made quick time back to the Center. As I walked in, I was already calling for Ronnie.

"Ronnie," I shouted. Three heads turned to stare me—Ronnie, Lam, and Harley. "Uh, I mean, Donnie. Sorry, I didn't know anyone else was here. What are you guys doing?"

"Shoot," Harley said. "We wanted to get these installed before you got back."

"We almost made it." Lam grinned. "But you can see what it's going to look like at least. Come here."

It was pretty obvious that they were building me more display space, but their design was ingenious. I edged around one of the large tables to where the guys were attaching a length of metal about four feet long against the wall at a height of about seven feet above the floor. Ronnie and Harley were on ladders, one on each end of the board, while Lam wielded a drill.

"One more," Lam said, depressing the trigger. The drill emitted a high-pitched whine and drove the screw deep into the wood of the log wall. "Okay, guys." He stepped off the stool and moved it out of the way.

Ronnie and Harley backed off the ladders, and the three of them wrangled a case, four feet wide and five feet tall but only about four inches deep, up the wall. Mostly, though, it was Lam and my handyman lifting the weight as Harley directed their efforts.

"Catch it on the cleat," Ronnie said, guiding his side to the proper position. "A little higher, Lam. Higher. Good." A solid thunk told us when the case settled into a safe position.

"Great design, Ron, uh, I mean Donnie," Harley said. "Sorry I couldn't help more, but this splint gets in the way of everything." He flashed the hand that had the metal splint wrapped with gauze.

At Harley's slip of Ronnie's name, I saw Lam glance at the handyman and then his eyes met mine. There was a questioning look on his face, but I just gave him a quick shake of my head. Lam nodded, and I knew I'd have to explain later but for now he'd remain quiet.

"Wow." I moved closer. "These are perfect. The whole display of JoAnn's recipes will fit here perfectly. and it hardly takes any room at all."

"That's the point. It was, well, we all thought of it. We were talking last week about how much you've gotten done. This place looks great," Lam said, "and we wanted to help. Right, Donnie? Right, buddy?" Lam slapped Harley on the back.

I could see that these two were determined not to wallow in the mud again. No more fights. I was glad that they weren't going to act like schoolboys ever again.

The bell over the door tinkled a merry tune. Before I could turn to see who it was, I saw both Lam and Harley get googly-eyed.

"Lam, you ol' sweetie." The syrupy voice dripped with sex appeal.

I had no idea who it was, but as soon as I saw them, I knew they were trouble. Two young women, both wearing miniskirts more appropriate to summer than November, stood on high-heels that made their legs look endless. The outfits were topped with fake fur jackets. Both women were colorful, reminding me of a candy store, and after taking in the outfits, I finally paid closer attention to the faces. They both looked about twenty and were very pretty. One of the two carried a cardboard box and started toward Lam. Suddenly, both men were all feet as they tried to get to the woman first to relieve her of the burden.

Harley won, lifting the box from her hands, and said, "Let me."

I couldn't help but notice how dowdy I looked in comparison to the two. Although I didn't go in for miniskirts, neither Lam nor Harley had seen me in anything but jeans for weeks. My nails were worked to the quick, and I was usually wearing more dust and dirt than makeup. No wonder the guys were impressed.

The other woman smiled at Harley and cooed. "Why you're just the most interesting man I've met in ages." She placed her hand on his arm and then noticed the splinted finger. "Oh, baby, you're hurt."

"Oh, it's nothing. Just, uh, a fight."

"A fight! Did you hear that, Nicole? I bet you were rescuing someone in distress," she said.

Nicole continued to fawn over Lam. "Oh, Missy, that's not how it was at all. These two were fighting, but now they're best friends." She twirled around like a child unable to contain her energy.

I strode over to them and took the box from Harley. "Is this a donation?" I tried to keep my voice professional, but a sharp edge was obvious. Lam gave me a look that said he'd heard it too.

"You must be Stacy. Lam and Harley told us all about you and this, uh, Heritage place." This came from Missy.

"It's Stella, and how did you all meet?" I twirled my finger in a circle to include them all.

"At the gas station. We drove up here to visit our cousins, and I just hate to pump my own gas," Nicole said, but then Missy picked up as if they were one person. "It makes your hands stink. Don't you agree, Stacy?"

Nicole started again before I could open my mouth. "We were lucky enough to find two real gentlemen—two of them—to help us out. Then they bought us a Coke."

"Before you know it, we're all best friends." Missy smiled,

showing dimples in slightly chubby cheeks.

"Oh, I can see that," I said, feeling that I should give a meow to punctuate my statement. I glanced from Lam to Harley, and they were looking like they had been caught with a hand in the cookie jar.

"So we asked our aunt if she wanted to donate," Nicole said.

Missy added, "And we wanted to see our guys again."

I slipped the box from Harley's hands. It was light as if it was empty but I heard a scratchy noise as something shifted inside. "That's very generous of you. And your aunt." Folding the cardboard flaps back, I gave a startled yelp as my eyes and brain finally figured out what the gift was. A stuffed rattlesnake, coiled, head raised, ready to strike.

"Auntie's first husband was bitten fourteen times over the years by mean ol' rattlers and lived. He was a preacher." Nicole grimaced and peered into the box. She shivered.

"What finally killed the man?" I asked.

"Oh, rattler number fifteen." Missy laughed. She turned to Nicole, and they bent their heads close together as they continued to laugh.

"You girls know what?" I sat the box onto a table. "Ol' Lam and Harley were just saying, right before you two got here, they were ready for a break and hungry enough to eat a whole cow." I paused to grin at both men. "I think I can tell they want to ask you to go with them, but they're just too shy to ask. Now don't go to JoAnn's across the street. No beer." I winked at Missy. "You make them take you over to the Honky Tonk. Best steaks in the state."

At that point I snorted a laugh when I caught sight of Harley's face. He'd gone from blushing to pale as snow. Lam didn't look much happier. In just a few steps I'd shuffled them toward the door, barely pausing to let the guys grab their coats. I shoved the panel closed behind them and burst out in a fit of laughter.

"Miss Stella, that was downright mean of you," Ronnie said. He'd come up behind me and leaned over to look at the stuffed snake. As cautious as if the reptile might still be capable of striking him, he lifted it out of the container. "Reckon it might appeal to the little boys."

"You know it's already grown on me. I think somewhere in a corner might be nice."

"How do you like the display cases? Lam and Harley really wanted to help out. They did most of the work."

"They're great. I mean, their idea and the guys. I'll bet you did most of the construction though. Hey, do you think we could get the second one up on the wall? And then we need to talk."

Ronnie sighed, and the weary look he'd been wearing for days settled back over his features. "Reckon we can. Let's get to it."

Thirty minutes later we dusted our hands on our jeans and high-fived our success, but we were so tired we didn't bother to climb the stairs to my office.

I glanced at Ronnie's watch. A little after four. "Ronnie, your life is probably in danger."

The words fell hard and flat between as I hopped up to sit on one of the tables holding folded quilts and Ronnie leaned against the wall. He didn't seem surprised at my statement but didn't speak. I should wonder if the poor man was anything but numb by now.

So far he'd been taken in by Debbie, only to discover that it was to a den and she was a dangerous snake. The stuffed snake sat across the room ogling me with glass eyes. Who would have even thought you could stuff a snake?

I rubbed my hand across the backing of one of the covers. The quilter had put as much attention here as she had to the front of the quilt. With a slight shake of my head, I pulled my thoughts back to the problem at hand. "I don't think Debbie is so in love with you that she'll let you live. After all, you are the only one who knows that she killed Donnie." I hopped off of my seat and paced the room. "I swear you were safer in prison."

"Yeah. I kept quiet and out of the way, and if Deb doesn't kill me, she'll surely send me back to that prison. This time it would be for life. So really it'd be the same punishment either way. I mean now that I know I have a son." Ronnie held his hands out staring at the palms.

I imagined the man was seeing his future empty or, worse, the loss of his life. He seemed the type that his biggest concern would not be those issues, but Jay. He'd already accepted that the boy was his and decided Jay's security was most important.

"Ronnie, you have to go to Gibb. Tell him the story. It's the only way to keep you safe."

His voice exploded. "I ain't worried about keeping me safe, and going to the sheriff won't keep the boy safe from that woman. She's been waiting ten years for that money. Sorry, Miss Stella, I can't do that."

Those words put a new spin on my thoughts. Could a mother, even one as bad as Debbie, hurt her own child? There were plenty of examples, and the woman was already holding her child hostage to make Ronnie do her bidding.

I stopped my pacing right in front of the snake and leaned down so that my face was level with the ominous fangs bared to strike. As if I were hypnotized by the sparkling eyes, I reached out a finger to touch the needle-point of the fang.

"Ouch." I sucked the drop of blood that rose to the puncture.

Ronnie jumped.

"Okay," I said, taking my finger out of my mouth. "First thing, who in your family was a quilter?"

"What? What's that got to do with anything?" he asked.

"Everything to do with the riddle and where I think the money is buried."

"Okay, although I still believe my brother would have already spent the money. Probably in less than a year and he wouldn't have spent a penny on his wife or Jay." He thought for a few seconds. "My grannie quilted but not my mom. Grannie, Dad's mom, lived with us for the last years of her life."

"The barn quilt block is called a Carpenter's Wheel."

Ronnie slapped his hand to his forehead. "I told Deb the money wasn't buried in the garage. It's out back of the house and has a dirt floor. She had me dig it up, and she even tore down half the walls. Can't even get a car in there anymore."

"We need to get Debbie to dig next to the barn under the painted quilt block, and we need to make sure she finds an empty jar. Or box. Whatever."

CHAPTER 27

The hay made my eyes water, and I had to keep sniffling and rubbing my nose to ward off the sneeze ready to erupt at any moment. But no matter how uncomfortable I felt, Ronnie and I had decided on a plan, and I couldn't let him down. His life might depend on me. Then, as if the need to sneeze wasn't a big enough problem, I heard a mouse scuttle across the floor, under the hay, and too close to my feet for comfort. I pressed both hands over my mouth to suppress a scream.

I'd been wrong when I'd guessed that the old Clark barn was not used. Right now a pet goat poked its head through the metal gate of its stall, and by stretching as far as it could, the creature kept nibbling at my woolen cap, knit for me by Mom of course. Flapping my hands would get the goat to jerk back for a moment, but the pesky critter would return to his tasty new treat the moment I turned my back on him.

I glared, but he practically shrugged. The animal must have been hand-raised and maybe bottle-fed to be so bold with a stranger.

"Aren't you pretty?" I whispered, thinking maybe flattery might help me. His head and long neck were the color of chocolate while the rest of his body was a creamy white. "Pretty, but leave me alone."

In my hiding place in the barn, half buried in hay, I alternated protecting my hat and twisting to press my eye to a knothole in the wall. I needed to keep a lookout for Debbie's arrival.

All I could see was a slice of the yard that fortunately included where Debbie would be parking when she drove up. It felt as if I'd been squatting in the cold barn for hours, but it probably had only been about forty-five minutes. I'd insisted on getting into position early so as not to take a chance on missing the opportunity. Ronnie was back at the Center waiting for Debbie to pick him up after work. They would soon be on their way here so I wouldn't have to sit in the cold much longer while fighting off a goat.

Earlier in the afternoon Ronnie and I had decided that he would call Debbie and send her on a mission to the pharmacy. He'd told her that he had a bad migraine attack coming on. Since Sewanee didn't have a pharmacy, she would need to drive down the mountain to the next nearest town. Evidently, from the side of the conversation I'd heard, Ronnie had to work hard to convince her to do this for him. Debbie wasn't a sympathetic person. While she, dragging Jay along, was away from the house, Ronnie and I had raced over to the barn and buried a large empty pickle jar which JoAnn had given me.

It wasn't an elaborate plan, but I hoped it would work. Ronnie was going to tell Debbie that he'd solved the riddle and had dug the jar up days ago, taking the money for himself. He was going to dig the jar up again to prove this to her. Then, while I was inside the barn listening at the knothole, Ronnie would tell her that there had been $60,000 in the jar, and he would trade the money for Jay.

Then Ronnie and Jay would be safe, since she needed them both if she wanted the money. We hoped he could get her talking, making a confession that I could overhear. I supposed it was a long shot, but I didn't have any better idea.

Even if I didn't hear her admit to murder, the plan still bought Ronnie some life insurance.

Once we'd buried the jar, I'd hurried to drop Ronnie back off at the Center raced back to the Clark place and my hiding spot. I'd had to take a stroll through the dark woods after parking the Jeep out of sight. Lately I'd done too much strolling in the woods at night.

Again the goat tugged at my cap, nearly pulling it off my head. "Drat. Stop that!" I jerked the wool from the goat's teeth and yanked the cap back on, dragging it low over my ears. The goat bleated in protest at losing it, but over the noise I heard a car pull up to the house.

Car doors slammed, and then shouting erupted. I believed I might have heard Debbie complain even if I'd been back in Sewanee and not just thirty feet away across her front yard.

"A headache? You're crying over a little headache," Debbie yelled. "Jay, get to the house. Your daddy and I got work to do."

Ronnie made some reply, but since he wasn't shouting, I couldn't make out his words. Following closely on the boy's heels, he disappeared inside, but only for a moment, and then he joined Debbie on the front porch again. Together they came out to the yard, and I saw him take her by the arm and urge her nearer to the barn.

"What do you have to show me?"

"See that up there? I done figured it out," Ronnie said.

"What? It's the barn, Ronnie. You ain't figured nothing since you got out of prison."

"That quilt painted on the barn," he said, gesturing upward. "That's a Carpenter's Wheel block. You get it? Who can build a wheel without wood? The answer's a quilter. And the rest of the riddle Donnie left says to dig under the wheel."

Debbie said, sounding for once excited, "Well, you finally win the prize, but I bet you didn't solve the riddle all on your own." She snorted. "I'll bet that goody-goody Stella helped you. Did you tell her about the money? Did you?"

Ronnie gasped, and I peeked out the knothole. He was rubbing his arm, and I guessed she had hit him. Then she slapped his arm while I watched.

"Debbie, stop."

"How much does she know?"

I shivered at the thought of getting on this woman's bad side, although she didn't seem to have a good one.

"Nothing," Ronnie said, with panic in his voice. "I drew out the block and asked. That's all. Let me get the shovel."

Ronnie trotted into the barn door and whistled low-like through his teeth, and I gave a soft reply note so he'd know that I was in place. I peered over the mound of hay but could barely see the shadow of his figure. Light from the security fixture, which lit the yard so well, barely penetrated through the spaces between the boards making up the walls of the barn. It was just enough light to make you think you could see. Ronnie grabbed the shovel and was gone.

The next noises I heard were the sound of the shovel's solid thunk against the ground. This time, though, Ronnie's work would be easier, as the ground was softened from the previous digging. The soil would not have had time to refreeze. For a few minutes, in silence, Ronnie dug, and Debbie stood aside. She pulled her coat tightly around her body and hunched her shoulders against the falling snow which now coated the ground. Every few seconds she bounced from foot to foot as if she couldn't bear not to be dancing. Maybe she felt this was finally her reward.

The thought made me feel sorry for the woman. Her figure was sharp against the view of the rundown little house. She'd been married to a handyman for over ten years, and he hadn't done much to make their lives easy. Ronnie had mentioned that he'd patched a leak in the roof since he'd been living here, and I could see that the three steps to the porch sat at an odd angle as one side had sunk into the ground. On my last trip I'd noticed how the barn needed major repairs.

I knew myself how unpleasant Donnie, the real Donnie, had been. He'd proven to be lazy, slow, and messy. One of the references I'd contacted told me that Donnie could be depended on, but only to show up at the local bar for lunch. I could not imagine living with the man as Debbie had.

I shook my head. Nothing was bad enough for her husband to deserve being killed unless Debbie had been defending herself, or Jay, from physical abuse. That did not appear to be the case.

"Anything yet?" Debbie's voice sounded like an anxious kid.

"No, you'll be the first to know."

We'd buried the jar deep, knowing that someone hiding money would have done so. Evidently Ronnie had decided to show her the empty jar first and then drop our plan on her. I heard him digging fast. It would only take a few more minutes.

I leaned back into a more comfortable position, trying to relieve some of the cramping in my calves. When the moment came, when the shovel struck the jar, I was sure that Debbie would alert me that it was time to pay attention again.

The scratchy sounds from the mouse told me it was far enough away that I could relax, and the goat seemed content right now with a mouthful of hay. His odd eyes, horizontal slits, continued to watch me, though, as if I were good television. Listening to his rhythmic chewing helped slow my frantic heartbeat. I didn't think I was cut out for spy work.

As I massaged my lower legs, I wished I could see the sky through my knothole and watch the snow. That would calm me, as I'd always loved this time of year. When I was little, I'd played a game of looking up into the snowy sky, picking out a large flake, and watching the snowflake's journey all the way to the ground. That and building snowmen were my favorite snow activities.

The sharp clank of metal against the thick glass rang out. I quietly knelt again and pressed my eye to the knothole. I watched as Debbie fell to her knees repeating over and over, "You were right. You were right, Ronnie. I don't believe it."

She began digging with her hands, and in seconds she tugged the jar free from its grave. In a scramble she rose and held it up to the light. A low scream escaped her lips. "It's empty," she said, voice rising as she threw the glass to the ground. "Oh, no, that jerk Donnie spent it. I wish I could shoot him again."

It had happened so fast that it took a moment to register in my brain, but there was the confession I'd hoped for. I didn't think that something like this could necessarily stand up against a smart lawyer in a courtroom, but it was a chink in Debbie's armor. She might crack and give a more official confession if this were used against her by Gibb. At this point I was anxious to find my brother and tell him the whole story.

Ronnie threw the shovel down so hard it bounced back out of the hole and fell to the side. "Debbie, I dug it up a few days ago. There was $60,000 in that jar. I've got that money now. You better listen to me."

"You, you did w-what?" The woman's words were a stunned stutter, almost unintelligible.

"You heard me. I ain't playing house no more."

I gasped and drew back when Debbie whipped a handgun out of her jacket pocket. It was small, but seen from the wrong side, it seemed huge. The black eye of the barrel reminded me of the last time I'd been held at gunpoint. My heart thudded with fear that she might have heard me, but Ronnie, taking a step backward, fell when he stepped into the hole he'd just dug. The noise of him falling covered any sounds I'd made. I was safe for now, but the woman was furious and screamed at Ronnie to get up.

He rolled to his knees and took his time standing. Maybe Ronnie was giving Debbie a few seconds to calm down. He needed it too, as I could see his whole body shaking, and when he spoke, his jaw didn't look as if it were working properly. The words sounded like those of a drunk.

"Debbie, I'm not going to back down. I promise you that. I want Jay, and you can leave here; otherwise, you're going to jail. If I have to, I'll say we did it together. I'll drag you to prison with me so that Jay can have a better life. I swear."

With those words Debbie's demeanor hardened. The woman could have been a statue there in the snow. Her face did not change expression, but her eyes narrowed.

"Okay, smart guy. You sleep in the barn, you rot, but you bring me that money tomorrow. If you try to come into that house," she gestured with the gun, "I'll shoot you dead."

Two things happened at the same time: Debbie turned on her heel to walk back to the house, and the phone in my pocket rang. It was Ronnie's cell phone that I was supposed to use to call for help if things went wrong. My phone still resided at the nursing home.

Debbie spun around pointing the gun, not at Ronnie, but at the barn wall. I didn't think she could see me watching through the small hole in the wall, but I leaned away. Thankfully, I could still hear.

Ronnie was a quick thinker, and he said, "I dropped my phone in the barn earlier. Couldn't see to find it and figured I'd get it tomorrow."

Debbie didn't reply, but I didn't for a second think she'd leave without checking. As quietly as I could, I scooted down into the hay, trying to cover myself. Then almost as an afterthought, I took the phone from my coat pocket and slid it away from the pile of hay, pushing it with my outstretched leg and giving it a hard shove. It continued to ring. The dim beam of a flashlight appeared at the door.

Scooped over my head, the hay now tickled my nose unbearably while, as I tried to breathe without sound, it made my throat raspy. Rather than watch the light come closer, I squeezed my eyes closed, but they popped open when I thought about my cap. The bright pinks and blues would be easy to spot whereas my brown hair would blend with the hay. I risked a quick movement to yank it off my head, but it was already gone. I glanced at the goat, where my hat hung from its mouth as he happily chewed and flipped it to and fro, waving it like a signal flag. I'd been so frightened, so focused on the story outside the barn, that I had not felt it being stolen.

In the long pause, one that felt a year long, the goat continued to chew. I could just see him and the satisfied but puzzled expression on his face. But thankfully now that he had the cap, he was beginning to figure out that it wasn't anything edible after all. He finally dropped it to the barn floor in the nick of time as Debbie paused, probably letting her eyes adjust to the lack of light.

The phone rang again guiding Debbie to its location. I heard her feet in the cheap sneakers I'd noticed earlier as they scuffed closer and closer. Then she must have bent and picked up the phone.

"Hello," she said, and then after a short pause, "No, I don't want to buy any magazine subscriptions." In her anger, Debbie threw the phone. It smacked me in the head, but I managed to stifle my startled scream.

CHAPTER 28

I sighed. I had failed to convince Ronnie, after Debbie had stalked off, to go straight to Gibb. When Ronnie had staggered into the barn, ghost-pale face visible in the darkness, he collapsed onto the rough plank floor. His breathing, ragged and irregular, had matched my own. I'd struggled out of the hay and together we sat for over ten minutes without speaking a word.

After calming down, we'd argued, in whispered tones, about whether or not to seek Gibb's help. Ronnie declared that it was too dangerous until he had Jay free from Debbie.

"Miss Stella, you saw how dangerous she is. There's no telling what that woman might do. Let me get Jay free, and I'll do whatever you want. I mean, you're right that I need to get Gibb's help, and it don't matter if he puts me straight in jail as long as he'll keep Jay safe. I reckon when you tell him that she pulled a gun and threatened my life, the sheriff won't send Jay back to her."

"Okay, but what are you going to do? You can't stay in this barn tonight. You'll freeze to death."

"No. There's a good sleeping bag in the van. I'll be okay, and I'm here if Jay needs me. Debbie might decide to run in the middle of the night. I'll lie out in the back seat of her old car, and it'll keep the wind and wet off me."

I knew that Ronnie was frightened out of his wits, but should I go along with him? Having left Ronnie, I'd made my way through the woods back to the Jeep. It wasn't until I was almost back to the spot where I had parked that my cold ears reminded me that I had not retrieved my hat. There was no way I was going back to risk Debbie seeing me. Not after everything I'd been through. Now I clenched the steering wheel, teeth chattering, while thinking, trying to make the right decision.

Would Ronnie's plan to get Jay away from Debbie work? It was simple. As she was walking away, he'd told her that the money was hidden at the Center. When she drove him in to Sewanee in the morning, he was going to have her wait in the car while he came in. He would carry a paper bag back outside and show her a few bills and then make her let Jay go before handing it over. It was my job to gather some bills and then fill a sack with some newspaper, placing the money on top.

No matter how much I tried to believe the plan would work, the sinking feeling in my stomach would not go away. That was my answer. I needed to tell Gibb. Tonight. With the crunch of the tires on the snow, I pulled onto the road.

When I turned into the driveway of Gibb's house, I was disappointed to see it dark. Maybe he was working late. I knew where he kept a spare key, and I decided to wait for him inside. I'd warm up, have some coffee to clear my head, and be ready to discuss the situation calmly. I hurried up the walkway, leaving footprints in the snow that was now about two inches deep.

With some trepidation, I slipped my hand into a decorative ceramic birdhouse that hung on the wall near the front door. It was never meant to shelter a live bird, but

I knew from experience that insects thought it was a great place to visit. Probably the cold temperatures had seen to all the bugs by now, and I had the key in hand without incident.

The lock turned smoothly, and I slipped into the living room, closing the door behind me. When I flipped the overhead light on, I saw Gibb and Arcadia, arms and legs tangled together, on the couch. Both stared at me with eyes wide. My brother leapt to his feet, his hair thoroughly tousled, the top buttons of his shirt undone, and his shoes kicked off.

"Stella, what are you doing here? What happened to knocking?" Gibb asked.

Arcadia was her usual cool self. "Stella, girl, I'm so happy to see you." She stood but was barefoot and her sweater twisted askew. After a warm hug she leaned back and looked me up and down. "Stella, why do you look like a scarecrow?" She picked a stem of hay out of my hair.

I hadn't made a sound, but her question broke the paralysis caused by my extreme embarrassment. I turned and ran, tumbled into the Jeep, and roared down the road. I was halfway down the mountain before I realized that I hadn't planned to leave Sewanee. I made an illegal U-turn and gunned the engine still with no idea of where I was going.

Only a few cars passed me on Main Street as I rolled down the two-lane. Without much thought, I guided my vehicle to the nursing home. I figured that Mom was still there, unless Alma's demands had been met. I'd been out on my spy mission since this afternoon so I didn't know if this elusive Mr. Tindal had ever shown up. I'd love to know what Gibb had found out about him.

Never in my wildest dreams would I have ever thought that Gibb would fall for Arcadia. I mean, I thought that my friend was wonderful, kind and exciting, thoughtful and adventurous, but I'd thought he would be totally irritated by her free spirit. The ways of the heart are strange and mysterious.

Mom's truck wasn't in the parking lot, which raised my hopes that the nursing home had returned to normal. I trotted directly to the front door but could see no one in the darkened lobby.

Oh, well, back to crawling in windows like a cat burglar. At the back of the building I found the window I entered through before still unlocked. The room was dark but not so much so that I couldn't see a few bundled and huddled shapes in chairs and beds scattered around in what had been the dining room. Now it looked like a dorm.

After pushing the window frame open as wide as it would go, I heaved myself up using the narrow brick ledge and thrust my head and shoulders through. Surprised at hearing a voice, I stopped my forward momentum, which left me hanging half in and half out, hinged at the waist.

"Dear, sweet, girl, why don't you ever use the back door?" Annaleigh's stage whisper caused several of those sleeping to rustle in their makeshift beds.

"What! I thought it was barricaded. The piano was in front of it." I huffed as the window ledge dug into my stomach.

"Not anymore. None of the police force have tried to enter from the backyard since the first day, and Jack went out earlier for a beer." She rolled her eyes. "Please try it." The actress swayed, silk dressing gown swishing, as she crossed the room to the door and held it open.

I shoved myself out of the window and dropped to the ground, tripping over the yew bush but regaining my balance.

When I entered, Annaleigh said, "Now isn't that easier? Your dear mama is not here at the moment if you were hoping to talk with our comrade."

"Comrade? Of course." I sighed. "Isn't this settled yet?"

Alma's strong voice answered as she rolled up to meet us, "No, and we'll be here until it is. We don't back down. By the way, we need more sugar."

I stared down at the old woman as I thrust my fists onto my hips. "No, no, no. You are not going to ruin my grand opening. You promised me a quilting bee tomorrow, and I'm going to get one if I have drag your skinny behind all the way to the Center."

Alma and Annaleigh stared at me with their mouths open until Alma recovered and her eyes narrowed.

"Uh, I mean, I'll give you a lift," I said. "All of you. And the quilt frame has to be there. I wish I had costumes. Does anyone here have some really old dresses?" I glanced around like I might find some draped over the dining tables.

Annaleigh, usually so upbeat, spoke in a tone that carried the weight of many years, decades even. "Dear one, everyone here has nothing but old clothes."

In spite of her sadness, I rubbed my hands together. "Gingham? Homespun? Maybe bonnets?" I wondered where I could find some this late and why I hadn't thought of costumes before? Then I remembered the more important event on the schedule tomorrow, although I certainly hoped that Debbie would be long gone—under arrest—by the time my Heritage Craft Center opened its doors at eleven sharp.

That's when I realized that I would have to go back to my brother's house and tell him the story. He was already mad at me, and this news would send him into orbit like a blazing comet. He didn't have red hair for nothing.

"Is Mom coming back tonight?" I looked first at Alma but then quickly turned to Annaleigh as the more reliable source of honest information.

"No, she said she needed to help you out tomorrow," the aging beauty said, "and I, although I cannot sew, would not miss this most grand of openings for the world. Perhaps I could sing?"

"Uh, I didn't know you sang, Annaleigh," I said.

Alma snorted. "I think we need to discuss a trade, Stella. Annaleigh, would you go and make me a cup of tea? No one makes a cuppa like you can." Alma smacked her lips and then gave me a big grin. "And, young lady, why do you look like a scarecrow?"

CHAPTER 29

"So you see, Gibb, I knew the right thing to do was to come straight to you," I said, trying to arrange my expression to look as innocent as possible at the same time that I squirmed in my seat.

Gibb, who'd sat across his kitchen table from me without saying a word for the last thirty minutes, now stood and grabbed a beer from the refrigerator. He leaned back against the counter. The pose and his bare feet with jeans and a white T-shirt made the subjects of our conversation—murder, blackmail, and ransom—seem normal. His prickly hair appeared more red than usual, but that was probably just my imagination. I could tell he was counting and probably not just to ten. Maybe a thousand.

"I could sure use one of those." I pointed.

Gibb asked, "Arcadia, would you like a beer?"

My good friend nodded that she would. She'd been holding an unlit cigarette between her lips, and somehow Arcadia made it seem as if Lauren Bacall were competing with her to look cool even with that bad habit.

Gibb dipped back into the refrigerator and came out with another can, but just one. He wiped the top with a paper towel and snapped the ring. Who knew my brother was such a chivalrous date?

"Uh, I guess you're upset," I said to him when he gave the beer to Arcadia.

"You think, Sis? And why do you look like a scarecrow?"

"Gibb," Arcadia drew the word out, "Stella's had a hard day and a dangerous one." She pulled several pieces of hay from my hair, letting them drift to the tabletop.

"That's the point. She shouldn't be playing detective because it is dangerous. She's not trained, and she doesn't carry a gun." Gibb gave me a hard glare as he picked up the hay and threw the pieces into the trash. "You didn't, did you?"

"'Course not. I was only armed with a phone. Oh, and a cap."

My brother and Arcadia both looked puzzled. "It's one of the ones Mom made ... well, of course, it was." I smiled, but I'm sure it was no more than a wary grin. "It was wool, pink and blue with these nice, nubby touches of violet. The color of your eyes, Arcadia."

I had always thought of Arcadia as one of my best friends, but now I was going to have to shift to thinking of her as Gibb's girlfriend too. I had the sneaking suspicion that this one was going to stick, and I was thrilled at the development. Tonight when I'd come to visit for the second time, ringing the bell, they'd been sitting on the floor in front of the fireplace. Her welcome had been warm and not the least bit embarrassed by me finding her still at my brother's house. Gibb, on the other hand, should never play poker.

"But you're talking about that cap in the past tense." Gibb left the words hanging to indicate he wanted more information.

"Well, that's where the goat comes into the story."

"Of course there's a goat in your story." Gibb smacked his forehead with the palm of his hand. "Let's hear the rest of it."

He tossed the remainder of his beer down in one swig and then sat back down at the table across from me.

"Okay, last night, wait, it was just a couple of hours ago. Shue, this day has seemed so long! So Ronnie and I had decided that we'd trick Debbie into confessing, and she did." I kept talking for another half hour, and to Gibb's credit, he didn't interrupt me once. Arcadia asked a couple of questions, but it was because she wasn't familiar with the Sewanee area.

"So that's how the goat got into the story," Gibb said, "and you're telling me that you've arranged a hostage-for-money exchange for eight in the morning."

"Uh, that sounds awfully formal when you put it that way," I said.

"There's no other way to put it, and I'm short of deputies. I still need one at the nursing home full-time in case someone there decides to die. Harold's mama is very sick, and he's out for a few days." Gibb walked into the living room and picked up his phone. "I can probably borrow one from Manchester." He tossed the words over his shoulder as he called up the number.

While he talked to the sheriff of the neighboring town, Arcadia and I put our heads together and discussed her relationship with Gibb.

In whispered tones, she asked, "Do you think Cele likes me? I mean, I think she's great. So cool." Arcadia rubbed a finger over the bee tattoo on her cheek as if it represented all the past mothers of sons who might not have liked her.

"She thought you were wonderful. I'm so happy, Arcadia."

My friend leaned back to take in my whole face. She seemed to read my every thought and then nodded. "It's just been a couple of dates. But I, well ..."

I leaned in close to her ear. "I know my brother." I squeezed her hand just as Gibb came back.

"Okay, I got lucky. He's giving me two guys since this should be short." He pointed at me. "This is the plan and I want you to listen, Stella. More than that, I want you to do exactly as I tell you. No improvising. No wild ideas. Just do as I say and don't get shot. Mom would never forgive me."

"Do you think I'm crazy?" I asked.

At first Gibb just stared at me, his face grim, and then he said, "Remember the goat."

After I'd repeated his instructions back to him, Gibb finally let me leave. I spent most of the night awake staring at the clock. The slow morphing of one number into the next did not help me to drift off. My fears for the events of the coming morning kept a stranglehold on my imagination, but the one thing I didn't worry about was my grand opening. A week ago I could not have thought of any event with the power to push that from my mind.

It was with great satisfaction that I recalled that every display was polished to perfection. Every speck of dust banished. I had no worries for the opening. In fact, this experience had been so rewarding that I could not conceive of doing any other job. If I didn't get the permanent job status … well, I wasn't going to think about it.

As for Ronnie's problem, before talking to Gibb I guess I'd been worried, but not for my own safety. As a professional, my brother was trained to think of all the possible outcomes, where I had only hoped for success. He had me imagining all manner of dangers.

Mostly I just knew that we had to be successful for the sake of young Jay. He could be physically hurt, but I feared that he would definitely be emotionally hurt. Regardless of how things went down, he was most likely going to lose his mother to a prison sentence. Gaining Ronnie might not make up for that. No matter how bad a mother Debbie was, a child has a way of forgiving.

At five in the morning, I threw the covers back with more force than necessary. "I give up," I whispered to Carly, who lay sprawled across the foot of my bed. She snored once and settled herself deeper into her dreams.

I made short work of a shower and makeup before tiptoeing through the house. Mom had promised to help me all day at the grand opening and, if she was sleeping, more power to her. There shouldn't have to be more than one of us dragging around like we'd been plowing all day. I left a note on the table asking her not to show up before eleven and telling her that I would need her all day until the seven o'clock closing. If she showed at the Center early, Gibb might have a heart attack, and frankly so might I.

The headlights of the Jeep had to slice through thick, icy fog so I kept the speed down to a crawl. Streetlights still lit Main Street with the halos of light piercing the darkness, although I could just make out dawn as a swipe of pink blush to the east.

I made note of each spot along the street where Gibb had told me a policeman would be stationed. The two from Manchester, who would be strangers to Debbie, were going to be nearby. They would be in work clothes identifying them as power company employees. Their work van would be in front of the jewelry store next door to the Center, and I noted that there were already bags over two of the parking meters with NO PARKING printed in neon orange. The van would be Gibb's hiding spot. He'd be able to see everything unfolding and rush out when the time came.

Deputy Mann would be in civilian clothes sitting in JoAnn's Café by the window. I imagined she would be lost without her holster and heavy belt, although her gun would be in a gym bag by her side. I wondered if this was going to be her first stakeout.

The town's one part-time deputy would also be in street clothes, pretending to wash the windows and sweep the sidewalk two doors down at Mimi's Quilt Castle.

Gibb had asked Lam to be standing outside of his business pretending to be busy with some task. Lam knew Debbie and would recognize her car. He was to call Gibb the second he saw her pass. It would give us two minutes of advance notice. I didn't know what I'd do with that time except maybe faint.

Somehow seeing the set-up and the careful although quick planning, made it all real, and my stomach twisted. I wanted to drive on out of Sewanee, perhaps all the way to Georgia. Maybe I wasn't as much of an optimist as I thought. Rather than turn to park behind the Center as usual, or in front, I continued on for a block. I didn't want any bullet holes in my vehicle.

I took a deep breath in through my nose and blew the air slowly out my mouth as Mom had taught me in yoga lessons. It didn't help.

With my hat, a forest green one today, scrunched over my ears and my muffler wound around my mouth, I scurried down the sidewalk to my beloved Heritage Craft Center. The snow had stopped sometime during the night and was now just a wet slush. It would soon be puddles when the temperatures rose even a degree. My shoes were wet, but it didn't matter. I'd worn work clothes and brought along a nice outfit to change into later for the grand opening. I left them in the Jeep.

Today was the big day in more ways than one, and I had to steady the door key with both hands to fit it in the lock. Once in the door, I paused for a moment before turning on the lights. I wanted to savor the moment when I would see all my hard work ready for the grand opening. Yesterday, with Ronnie and me racing around dealing with pickle jars, I'd scarcely had time to enjoy the view of my displays. I'd hardly noticed the colorful quilts hanging from the cathedral ceiling like floating stained glass windows with all the hues visible to the eye. I'd hardly glanced at the moonshine still boldly waiting in front of one window with its slight trace of the odor of hard liquor. I would light a stick of incense near it before Janice arrived. In the other front window Darla's well-worn quilt frame with the Tennessee Waltz quilt rolled onto it, partly stitched, waited patiently. It had held and released many quilts over a hundred years.

Over the last few days I'd carefully placed many display items just so in the cases. Each one had a card with its history, the story that brought it to life. I'd memorized most of the information, and I wanted to guide as many tourists personally through the Center as possible, telling them the history instead of having them read it. I'd tested the sound system and couldn't wait to show off a few clogging steps to the music of the mountain. There would be free recipes courtesy of JoAnn and her ancestors, and Mom was going to make sassafras tea, giving out bundles of the leaves for everyone to take home. She'd also worked hard beside me helping with a final cleaning and polishing.

I flipped the switch. The lights blazed, and after the darkness outside, I blinked. When my eyes adjusted, I did a double-take, unable to believe the chaos. My displays had been ravaged, strewn about, thrown to the floor. The quilts for sale which I'd left so carefully folded and stacked on the tables were tossed haphazardly around the room. The shock and horror of the damage robbed me of my voice. I wanted to scream, but nothing came out. It must be a nightmare, but the reality was solid, unwavering in my vision now clouded by tears. I fell to my knees and for a moment everything went dark.

CHAPTER 30

Lying on my side, I opened my eyes and relived the sickening feeling of my discovery. It was dark again, though, and I wondered what had happened to the lights. My faint had probably lasted only seconds, but my head throbbed. Other than knowing where I was, the rest of my memory came back slowly. It was early morning. Today was the grand opening. Today was also the day Ronnie would try to get Jay, his son by birth or love, away from his mother. Gibb was still angry with me because he was afraid for me. An alarm bell went off in my brain.

I didn't once ask myself who might have done this. I knew. Debbie. But the question I should have asked was when had the woman been here? When had she left? I knew she had come looking for the money she believed that Ronnie had dug up and then hidden here.

I sobbed and pressed my clenched fist to my mouth. My head hurt. I was going to be fired. More tears flowed with the thought of how I loved the Heritage Craft Center and this log building and all the crafts inside of it. I'd filled it with the hard work of crafters past and present, their skills, and, in some cases, their very means of survival.

The face of a young widow and mother of three swam in my blurry vision. She had come in last week asking in a quiet voice if I could help her sell the baby clothes she made. The woman wore a look of failure before I even opened my mouth, turning away without showing me the samples she carried in a paper bag. Greta, I learned, called the bag a sack. I had to urge her to open it, and then out tumbled bright colored sleepers and Sunday-best outfits with embroidered flowers and creatures dancing along necklines and hems. I told her how fantastic her sewing was and begged her to bring me more. As she walked away, I noticed that her shoes were falling to pieces, held together only with duct tape. I'd cried, and now with the thought of letting her down, I sobbed again, choking on my sadness.

"Well, I swear, I ain't never seen such a crybaby."

The voice, Debbie's voice, floated about my head but refused to settle into one spot. Oddly, I wasn't afraid because I thought I was imagining her words, but then I connected the destruction and the voice and my muscles quaked. I wished I could leap to my feet and run, but my head still hurt so badly that I wasn't sure that I was actually conscious.

"Git up. We got business. It's almost light outside." This time Debbie punctuated her words with a kick or punch to my side. It didn't matter which.

"I'm hurt. Oh, my head." I reached to feel the back of my head and felt sticky blood. When I brought the hand back to look, it wasn't the sight but the smell that bothered me the most. I gagged.

"Be sick if you want but hurry."

Now she walked around to where I could see her in the glow of the street lamps through the front windows. The tiny gun dangled from her hand, and then she used it to sweep a rack of CDs off a table near the door. The music of dulcimers, fiddles, and banjos clattered onto the wooden planks.

Her voice hissed at me. "You think you're special, don't you? This fancy place and being the boss and all. You know what I do for a living?"

When I didn't respond, a handmade pot burst against the floor when she threw it.

"When I ask a question I want an answer, Stella. Do you know what I do all day?"

"No, Debbie." I struggled to sit, cradling my head to keep it balanced on my neck. Would it roll away if I gave it the chance?

"I wash dishes and pots and pans at the high school from seven until two. Five days a week and even in the summer 'cause of summer school. Lots of days they ask me to work a second shift. Minimum wage and no benefits 'cause I'm just a contract worker. Do you think my son is ashamed of me?"

I flinched and backed up a couple of inches in case she wanted to kick me again.

"I guess so, but it's a job, Debbie. You should never be ashamed of hard—"

Her foot connected again and I howled.

"You were saying? What? I'm supposed to be proud of being poor? That it?"

My head bobbed up and down, which was a big mistake. I moaned again.

"Boy, you are simple, Stella." She dropped something in front of me. I instinctively jerked back, but the object didn't make a sound when it landed. I picked it up, feeling the softness, and twisting it to catch the available light. The colors, pink, blue, and a touch of purple, slowly coalesced into the form of knit fabric in my vision. I was seeing the tattered cap I'd left behind in Debbie's barn, the one the goat had stolen and chewed.

"Mmmm. I see you recognize what Dip Cone was playing with. He's Jay's pet. 4-H."

My ears heard Debbie's words, but something didn't make sense.

"Dip what?" I asked.

"Dip Cone. The goat's name. Jay loves those custard cones dipped in chocolate." Her hands made the motions of drawing a custard cone, flipping it upside down, and dunking it into the vat of melted chocolate. I'd eagerly waited on that very same desert myself many times.

I must have still looked confused though. Somehow the wonderful treat, soft on the inside with its crunchy chocolate coating, didn't remind me of a goat. Then the image struck me as I remembered the contrast of the milk chocolate color of the head and neck against the custard white on the body. Surely the name had been a creative choice by Jay.

"Ah," I said.

"Yeah, well, now we got that important business done, let's git going. Git up. I am running out of time and patience, and as you know, I don't have a lot of either."

Debbie bent down and started jerking on my arm. She was small, probably only about a hundred and twenty pounds, but she was strong and wiry like so many people on the mountain who worked physically hard. She dragged me to my feet and supported me for a few seconds until my dizziness subsided.

"Thanks," I mumbled without thinking about who I was talking to or my circumstances.

She laughed in response.

"What'd you hit me with?" I could feel a fine trickle of blood running down my neck.

"This gun's a good club, but I'll be happy to shoot you next time I use it." She prodded me forward into the room and away from the windows.

I knew without her telling me that Debbie wanted my help in finding the bank job money. Evidently Ronnie and I had done too good a job of convincing her that there was $60,000 just waiting for her to find. The fact that there wasn't any money would give her a good excuse to kill me. I didn't have any doubts she'd enjoy it.

As if she'd been reading my thoughts, she said, "You know where Ronnie hid the money." It was not a question, and she motioned for me to get it for her.

"I wasn't here when he hid it."

The color of anger flushed her face, and her mouth twisted into a grimace. "Stella, I am not kidding. I have to leave here real soon. I've been looking for several hours, but no one knows this place better than you. So where could Ronnie have put it?"

"Let me think just a minute," I said, my mind racing for ways to get the upper hand over this woman.

While I thought, I watched her take a crushed pack of Camels out of her T-shirt pocket under a sweatshirt and then dig deep into her front jeans pocket for a lighter. "Sure, take your time," she held the flame to the cigarette. "I'll just wait here." She took a deep drag and then dropped the lit cigarette onto the antique quilt spread across the brass bed.

Shock froze me for a second, but then I threw my body across it, rolling on the flames that flared in the dry aged fabric. It would not have taken a full minute for the whole cover to be fully engulfed and spread the fire across the room.

My breath, ragged and interrupted by hiccups, rasped from my dry throat. "My, Lord, you're crazy." I pushed my hair out of my face to stare up at her.

"No, I'm not. I am feeling a bit desperate though and rushed. Did that help you think of someplace we can look?"

"Maybe the storage room. There's some of those plastic bins, and I saw Ronnie digging in those a couple of days ago."

I struggled to my feet without accepting the hand that Debbie offered, so I was still staggering and unbalanced as we made our way to the back room. One after another I jerked the bins, seven of them, to the floor from where they'd been neatly stacked. The lids popped open to reveal supplies. There were tablecloths, plastic utensils, and plastic cups in one; clean rags, scrub brushes, and protective gloves in another; and office supplies in the last one. I knew what was here, but for Debbie's benefit I tossed items out and pawed through them to prove that there was no money. I moved as slowly as I dared, but once Debbie prodded me with her toe.

This morning I was supposed to have filled a paper bag with cut-up newspaper and then top it with bills that I'd collected. Gibb and Arcadia had both emptied their wallets, and on the way home last night, I'd gone through the bank drive-thru. I'd withdrawn my limit of three hundred, and it, along with the rest of the bills, was in my tote bag.

Would Debbie take that small amount of money and leave if I offered it? I was pretty sure I didn't want to find out what she would do if I told her there was no $60,000. I would have to play along and keep her occupied until I had some opportunity to escape or overpower her. I was sure it wasn't even six o'clock yet, giving her plenty of time to kill me. Mom would probably be the one to find my body. The thought brought acid to the back of my throat. I had to do something.

Rocking back on my heels, I asked, "Did you kill Ronnie?"

"I wish. What a dud. Prison really did rehabilitate that guy, and I never thought I'd say anybody was more boring than Donnie. If I ever hear one more stupid riddle in my life." She slapped her thigh. "Ronnie used to be so much fun, and he was always nicer than Donnie." She sounded wistful for her past and stared at the floor as if she were looking for some enjoyment to fill her life.

"I guess you dated both?" I asked

"Yeah, in high school and after we graduated. Then I was ready to get married. Yep, 'cause I got pregnant."

"Which one is Jay's father?"

"Well, now, I'm really offended, Stella." She gave me a dirty look and then threw her head back laughing. Once she'd gotten started, though, she couldn't seem to stop. I supposed the stress was getting to her also. The belly laughs, interspersed with gasps of air, went on for a few minutes, and then finally, wiping tears from her cheeks, she said, "I don't know. I really don't. Gawd, they're identical. Or they were. Ronnie's one of a kind now." Debbie crossed to the small refrigerator and studied the contents before taking a bottle of iced tea. "I could sure use a cup of strong coffee. Guess this'll have to do."

The sound of the vacuum popping when she opened the tea caused me to flinch. "Ronnie said that the bank robbery was your idea."

"Hmmm. You know, I don't really remember, but I suppose so. They don't give away those diapers for free, do they?"

243

"I'm sorry things were so hard for you, Debbie." When she didn't respond, I asked another question to kill time. "Why'd you marry Donnie instead of Ronnie?"

"Ronnie said no."

The look on her face made me afraid to ask any more personal questions. "Did you already look in those cabinets?" I pointed.

"Nope. Git to it."

"It would be quicker if we both do it."

The look she gave me would have withered even a strong person.

Rather than stand to cross the room, I just crawled the few feet. My head felt as if rocks were rolling back and forth banging against the inside of my skull each time I moved. I opened the first cabinet door and practically crawled in to pretend to check out the back space.

"Shue, I can't see a thing, Debbie. There's a flashlight in that drawer. Would you please get it for me?" My fingers curled around the handle of a pipe wrench that Ronnie, or maybe Donnie, had left in the cabinet under the sink pipes.

Debbie seemed to take forever to find the flashlight that I knew was in a drawer just a few feet from where I knelt. I used the time while she wasn't watching me to move the wrench out of the cabinet, positioning it next to my leg and out of sight under my pants leg. My hand continued to grip the handle and I tried to prepare my muscles for action, but I was feeling more like a limp noodle than a hero. I knew, though, that I wanted to fight for my life and not just let this woman shoot me or, worse yet, set the building on fire with me unconscious here on the floor.

When she stepped across my legs and as she held the light out to me, I swung the heavy tool. The noise as it contacted her ankle was sickening and her howl of pain speared my ears with its intensity.

If I'd thought Deb would drop helplessly to the floor, I was wrong. Maybe desperation gave her more fuel than my fear gave me. She did drop, but it was to wrestle me for the tool. It took her only a few seconds to snatch it from my hand. By then we were embraced in a fight for our lives. Only the fact that I hadn't found the money yet saved me from being shot.

At one point Debbie slammed my head against the floor, and stars whirled in a wobbly orbit. After that I wasn't sure how I managed, but I pulled away from her grasp. I scrambled across the floor, at first on all fours, but then gained my feet. I ran for my life.

As I hurtled through the front room toward the door, a sound caused me to stop dead.

"Help. Somebody, please help me." The scared voice of Jay Clark clearly called from upstairs. I changed direction and pounded up the stairs, although every cell in my body screamed to seek freedom. I'd been so close.

At the door of my office, I saw the boy huddled in front of my desk. He didn't rise, even when I called to him as I moved across the room to the window.

"Jay, hurry. You remember me. Stella. I'll get us out of here." The sash of the window banged upward as I heaved against the wood. A quick shove and the screen was out of the way. I turned and beckoned to Jay. "Hurry, please. We've got to hurry."

"I can't."

His voice was a soft whine through tears. He held one arm up as far as it would go, which wasn't but a few inches, because of rope tying his hands behind his back and to the leg of my desk. The boy's own mother had tethered him.

It would be easy for me to lift the corner of the piece of furniture to free him and untie the knots, but would I have time to convince him to go out the window? We would have to shimmy down the porch post, and I wasn't sure we both wouldn't fall the fourteen or so feet to the sidewalk. It probably wouldn't kill either of us, but Debbie surely would—at least in my case. I still wondered if she would actually hurt her own child. I couldn't take the chance.

"Jay, you're free," I said once I'd worked the knots loose. I didn't give the boy a choice but hugged him close and hurried him over to the window. I found myself muttering for him to hush while he cried because I could now hear Debbie climbing the stairs. There would only be seconds to get Jay to safety. If she heard him, my plan wouldn't work.

At the open window I shoved him through, half lifting and definitely using my greater weight to push him out to the porch roof. Even as he turned to try and come back inside, I slammed the window closed on him, almost mashing his poor fingers. I jerked the window shade down to cover the window with such force that I tore one screw of the bracket holding it in place half out of the wood.

"Crazy, crazy, girl," I said to myself. Now I was crying again as Debbie limped to a stop in the doorway, but thankfully all she saw was me cowering in the corner.

"You better hope you find that money in the next ten minutes." After those words she realized that Jay was not in the room. "Where's my son? What did you do to my boy?"

"Jay was here? The room was empty when I came up. I thought you were dead." I made my voice sound disappointed. "I came up to call 911. Gibb is on his way, Debbie."

She looked to the desktop, and I knew she'd see the portable phone there.

I added as I stood, "I don't have a cell phone right now."

"Where could Ronnie have put the money? I don't think you called your brother, but I don't have long. I swear I'm going to kill you if you don't find it. I'll let you live if you do."

"It's not up here, but I know where it is. I was just delaying before because I don't want you to get away with murder."

"You really won't want me to get away with the next one." She raised the pistol and fired in my direction.

I cringed and threw my hands up as if that would save me. I knew Debbie hadn't aimed at me but behind me only a foot away I could see a blackened hole in my quilt hanging on the wall. My poor double wedding ring quilt.

"Okay," I said, "let's go downstairs. That's where it is."

She dipped her hand into her pocket and fished out her lighter. Flicking it on, she warned me, with a growl, "You try anything ..."

I knew what she meant. I shuffled forward, not wanting to get closer, but I had to pass to get ahead of my tormentor. I knew she would want me to go down the steps first, and that's when I noticed the damage the pipe wrench had done to her ankle. Not only was there a wound and lots of blood, but the odd angle of her foot told me the bones were most likely broken. She wouldn't, couldn't let the pain stop her, but I might have a better chance now.

I went down the stairs on two good legs, well ahead of her. Behind me Debbie moaned in pain with each step. I knew that once I reached the bottom of the steps I should run for the door, but when I glanced over my shoulder, she flicked the lighter. The way that the staircase turned would give me some cover so I had a good chance of not getting shot.

But I couldn't do it. I felt that Debbie would follow through with her threat and drop her lighter onto a quilt. She'd torch the place. My career, my dream, my future would go up in flames. I had to try and save everything I'd worked so hard for.

Thin daylight bathed the showroom now as I started pretending to search.

"It's got to be down here," I said, picking up a couple of quilts from the floor to lay them back on the table. One was a traditional pattern and the other modern, looking sweet in its simplicity, but I knew it was a pattern best tackled by an expert. I remembered lovingly examining each quilt as I'd accepted them for consignment. Mom had relished each one too before instructing me on how she thought the quilter had tackled the project and, of course, throwing in her two cents on the color choices.

"What are you looking for?" Debbie asked, slashing my remembrances as she hobbled closer.

"There's a large ceramic pitcher. It was on this table, and I think Ronnie put the money in it. I was going to get it out this morning." In case she remembered, there really had been one here that I'd filled with bright silk flowers but no money.

"Yeah, it was here. You should be close." Her voice sounded her excitement.

I bent down again and fished my hands through the fabric, moving myself a few steps closer to Debbie. As I was trying to steel my nerves to grab Debbie and pull her to the floor, my hand bumped against an object under a quilt that surprised me. At first I couldn't place the odd, rough texture, but then the image of the awful stuffed rattlesnake popped into my mind. The prickly scales felt icky against the back of my hand.

Changing my plan, hoping to distract her with a glimpse of the rattler, I threw off the fabric covering the reptile. Debbie screeched and stepped back, but her feet became entangled in a quilt, and she fell backwards. The gun flew out of her hand and landed far enough away that she wouldn't be able to retrieve it.

Although I flinched at my own cruelty, I grabbed the woman's broken ankle and twisted. I hoped that the pain might make her faint or a least take some of the fight out of her. I was right because she went limp. I hated to touch her for fear that she might be playing opossum and attack me, but I rolled her into one of the quilts covering her from head to toe. Then I did the same with a second quilt. I raced up the stairs to my office for the rope and used that to secure her. By the time I'd finished, I could hear muffled moans and cursing.

CHAPTER 31

It might have been five minutes or it might have been thirty. I had staggered and stumbled to the door, and after swinging it open, I sank to the porch floor and leaned against the frame. Being this close to the rest of Sewanee made me feel safe enough. That's when I shut off, collapsed in a sobbing heap. I'll never be sure how long I cried because my brain shut down. It was completely blank of words or reason. There was only emotion, raw and deep. In the dawn light I breathed in the fact that I'd lived.

A small voice brought me back to the present.

"Stella. Stella, it's alright."

The sound came from above me, and I only wondered why my angel sounded so very young.

Then I saw a pair of sneakers, red socks, and then jeans drop down over the edge of the porch roof. The legs wrapped themselves around the stout tree trunk that had, over a hundred years ago, been fashioned into a post to support the porch roof. Finally, I realized that this was Jay. The rest of his body, and then his face, appeared as he moved downward as agile as a monkey.

"Stella, you saved me!" His voice was excited and happy, but then his face crumpled. "Is my mom dead? I heard a gunshot, and I thought you were dead. But you're not, so is Mom, is she, I mean, is she gone?"

"No, Jay. She's inside but ..." I said, grabbing at him as

he moved to go inside the Center. "Please stay with me for a minute. Help me, please." I didn't want the boy to see her trussed up like an animal.

I pulled Jay into a tight embrace. "Do you have a phone?"

His eyes were huge, dark disks staring up at me. He shook his head to tell me he didn't. A car passed on Main Street, and I felt like flagging it down but the fact was we weren't hurt. Also, I didn't think Debbie was going anywhere. I could hear an occasional faint moan, but the sounds of her struggles to free herself had stopped.

"Jay, is Ronnie okay? You know that he is your uncle and not your dad, don't you?"

"Mom told me a couple of days ago. She said that Uncle Ronnie killed Dad." He wiggled away from me but didn't try again to go inside. "I don't believe it though. My uncle is a good man." Tears streamed down the boy's cheeks.

I asked again, "Is your uncle okay? Do you know?"

"No. Mom said he attacked her." He watched his shoes as he answered, scuffing one against the other. "She woke me up and made me get in the car. A bunch of boxes with our clothes were in the back seat."

"Where is the car?" I'd assumed it was sitting at the back of the Center, but I was suddenly curious. "Out back?"

"No, it's through the trees back there." He pointed toward the back of the building and then continued the story. "We walked from the car, and Mom had a key so I didn't know we were doing anything wrong, Stella. Really, I didn't."

I realized that even if I'd parked in back like usual, I wouldn't have been forewarned. I had been feeling guilty that I'd walked into trouble because I wasn't paying attention. Debbie had been smart with the car, and she had used Ronnie's key to get inside.

Jay sounded desperate for me to believe him. "I know, honey, I do. What happened next?"

"We went upstairs to look, and she wanted me to stay there by myself but I wouldn't." He whimpered once and then pulled himself together. "That's when she tied me up. She tried to make it seem like a game, but I knew better. I wish Ronnie were here."

At that moment the fake power company truck drove up. When the driver, the undercover cop, stepped out, I could see he was puzzled. I motioned the man over and ran through the story, mindful that Jay was listening. "So you see it's not a covert operation anymore. Can you call Gibb, the sheriff, please, and we need an ambulance." I hugged Jay again. "It's just her ankle. I think it's broken, but she's okay. I swear, Jay. I would never lie to you."

"Looks like you need a doctor, too, ma'am," the man said.

"No, I'm okay."

With those words I had to swallow my own disappointment. I wasn't really okay, but it was not the small wound to my head. The real damage was to my Center. I had to face the fact that my grand opening was ruined, and I would surely lose my job today. But I was alive and Jay was okay, or he would be. Mom had taught me to face reality and look for the positive in hardship. I'd lift my chin and tell Janice the whole story. I'd accept her verdict.

The other officer had now joined our group, and I said to them, "If you guys don't mind, I think my friend and I could use some hot chocolate." I saw that JoAnn had turned the sign in her window from closed to open. She always opened early for all the people in town who had to start their work day with the dawn.

When they nodded, I put my arm across Jay's shoulders and led him across the street, telling him that he'd see his mom in just a few minutes. As we stepped inside, someone shouldered in the doorway behind us. I gasped and whirled around to find Deputy Mann on my heels.

"Ms. Hill!" The deputy's voice expressed her shock at seeing me. Her glance took in my condition. "Are you okay? Let me call the sheriff." The woman dropped the gym bag she carried and reached to heft her equipment belt, which she wasn't wearing.

We locked eyes, and I laughed. It took a few seconds, but she joined in and then said, "I guess you're feeling better than you look. I'll call the sheriff."

"One of the Manchester cops has already called. Have some hot chocolate with us." I stepped over to the table with the best view of the Center across the street and dropped into a chair. I scooted another chair out and patted the seat for Jay to join me.

"Maybe coffee." Deputy Mann took in the expression on Jay's face, which was a mix of fear and awe at this woman who looked like a super hero out of a graphic novel. "You know, a cocoa would be good." She pretended to hitch up the heavy belt, getting a laugh from me as she'd intended.

We'd barely had time to sip from our mugs after blowing away the steam when the sound of a siren grew so loud that Jay slapped his hands over his ears. When the car squealed to a stop in front of the Center, Jay hopped to his feet.

"Can I go and see the car?" he asked.

I just nodded, as he was already running out the door. My brother caught him in a hug and knelt beside the boy, where they talked for several minutes until the ambulance arrived. Gibb casually held Jay back while he spoke over the boy's head to one of the borrowed officers, leaving the other cop and the medical technicians to do their jobs.

To her credit, Deputy Mann sat through all of this, watching with me, and not badgering me for the story, although I was sure she burned with curiosity. Twice she opened her mouth but didn't speak.

I placed my hand on her arm. "I hope you don't mind, but let me quickly tell you what happened." I ran through the story.

"You did good, Ms. Hill." Her blue eyes smiled when her mouth didn't.

"Stella," I said, but she just nodded.

JoAnn slipped up beside us carrying two mugs of coffee and several ice cubes sealed in a baggie. "Stella, honey, you look like you could use something with more caffeine and some ice for that bump on your head. On the house if I get to hear the story in a few days." JoAnn turned to go back to the kitchen but then stepped back, giving me a quick hug. "Looks like you had some trouble, and I'm sorry. I promise you that Sewanee is going to hear about this and be there for you." She rushed away back to her kitchen.

"What's your place look like inside?" the deputy asked.

"Oh, like a storm came through. Hurricane Debbie." I sighed.

We enjoyed the smooth bite of the coffee for a few more minutes in silence as we watched the EMTs bring Debbie out of the building on a stretcher. She was covered with a blanket, but I could tell by the way that she could only lift her hands, and not her arms, that she was restrained. Jay rushed to her side and buried his face against his mother.

Just as I'd guessed, Jay might realize the bad things his mother had done, but she was still the only mother he had. He was young enough to forget that only an hour ago she had tied him to a desk, and that she was willing to go on the run with him.

Through the window I saw Gibb gently take Jay by the shoulders and say something to him while Debbie, on the gurney, was loaded into the back of the vehicle. Then Gibb helped Jay into the back beside his mother, which surprised me. Surely he wasn't going to allow a child to go alone to the hospital. I didn't suppose Debbie was much of a threat at the moment, but I wouldn't trust her.

Then Gibb hurried across the street toward us. He stuck his head in the doorway. For a few long, searching seconds he looked me over and then nodded. "Mann, grab your bag. You're going to the hospital, and you can change down there. First, guard Debbie but second, don't let anything happen to that boy. I'll have someone down to help out within an hour."

He went back to the ambulance without seeing if his deputy was following while she jumped to her feet as if she'd been scalded. She rushed out the front door with her gym bag in her hand, beating her boss across the street.

I knew Gibb would be back to me in seconds. With the ice pack pressed to my head, I took several drinks of the coffee and prepared myself. Maybe he'd be mad and maybe not. I continued to watch the show through the window as he used his phone two more times and then walked back toward the restaurant. The purposefulness in his steps reminded me of how I admired my brother. He was a good man and a great sheriff for this community. He was the best mountain man I knew.

Gibb dipped and kissed me on the top of the head. It was a move he'd made many times, never afraid who saw him kissing his sister, but today it was accompanied by a hug. I'm sure he imagined, during those sweet seconds, many different endings to this story. When he finally sat down, it was with a sigh. He'd resolved his fear and knew that the story had a happy ending. There was no reason to dwell on what had not happened.

"Okay, Sis, most important thing first. Thanks for Arcadia." He grinned to let me know he was pulling a small joke on me. "How bad?" He pointed to my head where the lump was growing despite the ice, and where I knew that blood had now dried in my hair. Washing wasn't going to be fun, but I didn't think it was really that bad.

Pretending that I had not been a quivering mass of nerves only fifteen minutes ago, I shrugged. "Will I be in trouble for breaking Debbie's ankle?"

"Hardly. Tell me the quick version." Gibb glanced over his shoulder as four men in work clothes came in wanting a hearty breakfast that would sustain them through the cold morning hours working outdoors. They were soon followed by a woman dressed for a day at an office and another woman in a forest ranger uniform.

With my voice lowered, I gave him a quick version. "Gibb we need to get out to the Clark place and find Ronnie. At least Debbie told me she didn't kill him, but I don't know if we can believe her or not."

"We'll find out." His jaw set.

Then we were distracted as Harley's truck, moving well over the speed limit, barreled up to the Center, the brakes applied and squealing at the last moment. He stopped just behind Gibb's police car, which had the siren off but the lights still flashing. It served to warn others to move on and not park near the Center, but Harley ignored it. I wondered how he knew something had happened to me.

Before he was out of the truck, Lam's SUV roared in to park directly behind the Trickster. Both men started into the Center. Gibb and I stood, wanting to get to them quickly to let them know I was okay. Gibb and I had a good view as both Harley and Lam reached the front door at the same moment. For a second they tried to push in ahead of the other, wide shoulders banging together, but then both backed up and Lam surged in first.

CHAPTER 32

I'd always enjoyed my few rides with Gibb in his police car with the siren and lights clearing a path. It made me feel like an actor in a movie or TV cop show. Today though, I mostly felt the headache pounding at my temples as the siren screamed.

"So there really was no money?" Gibb's question broke into my thoughts.

"Uh, no. I mean, yes, the robbery got just what the news stories said it got them, close to fifteen thousand. I talked to the former bank president."

"Good detective work."

At first I thought my brother was being sarcastic, but then I decided that his tone was genuine. The car slewed on gravel scattered across the asphalt, and he man-handled the wheel to bring us back into the lane. I clutched the edge of the seat, but Gibb didn't bat an eye.

I swallowed. "I talked with the former bank guard, too. The one that got shot. He's a preacher now and is really a nice old guy. It was Donnie that shot him and not Ronnie. Oh, you were asking about the money. Debbie thought all these years that there was a lot more than fifteen thousand buried somewhere on their property. Donnie told her there was more and that he buried it to save and split with Ronnie. He talked Ronnie into taking the rap for them both since Debbie was pregnant."

"Donnie was a smooth liar and lazy as a hound."

"Yep. He loved those stupid riddles he was always making up. The one for the money was 'Who builds a wheel without working with wood?' And then he said to dig under the wheel." I laughed. "Ronnie said that Debbie had him dig up the dirt floor of the old garage. But their barn has a quilt block painted on it. A Carpenter's Wheel."

Gibb whistled low-like. "My guess would be that Donnie spent the money. Probably bought that van for the business. It's about ten years old. I guess she believed him about burying it, but I know it was hard on her sticking with Donnie."

"What do you mean?"

He said, with a sigh, "Over the years I was called out to their house several times for domestic abuse."

I mumbled as I touched the side of my head, "I bet it was her beating on him."

"You might be right. It seemed like he had as many black eyes as she ever did."

We made the twenty-minute trip in half the time. At the turn to the driveway, he slowed and turned off the siren and lights. As we approached the small house set back into the woods, it looked dead and uninviting. This cop movie was turning into a horror show. My brother turned the vehicle around so that it was facing back down the driveway and blocking the path for any other vehicle.

"You stay. If you get out of this car before I give you permission, I will give you so many tickets that you'll never drive again in your life." He said the words while jabbing his finger in my face.

"I don't understand. Ronnie might need our help."

"Until I'm sure what's going on, you stay."

He swung out of the car and moved quickly toward the cover of the barn. At first I could see him in the side mirror and watched as he pulled his weapon. With slow and cautious steps, he disappeared into the barn and didn't reappear for over five minutes. I guessed that he'd done a pretty thorough search in that time, given that it was mostly a big open space plus Dip Cone in his stall.

Next, Gibb made his way entirely around the house, and then he examined the inside of the van. Even though I knew that the van doors, all of them, squeaked horribly, I still jumped as I watched from the car.

I hadn't wanted to tell Gibb that I was perfectly happy to sit still and let someone else do the work for me, especially if my brother felt there could be some danger. He was right that he had the training and the experience. For my part, I wanted to retire from catching criminals.

His extreme caution did surprise me, though. Gibb hadn't gotten to know Ronnie over the last week as I had, and I felt sure that he was the victim here and not the criminal. I only hoped that Ronnie wasn't hurt or, worse, dead. I knew he wasn't waiting to waylay the sheriff.

Not finding Ronnie in the van, he headed for the last place left to look—the house. I waited, twisting repeatedly to look back over my shoulder. It seemed a long time, but finally Gibb stepped back onto the porch and motioned for me to join him.

Gibb held the screen door open for me and crossed the living room with long strides. I felt the skin on my neck prickle and hunched my shoulders like a turtle as I shuffled along on the carpeting. He led me into the kitchen, where the door of a pantry stood open. Inside Ronnie was on the floor twisted like a pretzel. He seemed stunned.

"Found him like this." He pointed to a kitchen table chair sitting near. "The chair was jammed under the door handle. Talk to him, Sis. I don't have cell reception here so I'll have to use the car radio. Be back as quick as I can."

I knelt on the linoleum as if I were going to pray. "Ronnie," I reached out to touch his arm, but he flinched, "are you hurt? Are you shot?"

It took a full minute but slowly life returned to the man's face which had been vacant. He moved in jerky starts, crawling out of the pantry. I had to scoot backwards inch-for-inch to give him room. When he had freed himself of the confinement of the closet, he collapsed onto his side and rolled over onto his back. As I listened to his ragged breathing even out, I sat back on the floor and took time to look around the kitchen. Dirty fingerprints decorated the refrigerator alongside a school report card held up with a magnet shaped like a football. At least Debbie was proud of her son.

I sure wouldn't want to have to cook or eat here. A dark, wavering stain marked a water leak in the ceiling at the corner, and the paint behind the stove looked greasy and dark. I knew if I stood and peered down into the sink, I'd find the porcelain chipped and stained, that is if I could see the sink. The top of a mound of pots and plates rose above the height of the counter from my viewpoint. Evidently she'd had enough of cleaning pot and pans at work to do more at home. I couldn't find it in my heart, though, to feel any sympathy for Debbie. Not yet, but maybe, with what Gibb had revealed to me, I could be more generous once my headache subsided.

Ronnie's hazel eyes gazed up to the ceiling as he said, "I don't do well with tight spaces anymore."

We stayed like this, silent now, as color returned to his face. Although I wasn't sure, he seemed unhurt.

His memory must have been returning as, with a start, he sat up and grasped both my arms. "Jay. How's my boy? Is he safe?"

"He's fine, Ronnie, but Debbie's the worse for wear. Gibb sent Jay to the hospital with his mama." When Ronnie looked alarmed at those words, I added, "With a police officer who will keep him safe. I promise."

He relaxed.

That's all the conversation we had time for before we heard Gibb moving back through the house. He stopped in the doorway and stood with his hand on the butt of his gun.

"You hurt, Ronnie?"

"No, sheriff," Ronnie struggled to his feet with stiff limbs. "Miss Stella said my boy's safe and that's all that matters. I'm ready." He stuck his arms straight out in front with the wrists close together.

I expected Gibb to say something nice, waving away the suggestion that this man should be arrested. I did a double-take as I watched him pull handcuffs from the back of his belt. With quick, efficient motions he twisted Ronnie's arms toward his back and snapped on the bracelets. Clicking noises marked the tightening of the cuffs.

I gasped. "Gibb, you can't do this. Ronnie's the victim, not a criminal."

"Hush, Miss Stella," Ronnie said. "The sheriff knows what he's doing. He can't be sure until this all gets sorted out. I'm an ex-con, and he's got to be careful. Don't blame him a bit."

"Don't argue," was all Gibb said to me with an unsmiling glance.

We walked out to the car, Gibb guiding Ronnie with a hand pressed to the middle of his back. He helped him into the back seat. I followed, dragging behind, and took my seat in the front without a word. Fatigue had settled into my mind now like an impenetrable blanket of fog. All the words I might have said seemed to have frozen, but Gibb began gathering information.

"Ronnie, did you shoot your brother?"

"No, sir, Debbie did, but you'll find my prints on the gun. When you do find it. The crazy woman put something to make me sleep in my food or drink. Then, she put the gun in my hand while I was sleeping. That was after she shot Donnie, but she's smart. Debbie'll be happy to tell you where it's at."

Gibb only grunted.

I needed to speak and defend the man, but my tongue felt as if it no longer worked, along with my brain. With great effort, I summoned my strength. "I heard her confess, twice."

"That will help," Gibb said, "but sometimes these things aren't as simple as you think. What were you doing that two weeks between when you got out of prison and when you showed yourself to your brother?"

Ronnie told the same story to Gibb as he'd told me days ago. I could hear his regret in the words. "I ain't proud of myself, sheriff, but I'm not a murderer. Debbie shot him in cold blood, or that's how she told it. She sent him out to steal that copper, just like they had planned. She followed and waited until he'd got the job done, and then she jumped in the van and pulled the trigger without a word. That's what she told me. She was just setting it up to look like me getting killed while doing something wrong."

"Oh, that gun's already in the evidence room. Somebody," Gibb emphasized the word, "left it anonymous-like outside the police station last week. In a paper bag. Caused quite a stir until we decided it wasn't a bomb."

"That seems kind of dumb," Ronnie said.

"You bet. How could Debbie not guess that we have a camera there? Maybe it's not so dumb, though. It gave a reason why her prints were on the gun too. Like I said, it will all get sorted out."

I watched the trees flow by outside the window, unable to figure out the riddle of what Debbie's defense would look like or how Ronnie might be saved. It was beginning to feel like we'd gone to a lot of trouble and risked our lives so that Debbie might go free, and Ronnie might end up in prison for the rest of his life. It made my problem, that I was almost certain to lose my job today, seem petty in comparison. That didn't stop a few tears from slipping down my cheeks. I kept my face turned to the window as I rubbed them away. I was not going to complain.

Gibb continued to talk. "'Course, I've been following her these last days and her actions don't seem like someone who is innocent. Maybe my testimony, along with Stella's, can keep you out of prison, Ronnie."

From the back seat came a strangled thanks, and then we rode on back to Sewanee in silence. I reached across the seat and patted Gibb on the hand.

CHAPTER 33

When the county road changed to Main Street, I asked Gibb if he could drop me at work and let me come by to make a statement later.

"If you promise to get that cut looked at," he said.

"I will." I spoke the words Gibb wanted to hear, but I wasn't going to do it. I didn't have time. Maybe the cut needed a stitch but it had quit bleeding, and I didn't think I had a concussion. I knew I was just telling myself that because I had a lot to do. First thing was to make a sign to go in the window. I pictured myself marking *Closed Until Further Notice* in thick, black lettering.

Worse yet was the phone call I'd have to make to Janice. Time was running out, as I needed to phone her before she set out from Nashville to drive up to the plateau. Over the last few weeks she'd already pegged me for a bumbling fool, and I had to admit that the description fit. I should have never thought that I could go from being a cubicle nanny to creating the Heritage Craft Center, which I dreamed of being half museum and half a retail opportunity for the crafters of today.

I just loved my Sewanee Mountain and its people so much. I'd wanted to be a part of it again and give back, and being the director had seemed such a perfect opportunity.

"What the ..." Gibb slowed the car, and I focused on the road instead of my thoughts.

"Is there an accident?" My voice was small, so small that I didn't think Gibb heard me.

In front of the Center cars and a truck were double parked. For some reason, Larry Hargrave was in the middle of the street directing traffic while two guys unloaded an antique stove from the cargo space of a box van. Next, I noticed JoAnn and her assistant standing on the sidewalk handing out cups of coffee and muffins. Near them Esther's car was parked, and the trunk yawned open. Harley was in the act of unloading something while Esther talked on her phone.

A familiar mountain in the form of a man, Earnest Carter, hurried into the Center carrying two mannequins, one under each arm. For a confused second I'd thought they were live people. He almost wiped Lam out as he trotted through the doorway. Ducking his head, Lam danced past the obstacle and stepped into the only open lane for traffic. He let loose an ear-splitting whistle. At his direction, a car pulled forward and stopped. A lane that had appeared to be open was now blocked. The driver jumped out and helped Lam unload a couple of boxes. They both disappeared inside.

"There's Mom." Gibb pointed. "I don't know what's going on, but she will. I'll have to turn around, and I'd better get someone out here to direct traffic better than Larry's doing." He prodded me with a poke in the side. "Go on. I've got some idea of what's happening, but you look dumbfounded."

I eased from the car as if I expected to be attacked at any moment. From the back seat Ronnie called to me. "Miss Stella, I almost forgot. There's a box upstairs in the utility closet. I was going to surprise you today. It's full of those little whistles I carve that you like so well. It's a gift for you."

I didn't trust myself to speak but lifted my hand for a wave. As Gibb turned the car around and drove off, I watched Ronnie's bowed head through the back window. When I turned, I plowed into Will Chastain, better known in these parts as Wailin' Willy. He tipped his hat, as did the male members of the Four Plucked Angels following him. Elderly Norma Gill raised her mandolin in a salute to me as the band trooped into the Center. My mouth dropped open, but before I could move, Mom snatched me into a hug as ferocious as any mama bear could give. She planted kisses all over my face before pushing back. That's when she finally saw the blood in my hair and let loose a little scream. I went through a lot of explanations and reassurances before I could wiggle out of her grasp. Even then she hovered.

"Mom, what's going on?"

"Stella, the whole town is here for you. JoAnn got the ball rolling, and I think, well, I've got to admit, that JoAnn's coffee is good. Everybody she phoned started calling friends and," she threw her hands wide and turned in a circle, "here you have it."

Harley noticed us then and rushed to my side. "Stella!" He trapped me in another hug, this one lifting my feet from the ground while he spun around. "Oh, Stella, I can't believe what happened to you. You're the bravest woman I've ever met."

"Harley, Harley," Mom said. "I think you're making her dizzy."

"Oh, right." He sat me back on my feet.

"Harley, how did you know to come here? Early this morning, I mean." I was still puzzling over how Harley had known about the trouble here.

"My friend called. Lam." Harley smiled.

"I'm glad." It was all I could think to say. The surprise of them both coming to the rescue had me almost speechless.

Harley glanced at his watch. "Let me show you what we've done so far, but we've got to hurry. It's 9:40. We've still got over an hour left, but none of knows when your boss is expected to arrive." He waited for me to answer.

"Uh, she said not until eleven, when I was going to open the door," I choked on the words before I could continue. "But Harley …"

As I talked, Harley had been dragging me toward the door. Each foot closer made my stomach churn. I'd seen the destruction in the dim early morning light and wasn't sure I could face seeing it again. Not yet. I wanted to turn and run, to hide away until I was old enough to manage a job like an adult. I'd failed, and what he was going to make me see was the proof of my failure. I threw my hands over my eyes.

Someone pried my fingers away one at a time. "Baby," Lam coaxed. "Come on."

The vision made my legs collapse under me. If not for Lam on one side and Harley on the other, I'd have fallen to the floor. They kept me upright while Mom, behind us, rubbed my back. My Heritage Craft Center was almost back to what it had been before the destruction caused by Debbie.

Old Soldier marched up, stopping in front of us with a clicking together of his heels. He saluted. "The glass truck called. ETA is five minutes. Shall I direct the work, General?" He asked, looking unblinkingly at me.

I felt prodding against my hand from Harley, and I raised it in a return salute to Soldier. "Uh, yes, that would be good. Carry on, Sergeant." I whispered to Lam, "What's broken?"

Lam pointed to one of my cases where the front panel of glass was cracked.

Soldier executed a wobbly about-face, and when he regained his balance, he crossed the room to talk with Annaleigh. She was hanging onto Wailin' Willy's arm while cooing in the man's ear. I supposed she was wrangling an opportunity to sing.

Then I saw Alma enter the room from the back and stomp across to where the quilting frame had been erected. She was walking!

"When did Alma get out of the wheelchair?" I asked Mom.

She said, "Alma's been up and down a bit during the strike."

"And how's that going?"

"I promised to let her tell you the news."

"Can't wait," I said, not at all sure I wanted to be involved anymore.

The ladies of the quilting bee were in place and already sewing. The needles flashed in the light as they dipped in and out of the fabric, and I noticed the women were all in dresses from the past. Esther was going around placing bonnets on their heads. The costumes gave the impression the quilters had walked straight out of the past.

I heard Ernest's bass voice boom. "How's this?" He was arranging two mannequins in a tableau to show the moonshiner hard at work by his still, imbibing from his jug, while a revenuer in a black suit came up behind him.

Mom said, "Oops, it's my job to help Earnest." She hurried over to admire his work and straightened the tax man's black hat.

I looked from Lam to Harley. "I see it, but I don't believe this much work could have been done so quickly."

"The whole town's been in at one time or the other," Lam said. "Everybody's pulling for you."

"And when Lam says everybody, he means the whole mountain," Harley said. "If I hadn't seen it myself, I don't think I would have believed it either. Esther collected more antique quilts and found the clothes. The high school used them in a play a couple of years ago. Earnest heard that the still had gotten knocked over, and he fixed it right up. Plus, he brought a jug of new, uh, I think you just call it 'shine."

"Don't worry, baby, I hid the jug. Don't want this crowd drunk." Lam flashed his signature devilish smile.

Harley touched my hair lightly. "It's time for you to go home and get cleaned up. Cele will take you and get you back in plenty of time. Is there anything that needs to be done that you think we might not know about?"

"Just keep your eyes on Alma, and, shue, somebody get my phone back."

Mom pampered me over the next hour and arranged my hair into an artful pile on top of my head. It hid the cut and lump and even made me look more grown-up. The headache was a whisper now, and my hands had finally stopped shaking. We got back in plenty of time to make a last check, where I found that the Center was in even better shape than it had been.

Annaleigh leaned over and whispered in my ear. "It's like a surprise birthday party. I haven't been to one in years." She clapped her hands together and sang the first lines of the song.

Alma stood at my other side. "Well, your boss better appreciate all our work. If she doesn't, I'll have to twist her ear till she does."

I turned to Alma, probably wearing a horrified look on my face.

Across the showroom, standing by the antique stove Larry had donated, Mom flashed me a concerned look. She'd been watching me like a hawk as she arranged the drinks—punch, coffee, and sassafras tea—and the cookies on top of the stove. The massive appliance stood beside the display of JoAnn's recipes and was the perfect place for Mom to serve the refreshments from.

I pointed to the old woman to let Mom know it was just something Alma had said and not that I was feeling bad. The worry frown on Mom's face eased, but Alma poked me in the side.

"Pay attention." The woman was dancing from foot-to-foot in her sensible shoes. "I've got big news, Stella." Her thin chest puffed up so that she looked like a tiny game cock in a jumper. "I bought the nursing home."

"Wow, that's amazing news! I'm sure you'll have everyone whipped, uh, I mean, well, taken care of. I mean it." I guess she'd been saving her money through the years. "I'm happy for you. I guess there are big changes coming."

"To put it mildly." Annaleigh sighed. "Our Alma brings to mind the very definition of tenacious. Most dedicated and definitely in charge. Chocolate chip cookies every day. I'll leave you two to your conversation," she said and headed off toward the band.

Alma glared but then grinned. "I'd better go and check on the quilting bee. Got to keep my ladies working. You mark my words, young lady, before this day is over, you'll be happy I was here for you." She turned away, mumbling. "Girl can't do without me."

"Wait," I called to her back. "Where's my phone?" I started after her but Earnest's voice rang out.

"She's here. She's here," Earnest shouted at the top of his lungs, making considerable noise. He'd been kneeling in the front window among the parts of his moonshine still display. I believe the man thought he was hiding, but he'd need something larger, like an elephant, to conceal his bulk. He blended in though with the moonshiner mannequin wearing identical denim overalls with long johns underneath and a floppy-brimmed mountain man hat. I guess that told me where Earnest had gotten the clothes, but I was wondering where the actual dummies had come from.

At that moment I pasted a smile on my face as Harley held the door for Janice to enter.

Harley had taken it upon himself to wait unobtrusively outside to be our lookout and to practice smoking the corn cob pipe he'd bought to be my first sale. He had been sitting on one of a half dozen oak whiskey barrels that someone had donated and lined up across the porch. They made a great decoration and pretty good seats. Earnest had assisted Harley, showing the city lawyer how to pack in the tobacco—straight from a pouch that hung from his belt—and draw the flame into the bowl. Now Harley looked a bit green.

My heart danced a skippy-beat as Janice stopped and took in the whole of the Heritage Craft Center. It was amazing to behold, and I knew from the expression on her face, that she was impressed. The walls were now decorated with many more antiques and framed photos of times gone by. I hadn't even seen all of the images myself, but those I had seen showed mountain living as the pioneers had experienced it. The photos skipped from loggers with their axes, farmers plowing the fields with the aid of mules, to weavers, moonshiners, a blacksmith at his anvil, and, my favorite, the quilters.

When Janice tipped her head back, I let my gaze travel upward as well. The quilts Mom had helped me select to hang from the cross beams were delightful banners of mountain life. They really did make my Center seem like a cathedral with beautiful stained glass. My quilts were better though than any colored glass as they brought their own warmth to the room.

Tears rose in my eyes and my throat tightened for a moment, but instead of being frightened that I was going to lose all of this, it was now pride that stirred my emotions. Not only was I amazed at what I'd accomplished, but how it all had been multiplied over and over by the mountain people of Sewanee. They'd been there for me all along when I'd been too busy to see. When the time had come, when my need had been greatest, they had carried me through. In one way it didn't matter what happened with the job or the detail of being a permanent employee. I'd moved beyond that. I laughed. Of course, I wanted the job, too.

In long strides, I crossed the rough plank floor, my hand out, and for once a genuine smile on my face welcomed Janice. Before I could reach my boss, Wailin' Willy started up the band, and Earnest came up from behind to grab Janice in an embrace, whirling her around his own impromptu dance floor between the displays. Annaleigh's high soprano joined Willy's falsetto for a pleasing duet as the music filled the large room. Everyone started tapping their toes, and a few couples began to move to the beat. Earnest even proved to be a good dancer.

While the music worked its magic, I stepped back, first watching over the crowd, but Alma caught my attention when she brought a pitcher out of the back room to replenish the punch bowl. It really wasn't like the woman to pitch in with actual work, and she had a broad smile on her face, making me suspicious. She ladled some of the drink out into a plastic cup and, when the music ended, gave it to Janice. I smelled a rotten fish, but as I again moved to greet Janice, the music started back up and Lam moved in to tap Earnest on the shoulder. Janice took one look into Lam's sultry eyes and began moving to the beat. She kept the drink, though, and sipped when she could. I stayed busy as a few of the locals left but were being replaced by tourists. I believed the townsfolk had intended to create the appearance that the Heritage Craft Center was the most popular place in Sewanee, but it seemed to be doing pretty well on its own.

I rang up a sale and then noticed Alma's doctor from the day at the hospital emergency room. He held one quilt up and then another and shifted back the first.

"Can I help you decide, doctor?"

"How'd … Oh, hello. You came in with the elderly patient who was, well, uh, I'll just say rather opinionated. I thought you were her granddaughter."

"That's me, well, not the granddaughter part, and there's your patient." I pointed to where Alma was still serving punch.

"I guess she doesn't normally dress like that. In a bonnet. She looks well, but I told her she'd be up and around in a day, two at the most."

"Really." My eyes narrowed. "So she only needed the wheelchair for a day?"

The doctor hooted, "Wheelchair! She only needed an ace bandage and some aspirin. She was pretty insistent, though, so I figured a day wouldn't hurt."

"That's good to know." I stared across the room, but Alma wasn't looking our way. "Whom are you buying a quilt for?" I asked the doctor.

When he told me the quilt would be a gift for his teenage daughter, I steered him toward a table of modern quilts rather than the traditional patterns. I left him deciding.

I was now determined that it was time to talk to Janice. I waded into the couples, weaving between the displays, and tried to follow Janice. After another quick spin by Earnest, I tapped Harley on the shoulder and freed my boss.

I linked my arm in hers. "Hi. I hope you're having a great time. What do you think?"

Janice swayed on her feet and burped. "Oooops. This is the bestest opening ever, Stel. And thisss some great punch. Need the recipe." She tried pointing at her cup but missed by several inches.

"Shue, Janice, you're totally sloshed."

"Really?" Janice overbalanced and tipped backward. It was only by grabbing her that I saved the woman from a fall. I led my boss to the staircase, which was the closest place to ease her to a sitting position.

"I take it you aren't much of a drinker." I tugged the plastic cup from her hand and took a whiff. It smelled vaguely like paint stripper.

"Nope. I'mmm proud to be a toptotaler. I mean teetotaler." Janice pressed two fingers to her mouth. "Never pass these lips." The touch wiped her lipstick from the middle of her lips, giving her a strange look.

"I think we'd better go to the back and sit down." I tried to hoist her to her feet but the height difference between us plus the low step made it difficult. The fact that she kept reaching around me for her drink wasn't at all helpful.

I sat beside her to catch my breath. With a huff, I asked, "Janice, do you really like what I did with the place?"

"Beautiful."

"Do you think you'll keep me on? I mean, I'd love to get off this probation."

"Okey-dokey, no problemo." She pulled her phone out of her bag, still draped over her shoulder, and entered a few numbers. "Cheryl, fix up that permanent employee form for me. Oops. I'm already one. For good ol' Stel here in Sewanee." She waved her hand. "No, no. Just sign it electrically, I mean, electronically. One less thing for me. I'm feeling sleepy. Nighty-night."

I waved Earnest over and explained what I needed. He hoisted Janice to her feet and over his shoulder in a swift movement. She giggled as he hauled her to the back room as if she weighed no more than a child. I'd leave her to sleep it off in a chair that was a little more comfortable than the stairs.

The rest of the day flew by with good music, great sales, dancing, and plenty to drink, except no more 'shine.

CHAPTER 34

I signed the electronic tablet the UPS driver held out to me.

"Looks like you're doing real good here with this store," he said, stacking up the boxes he was delivering.

"It's going great. I've only been open two weeks, and we've beaten the other Centers in the state by double. It's not just a store though," I said. "It's really more a museum of the craft heritage of the area. Are you from the local area?" I asked.

"No. Down south of Atlanta."

"Stop by when you have time to poke around. Bring the family. I promise you'll be amazed."

"I will." He tipped his hat to me and jumped back into the double-parked truck to continue his rounds.

None of the days had equaled the sales during the grand opening, but the receipts added up. So far I had worked twelve hours every day and couldn't have been happier. I'd even been given extra budget money by Janice to hire help.

I'd briefly wondered if the extra funds—offered the day after her teetotaler lapse—was her way of trying to make sure I never talked about the incident. Janice didn't have to worry whether her secret was safe with me. There was no way I'd ever bring the subject up, as I loved my job too much.

I leaned my head around the front door. "Earnest! Help me, please." I gathered up a couple of the boxes.

Earnest appeared, peeking around the door frame. "What do you need, boss?" He saw the stacks of packages and hurried to help me. "What'd we get?" he asked. "It's like Christmas every day working here."

I glanced at the shipping labels. "Postcards and shopping bags. Not much fun there. Wait. Here's the coloring books that I bought from Norma Little. Original drawings showing life on the mountain. Hot off the printing press."

"My niece would love one. I'll get it for a Christmas gift. I already bought her one of those carved whistles. We should get more of those. They're really fun." The mountain of a man gathered most of the boxes into his arms and carried them in to begin unpacking. He popped back out and took the rest from me.

"Why don't you take a break? I swear that I never did see a missy work as hard as you do."

"Thanks, Earnest. I believe I will." I hoisted myself onto one of the oak barrels and leaned against the log wall. Today was one of those beautiful winter days that looked, from the window, like summertime with a gem blue sky, but the temperature caused me to rub my hands up and down my arms. I could enjoy it for a few minutes.

I thought of the carved whistles that Ronnie had made for me. Shaped like little birds and playing two notes, they'd sold out in two days. I'd love to have more. Mostly, though, I'd love for Ronnie to be free and clear of the problems haunting him. His defense, courtesy of Harley, looked promising. Debbie was being held in jail until the trial as she was considered a flight risk. It helped that a witness had come forward who saw Debbie driving on Main Street the evening that Donnie was murdered. The man swore he didn't see Ronnie in the car.

Jay said that his mom went out that evening, leaving him with his uncle, who was sound asleep. But Ronnie didn't want the boy to be involved with sending his own mother to prison. I agreed with him on that. Harley kept telling me not to worry.

The good news was that Ronnie could continue staying at the Clark home. Ronnie and Donnie's father had originally left it to the two of them, and Ronnie had never sold his half to his brother. Maybe Donnie had a conscience after all, as he'd left his half to his brother and everything else to Debbie, which didn't add up to much at all. Now Ronnie was fixing the place up.

Jay had to move, by court order, in with an aunt of Debbie's, but she let Ronnie visit and had really taken him under her wing. Ronnie had told me he needed to look for a job soon, but he wanted to spend some time to himself. Who could blame the man?

A horn honked, and I jumped, rousing me from my thoughts to wave at Larry as he drove past. He was laughing at me. Shue, it was good to have a home like Sewanee.

A bus, designed for about twelve passengers, pulled into a parking space directly in front of the Center. It looked newly painted with the words *Home Sweet Home* in red on the side. The door swung open with a hiss of hydraulics, and Soldier slid from behind the wheel and hopped with the spring of a kid down the two steps. He helped several ladies off the bus. They moved single file inside. Last off the bus were Annaleigh and Alma.

"So good to see you, dear." Annaleigh placed a gloved hand on my arm and leaned in to allow me to give her a peck on a rouged cheek.

"Did the nursing home get a new bus?" I asked.

"Oh, yes, and we're Christmas shopping today since we have wheels. The real excitement, however, comes next week when we are putting on a production of It's a Wonderful Life starring, who else?" She placed one hand on her chest. "You will come, won't you, and bring that handsome blond fellow of yours?" She swept into the Center, leaving a scent of lavender on the brisk air.

"What's up, Alma? I think you've been avoiding me these last two weeks."

Alma stared hard for a second but couldn't contain her grin. "So did your boss lady do right by you?"

"My wildest dreams." I threw my arms wide. "I'm so happy. If I just had a phone ..."

As if my words had summoned a call, a ringtone—my ringtone—sounded from Alma's coat pocket. She blushed, something that I'm not sure had ever happened in the history of time.

She dipped her hand into her right pocket. "Well, well, look what I found. Your missing phone, Stella. Here you go."

She dropped my smartphone into my hand, and I answered the call. It only took a moment to get the good news that I'd been awarded the grant which I had applied for. I could hardly wait to call Janice. After so much bad news to pass along these last weeks, it would be fun to tell her as I'd developed a good relationship with my boss.

Alma turned away. "Got to go. Christmas shopping, you know."

I reached out and touched her shoulder. "Alma, I have to know. When did you find out that you'd been retired? I've felt so guilty." Saying those words felt like lifting a piano off my shoulders. I'd never been good at keeping secrets.

She laughed. "Oh, I called the district boss and resigned the day I fell. Just decided on the spur of the moment. You never know how long you have to enjoy, and going to the nursing home was the best thing that's happened to me in a long time. I have so many good friends now. How could I not buy the place?"

"Shue, you used me! You made me feel so guilty." I hopped off the barrel.

"Got to shop." Alma darted into the Center, her cackle lingering.

I started to count to ten but stopped at two and just laughed.

Enjoy these and more from AQS

AQS Publishing brings the latest in quilt topics to satisfy the traditional to modern quilter. Interesting techniques, vivid color, and clear directions make these books your one-stop for quilt design and instruction. With its leading Quilt-Fiction series, mystery, relationship, and community all merge as stories are pieced together to keep you spell-bound.

Whether Quilt-Instruction or Quilt-Fiction, pick one up from AQS today.

AQS publications are available nationwide.
Call or visit AQS
www.shopAQS.com
1-800-626-5420